Praise f

The Trouble with Spells

"Wow! I am so impressed! I was IN from the very start. The characters are beautifully written and the story is fantastic. I was on the edge of my chair, turning pages as fast as I could read them! Couldn't get enough of this book! It has all the elements of a must read. It has non-stop action, daring deeds, good vs. evil, danger and suspense, as well as being an all-out love story."

– Beverly Sharp, The Wormhole Reviews

"*The Trouble with Spells* has everything needed for the making of an amazing series and has quickly become my new favorite. Vance and Portia will be giving other YA couples a run for their money!!"

– Lyndsey Rushby, Heaven, Hell, and Purgatory Book Reviews

"*Of Witches And Warlocks: The Trouble With Spells* is a definite must read and will have you hooked from the beginning. Lacey Weatherford writes an amazing love story that will leave you addicted and craving for another hit of action, romance and an extra dose of the local bad boy, Vance Mangum."

– Naomi McKay, Supernatural Bookworm Reviews

"I fell completely, head over heels in love with *The Trouble With Spells*. The charged relationship between Portia and Vance in this electrifying novel leaves a lasting impression."

– Susan Mann, Susan K Mann Book Reviews

Of Witches & Warlocks

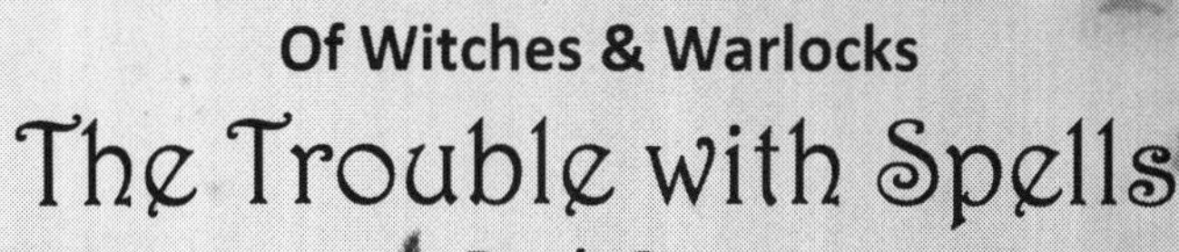

The Trouble with Spells

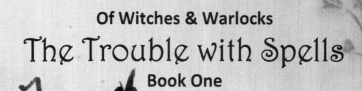

Book One

By Lacey Weatherford

Moonstruck Media

Arizona

ISBN-13:978-1466209770
ISBN-10: 1466209771

Published by

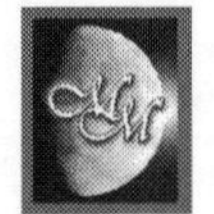

Moonstruck Media
Arizona

This book is also available in ebook format.
http://www.ofwitchesandwarlocks.com

DEDICATION

To my darling daughter, Kamery, whose ever-changing hair color first inspired me with the idea, to Connie and Larissa who loved it enough to encourage me to go for it, and to my husband James, who put up with everything else so I could write.

ACKNOWLEDGMENTS

Just a quick thank you to everyone who has been so helpful in getting this book out there. To my terrific beta readers—thanks for all your time, effort, input and encouragement. Your suggestions and support are always worth their weight in gold! To my wonderful family—thanks for being so good to help out and take care of running day-to-day things so I can have more time to write. To the awesome "Vance Fans" out there—thanks for everything you do to help spread the word about this series. To my business partner and best friend, Belinda—thanks for all your continued encouragement!

Sincerely,

Prologue

Vance Mangum - Two Years Earlier

I was sitting under a tree at my new school during lunch, trying to avoid the silly giggles and laughter from the endless parade of idiotic girls who were trying to catch my attention. Pretending to be oblivious seemed to work best for me, so I focused on pulling random blades of grass out of the ground while I bit into the apple in my hand.

It's not like I wasn't interested in the girls—I definitely was. I was just tired of not being able to really get to know the ones I liked before I had to move to a new place again. I already missed the girl I'd been hanging around with at the school I'd just left. Amber was amazing, and she could kiss like ... well, there just wasn't any point in thinking about her kisses because I wouldn't be experiencing them again.

I hated running. I despised constantly looking over my shoulder for him, always getting so close to being found. It was totally messing up my life. While I was already sixteen, I was only a sophomore. I should've been a junior, but being on the run and having to go into hiding put me a year behind in school. Hopefully, this time would be different. I didn't know if I had the same faith in this new coven that my Aunt Marsha did.

She seemed to think they might be able to help protect us better than we'd been able to protect ourselves. I guess, deep down, I really hoped they could—I was so tired of running.

I took another bite of my apple, while focusing on the doors to the school, successfully redirecting my gaze away from the group of girls who were twittering together off to my left.

That's when I saw her.

She stepped out of the door, walking next to some other girl, but my attention was instantly riveted on her. Every emotion she was feeling at that moment washed over me. I sucked in my breath, having never experienced anything quite like it.

This girl was different. She was magical. Literally.

The warlock inside me lifted his head in curious admiration. She was young, probably only a freshman, but she was beautiful in a totally understated way. I was instantly drawn to her, and I glanced over her small, petite form as she moved toward the cafeteria.

A light breeze caught her black hair, stirring it slightly away from her face, and she smiled at her friend. The music of her laughter carried to me through the air, with the high and low notes blending in my mind in perfect harmony. She was ... content, happy, secure, and amused about whatever her friend was telling her. She was everything I was not, and I knew I had to know who she was.

“Excuse me,” I said, turning to one of the girls hovering nearby. She looked down at me with a hopeful expression. “Do you know who that girl is?”

I glanced back toward the beautiful girl, but not in time to miss the crestfallen look on this one's face before she lifted her head to follow my line of sight.

“Who? The blonde?” she asked icily.

"No. The one with the black hair," I replied, not taking my eyes off her while she walked.

"Her?" she replied with an incredulous tone in her voice. I turned back to look at her, narrowing my eyes cynically. She shrank back for a second before squaring her shoulders and flipping her hair with one of her hands. "That's Portia Mullins," she replied, looking away from me to whisper with her friends again.

Portia Mullins. Oh, the irony.

I knew exactly who she was. She was the underage daughter of my new benefactor who had sworn to help protect me. She was the girl I'd been instructed not to interact with because she had no idea she was a witch, or that her family was part of a magical coven. I wasn't to have any contact with her until she turned sixteen and found out her true heritage. That was when she would be inducted into her coven. My coven. The coven I willingly bound myself to and could not betray.

She lifted her head and looked right at me. I had to fight for control while I turned my eyes away from her, with what I hoped was a bored, uninterested glance. But my heart raced slightly when I felt her emotions—her pulse picking up at the sight of me. She felt ... intrigued, perhaps even attracted, but that was immediately replaced by deflation. She didn't feel worthy of my notice. If she only knew.

Portia and her friend entered the cafeteria. Even though she was gone from my sight, I could still feel her.

Unexpectedly, I became very angry. I'd found a person I connected with on a level I never experienced with another living being, and I couldn't even get to know her. I felt the need to punch something.

I stood up and strode across the parking lot to where I left my motorcycle, knowing full well I was going to get in trouble for ditching on my second day of school, but I didn't care. One thing was for certain, I was going to stay in this place and get to know Portia Mullins … even if it got me killed.

Chapter 1

Portia Mullins - Present Day

I thought I was the typical teenager—a normal fifteen year old, eagerly awaiting my sixteenth birthday, which was in just three days. I was mostly excited because I could finally get my driver's license and, of course, the dating thing.

My family had a strict no dating policy until I turned sixteen. It didn't bother me too much since I'd seen some sad results from other girls who were allowed to date before then—not that those stories were always their fault. It just seemed like guys who didn't respect girls had an easier time taking advantage of them when they were younger.

Even though I hadn't hit the official dating scene, it wasn't like I didn't have guy friends. I'd always been a happy-go-lucky girl, and cute too, in a sort of Goth girl way. The funny thing about that is I wasn't Goth at all. I just happened to have naturally straight black hair that flowed down past my shoulder blades. My sweet, little upturned nose matched perfectly with my bow-shaped lips, but it was my big, nearly black eyes, with thick dark lashes, against my almost translucently pale skin that set off the entire look.

I tried tanning, but somehow only seemed to be

able to turn a beautiful shade of lobster red before my skin puckered, peeled off, and revealed a lovely, new white skin beneath.

My best friend, Shelly, whom I happen to call Barbie behind her back, tried to make me over many times without success. My hair wouldn't hold a curl, and the extra makeup made me look a bit like a hooker. Since I'm so style challenged, I religiously tried to avoid wearing too much black, sticking to jewel tones and that shabby chic kind of look I adore. That, perhaps, makes me come off as a gypsy of sorts, which is a taste in fashion I've picked up from my grandma, of all people.

Grandma Mullins was my most favorite relative in the world. She's an eccentric, sixty-something, free-spirited individual—the kind of lady who's always smiling, but you feel like you might be missing the big secret behind it.

Grandma's tall, slim, and graceful. Her hair is straight like mine, but it's a beautiful chestnut brown, and it looks like it was purposely streaked with gray highlights. She always dressed in light flowing clothes with way too many layers and styles of jewelry on at the same time, but somehow it works. She was going to be throwing my birthday party for me this week.

"Portia!" my mom called from downstairs. "It's time for breakfast!"

I groaned, hearing my name. I didn't hate it exactly, but my dad goes on and on about it. He's the one who chose it. It was sort of a joke he did, using a play on words.

My dad and his buddies were really big into cars in high school, and according to the many stories I've been told, they used to have some heated verbal disputes over whether their favorite car was called a "Porsche" or a "Porscha" in their pronunciation. My dad promised his buddies someday he would "own a Porscha." After college, though, he had a hard time finding work in his field of expertise. He ended up becoming an encyclopedia salesman and working his way up through the company, but he quickly began to see his car dream fade. Then I was born, and he suddenly found a way he could own a "Porscha" once again. He wanted to even spell my name like the car, but, thankfully, my mom put her foot down.

"Hey, Mom," I said, dropping my backpack at the foot of the stairs.

I gave her a quick peck on the cheek before grabbing a piece of toast from the stack and slathering it with jelly.

"I have to work the swing shift again, so I won't be here when you get home from school," she said.

My mom was a nurse at the Verde Valley Medical Center. I figured she was most likely the reason our family stayed afloat financially, since I didn't think there were really many people out there buying encyclopedias in mass quantities.

"That's okay," I said, looking at the cartoon-covered scrubs she often wore to work with her pediatric patients. "I'll go hang out at Grandma's after I get my jobs done."

"That's fine," Mom said. "Just remember to take out the trash this time before you go."

I sighed heavily. I'd only ever forgotten to take out the trash once, and that was over a year ago. She'd never forgotten it.

I quickly finished the scrambled eggs she gave me, while she rattled on about some of her patients, before carrying my dishes to the sink.

"I need to go, Mom. Shelly will be here any second."

"Okay, sweetheart. Have a nice day," she replied while I grabbed up my backpack.

"You too." I sent her a quick smile before I turned to leave.

I ran out the door to see Shelly pulling up in her pink Mustang convertible. I shook my head at her color choice every time I saw it. Her parents bought it for her sixteenth birthday. It totally set off her Barbie doll persona—big blond hair, bright blue eyes, perfect figure dressed in the latest fashions. Not to mention she's dating Brad, the captain of the football team. The two of us were complete opposites, but we'd been friends since kindergarten.

"Hey, girl!" she called out to me, while leaning over to pop open the passenger door. "Hop in!"

"Morning," I said absently, climbing into the car as I licked some jelly off one of my fingers.

Shelly immediately launched into her fabulous date Brad had taken her on over the weekend. I "ooh-ed" and "aah-ed" in all the appropriated places, while I watched the scenery rush by.

I enjoyed the air, which had almost turned fall-like. It wasn't cold yet in Sedona, but the weather had started getting a little of that nice crisp feel to it. That was one of the things I loved about the Arizona climate, the warm seasons hung around for a lot longer than most places. Of course, a nice snow in the winter was always fun too, just to break things up a bit. It could get very hot in the summer, but that was usually when a group of us would take the short drive up into Oak Creek Canyon to go for a swim at Slide Rock State Park.

This year's excursion had been especially fun, since the water was high from a good snow run off. When the water is low you tend to get a lot more bumps and bruises on the rocks, and there is always the occasional swimsuit blowout from those tourists who don't know they should wear cut offs or board shorts to keep that from happening. That's always a good laugh.

My attention drifted back to the present when the car turned into the campus parking lot. Sedona Red Rock High School isn't a large school by any means. It only has about five hundred students. Its red brick buildings were designed to blend in with the giant red rock cliffs that surround the area.

The whole town has a strict color code ordinance. Everything has to blend in. Even the lamp posts are brown instead of silver or green like anywhere else. The color thing can sometimes be a source of controversy. People either love it, or hate it, but it does lend the town a nice sense of ambience, I guess.

Shelly parked her car in the closest space she could find and put the top up. We grabbed our books and walked into school.

There were posters plastered everywhere in the halls with giant scorpions on them, which is our school mascot. The first football game of the season was coming up this weekend. It was a non-conference game against the Snowflake Lobos. Their team had creamed us last year, and everyone was determined to get hyped up so it didn't happen again.

The game also happened to coincide with my sixteenth birthday. Since everyone on this mountain is freakishly insane about football, my party was being held after the game at my grandma's, so more of my friends could come.

I coasted through the school day. The only exciting thing that happened was when Mrs. Skipper lost her glasses and couldn't read our English lesson to us. The glasses were actually on top of her head, which I thought she should've figured out immediately since the whole class was snickering at her under their breath.

Shelly met me in the hallway after last hour, and we headed out to her car. She rambled on about all the unfortunate kids who had to ride the bus home. I wanted to remind her that most kids around here don't have parents who own a multi-million-dollar spa resort like hers.

Her family's resort, which was named after them, was located on top of one of the town's big red rock cliffs. It was called The Fountains at Fontane, and it was a really nice place. I'd dubbed it my third "home away from home," Grandma Mullins's being the second.

Shelly pulled up in front of my house, which was situated at the bottom of the red rock cliff in a Spanish-styled neighborhood. It was a small but pretty adobe-looking home, complete with wooden beams and an interior courtyard, graced with a bubbling fountain. It wasn't anywhere near as fancy as Shelly's, but I loved it.

"You want to come over later?" Shelly asked as I exited the car.

"Thanks, but I'm going over to my grandma's this afternoon," I said, shaking my head.

"Oh. Well, tell Grandma Milly I said hi."

"I will. She'll be sad you didn't come with me." I smiled at her.

"I would, but I have a ton of homework." She gave an exaggerated eye roll. "Apparently, my teachers feel I have way too much free time on my hands."

"Yeah, I have some I need to do too. I'll call you later." I stepped away from the vehicle.

"Okay. Talk to you then!" She drove off, waving her hand in the air behind her as she sped up the hill.

I turned and went inside, dumping my books on the kitchen table before I began doing my list of after-school chores. I was done quickly, and a short time later polished off the minimal amount of homework I had to do.

Grabbing an apple out of the fruit bowl on the counter, I headed out the door and walked up the street toward the highway, where my grandma's shop was located.

Grandma owns one of those metaphysical shops that are popular in this area. It's called Milly's Lotions, Potions, and Notions. It's a fun place to hang out, with books on all sorts of subjects, as well as an assortment of crystals and candles for purchase.

Grandma was very good with herbs too, so she made her own lotions, soaps, shampoos, and other ointments. She packages them up for sale in trendy brown bottles with green labels. She also likes to read auras for people with this cool camera she has. It takes pictures of people and shows the colors surrounding them. Then she reads the image and tells her customers what the colors in their auras mean.

She also held meditation classes once a week where she taught people how to achieve a deep state of relaxation. These classes were conducted in a very calming room in the back of the store. I used to go to them with her, but she started paying me to run the register on those nights instead.

She had another small room added on to the rear of the store after she met Babs, a local massage therapist, and they decided to partner up together. Babs is a wonderful person, and she and Grandma fast became best friends.

I arrived at the store, stepping inside. The soft lighting and mellow music, along with the pleasant herbal smells, always felt serene to me.

"Hey, Lollipop!" Grandma called out from behind the counter where she was rearranging merchandise.

Lollipop had been her nickname for me as long as I could remember. I asked her how she came up with the name, and she told me sometimes kids are sweet, and sometimes they just need a good lickin'. I thought that was funny.

"You want to help me stack these new lotions I made today? I've cleared a spot for them over on the shelf in the corner." She nodded in the general direction of a large box filled with bottles.

"Sure," I said. I hefted the heavy box onto my hip and hobbled over to the shelves.

"I also got a new batch of antique jewelry I thought you'd be interested in looking at."

Grandma often purchased antique crystal jewelry which caught her fancy and sold it in her store. She also collected several beautiful pieces for herself. For as long as I could remember I'd always been fascinated by them.

"That sounds great!" I replied enthusiastically, excited to see what she had acquired.

"I thought maybe you'd like to pick a piece out for your sixteenth birthday."

"I'd love to!" I replied with a grin.

I hurried to continue my shelving until all the bottles were neatly arranged in perfect rows. When I was done, I gathered up the box and headed toward the storeroom.

"I'll meet you back there as soon as this customer is finished," she whispered as I passed by, tipping her head toward a woman who had entered the shop.

I nodded and stepped through the funky beaded curtain separating the backroom from the rest of the store.

I broke the box down and stacked it in the corner, where we kept the others waiting for recycling, then went over to sit at the table in the middle of the room. It was large and had bowls and bottles of different sizes scattered across it that were used for grinding and mixing herbs. I studied some of the containers for a few moments before Grandma breezed in.

"Sorry to keep you waiting," she said, moving over to a counter against one wall. She picked up a large, flat wooden case.

"No problem."

She brought the case to the table, popped open the latch, and lifted the lid.

"Wow!" I exclaimed, as the beautiful pieces came into sight. There were pendants, rings and bracelets of all sizes and colors. I greedily took it all in, my eyes flitting over the beautiful craftsmanship of an era gone by.

"See anything you like in particular?" Grandma asked, the same light of excitement in her eyes.

"There are so many choices." I ran my fingers over piece after piece, taking in each design.

The chime on the door in the front of the store jingled, alerting us to the arrival of another customer.

"Keep looking. I'll be right back," Grandma said, heading out of the room.

I continued my perusal of the gems until my eyes rested on a lovely violet pendant. Gently, I lifted it out of the box, letting the heavily tarnished chain fall through my fingers as I held the scrolling silver filigree surrounding the purple crystal. I slowly ran one finger over the smooth and rounded oval stone. It sparkled in the light so beautifully it was almost hypnotic.

I turned the piece over to examine the back and noticed a small symbol etched into the bottom. It was the letter P, in the middle of a tiny heart.

Well, that's convenient, I thought. It was like it was engraved just for me.

Grandma broke the silence when she entered the room again.

"Did you find something that speaks to you?" She smiled, her eyes flashing.

I held up the purple pendant, and Grandma laughed.

"You have good taste. This is the most expensive one in the bunch."

"Oh," I replied, a little downhearted. "I can pick another one."

"Nonsense," Grandma said, patting my shoulder gently. "I'll let you in on a little secret. You don't choose the jewelry. The jewelry chooses you." She reached out and took the pendant from me. "You may have it on your birthday," she added with a smile.

I stood up and gave her a big hug.

"Thanks, Grandma. This is more than I would've imagined."

Grandma laughed again. "It's only part of your present." Her eyes twinkling in secret delight, and I looked at her with anticipation. "No more hints!" she said, shaking her finger at me. "I've said too much already."

Chapter 2

It was Friday and my birthday.

Shelly and I pulled into the parking lot, grabbed our bags, and headed toward the school, chatting between ourselves about my party, which was to take place that evening. I smiled at the few birthday greetings called my way by friends and students heading in the same direction we were.

"Well, that's interesting," Shelly said with a little smirk.

"What is?" I said absently, not following her.

"Vance Mangum is staring at you." She gave an almost inconspicuous nod over her shoulder.

I couldn't help myself, turning my head to look.

She was right. My heart skipped a beat.

Vance Mangum was leaning up against his jet black motorcycle looking straight at me. For a moment our eyes locked, we just stared at each other. I couldn't seem to break my gaze away from him, until I tripped over the curb. Thankfully, Shelly caught me before I fell all the way down.

I couldn't resist a quick peek again to see if he was still watching. He was, of course, and I was mortified. I turned and hurried into the school.

All day long, I found my thoughts drifting back to

the incident.

Vance Mangum was in a class by himself. He was a senior who had the reputation of resident bad boy, yet despite that, every boy in school aspired to be like him in one way or another.

They were always trying to copy his cool messed up hair or getting their holey Levis to look just as good. Some even attempted doing extra workouts to build their muscles so their t-shirts would stretch across their chests like his. But no matter how hard they tried, none of them managed to pull it off quite the way he did.

Of course, the girls adored him. He was totally gorgeous, sporting the looks that went with the physique—luscious, dark brown hair and chiseled features, set off by bright blue eyes lined in thick lashes. The parking lot would come to a virtual standstill whenever he would ride up on his motorcycle, decked out in a black leather jacket and helmet. All the girls would cease whatever they were doing and begin chattering about him together.

I definitely hadn't been immune to him either—often catching myself joining with the masses to watch. In fact, if I were being truthful, I'd have to admit to the secret crush I had on him since I first noticed him.

Vance never had a girlfriend that I could remember. He'd only lived here the past couple of years, and plenty of girls had paraded themselves in front of him hoping to catch his attention, but he just seemed oblivious to them.

His aloofness spawned many wild tales. Stories were told of how he was a drug dealer, or how he'd been in juvie because he had beat up a guy in a bar fight. Another one said he'd gotten some girl pregnant and been forced to leave home to come here to live with his aunt. But the truth was no one really knew anything about him because he stayed to himself.

Shelly had a couple of classes with him. She said he always sat in the very back of the room, and he never said anything unless the teacher called on him specifically, but he always turned his work in on time and never harassed the teachers in any way.

"Do you agree with that, Miss Mullins?" Mr. Harkins's voice popped into my head, breaking me out of my reverie.

"Huh?" I said absently, before realizing I had no idea what the question was.

"You better start paying attention in math, instead of doodling in your notebook." Mr. Harkins frowned.

"Yes, sir." I sat up a little straighter, staring ahead at the problem he was going over with the class.

When Mr. Harkins turned back to the chalk board, I glanced down at my notebook and saw I'd written the name Vance Mangum all over it. I spent the rest of the class furiously scribbling it out before anyone else saw.

Later in the day, Shelly and I were sitting in the lunch room. She was talking away about her frustration with an assignment her honors English teacher had given her, while I glanced inconspicuously around at the other students. I mentally kicked myself over looking for Vance here, since I knew he never ate lunch in the cafeteria. I just couldn't figure out why he'd been staring at me so intently this morning. Frankly, I wanted to see if it would happen again.

I tuned Shelly out, but my attention was immediately averted back to her when she suddenly winced and grabbed her mouth.

"What's the matter?" I asked, concerned at her look of pain.

"I think I just broke a tooth," she replied, throwing a half-eaten cookie with nuts back on her tray then reaching for her cell phone. She leaned over to show me, and sure enough there was a chip out of one of her molars.

She called her mom and told her what had happened. Her mom said she would call her right back, and when she did she told Shelly to leave school and go directly to the dentist.

Shelly asked if I'd be able to get home okay, and I told her not to worry I'd catch the bus, and I sent her grumbling out the door.

The last two hours of the school day passed quickly. I had my art class, which I loved. We were working on creating clay sculptures. Mine was turning out to look something like a pencil holder made by a kindergarten kid, but it was still fun to do. I enjoyed the creative outlet it gave me.

The bell rang, signaling school was out for the weekend. I quickly put away my supplies and washed my hands before venturing out into the hallway. I made the trip to my locker, organized my bag, and then headed toward the girl's restroom.

It was then I remembered Shelly was gone already, and I was supposed to catch the bus. I let out a groan of dismay, quickly turning to run out the door and down the long hallway which led to the boarding gates.

I was almost to the exit when someone rounded the corner and we collided. I dropped my book bag, scattering the contents everywhere. I scrambled about in a rush trying to gather up my things.

"Why don't you watch where you're going?" I said, mostly under my breath. I didn't even look up, but I was completely irritated.

"Hey now. You ran into me," a soft, sultry, male voice returned. I froze. I moved my gaze slowly to the feet in front of me. My eyes continued to travel up—over the black laced-up boots covered by tattered Levis and past the black belt with the silver buckle to the ever-present, tightly stretched t-shirt with a leather jacket slung casually over the shoulder. I noticed the pulsating veins in his neck, and I paused at the soft wide-set lips before looking straight into the piercing blue-eyed stare of Vance Mangum.

I swallowed hard, and my entire vocabulary was suddenly reduced to only one word. “Sorry.” It came out like a whisper, and I wondered if he even heard it.

Vance slowly squatted down to my level with a slight smirk on his lips.

“Where were you going in such a hurry?” he asked, picking up one of my books and handing it to me.

I threw a glance out the glass door just in time to see the last of the buses leave the lot.

“I was trying to catch the bus,” I explained feeling more than a bit dumb. “I forgot my friend, Shelly, had to leave early today.”

“Ah,” was all he said. I was surprised when he continued to help me pick up my things.

He handed me my last book and stood up, reaching a hand out.

I was shocked by the gesture, but I took it, feeling sparks shoot up my arm at the contact when he pulled me to my feet.

“I can give you a ride,” he offered, letting go of my hand, and I felt a little sad at the loss of it.

I couldn’t speak. Vance Mangum had just offered me a ride home. What should I say? I must have stood there looking bewildered because he spoke again.

“Of course, if you’re afraid of motorcycles ....” He let the sentence trail off, almost like he was accusing me of being scared.

"No. Not at all," I replied with a bravado I didn't really feel. I raised my chin a notch, determined not to let him see how nervous he made me. "I'd be happy to accept a ride."

"Great," he said smiling widely, and I almost choked.

I suddenly realized I'd never seen him smile before, and it was devastating to my girlish heart. I'd never seen anything so beautiful—all perfectly straight, white teeth, framed in by those great lips, and masculine dimples that suddenly appeared in his cheeks.

The guy should be a model, I thought to myself. *He'd make millions.*

Vance took off down the hall, and I slung my backpack on, trotting after him like a willing little puppy.

When we reached his massive motorcycle, he took his helmet off the seat and handed it to me.

"Safety first."

"What about you?" I objected, reaching out to take it from him.

"I'll be fine," he replied, swinging his leg up and over the seat while knocking the kick stand up in one fluid motion. "Just hop on behind me and hang on around my waist."

I stood there for a moment struggling to adjust the strap on the helmet after I put it on. Vance reached over to help me with it, tightening it nicely around my chin.

"There you go. Perfect," he said, and he jump-started the engine.

Yeah right, I thought. I probably looked like an idiot with my hair stringing out of this thing and hanging down over my geeky backpack. Thank goodness I'd worn pants today!

I threw my leg over the seat, settling on it comfortably, and wrapped my arms around Vance's waist. I didn't know what to do with my feet though. Vance patted my leg and gestured to me over the roaring engine to put my feet on the pegs next to his.

As soon as I was situated, he took off, catching me by surprise, and I found myself grasping his waist tightly with both arms. I couldn't help but notice the stares of many onlookers as we passed by them on our way out of the parking lot. I didn't blame them. I was in shock too.

The next surprise I got was when Vance dropped me safely off at my front door without me telling him how to get to my house. I hopped quickly off the bike, even though I was sad to let go of him.

Vance helped me again when I struggled with the chin strap. When he was done, I took the helmet off, handing it back to him.

"Thanks for the lift," I said, trying to casually straighten my wayward hair while hoping he didn't notice how horrible I must look.

"No problem," he said, not breaking eye contact with me.

We waited there awkwardly for a couple of seconds, not knowing what else to say.

"Well, I guess I'll catch you later then," I said, feeling dumb because I knew that wasn't a likely thing to happen.

He nodded, and I turned away, tempted to run up the sidewalk to escape further humiliation.

"Hey!" Vance yelled after me when I'd gone only a few steps.

I turned around.

"Happy birthday!" he said with another devastating smile, and then the engine roared to life and he was gone.

I stood there, staring down the street after him, until I couldn't even hear the engine anymore. With a silly girlish giggle, I turned and ran into my house hoping Shelly would call me soon.

The football game was in full swing by the time Shelly and I finally showed up. She had been at the dentist for a long while, so when she came to pick me up we were running late.

We quickly made our way around the field and squeezed into the standing student section near the pep band. Everyone was intensely following the game as the score was now tied at fourteen early in the second quarter.

I shook my head in amazement at what some of the kids were wearing, or not wearing to be more accurate.

We had the typical row of guys with their shirts off, showing their purple-and-black painted chests. Next to them were the girls in their sports bras with their stomachs painted too. What were they thinking? Hadn't someone in the faculty noticed this yet? I was fairly certain this went way beyond the realm of the school's dress code. That was something I'd always found crazy about sports. People think they need to be half naked to show their enthusiasm. I just didn't get it.

The crowd suddenly roared its approval when one of Sedona's players intercepted a pass from the Snowflake team and ran it in for a touchdown.

"It's Brad! It's Brad!" Shelly screamed into my ear over the deafening sound of the pep band.

"And the extra point is good!" the announcer's voice came over the loudspeaker a few moments later, making the crowd roar again.

The score was now twenty-one to fourteen, in favor of the Scorpions. The rest of the quarter was a tough struggle between both teams without either one scoring. When the buzzer finally sounded announcing it was halftime, each of the teams ran to opposite ends of the field to huddle and talk things over with their coaches.

Shelly and I walked out of the bleachers and headed up the hill toward the concession stands.

"Brad's doing so great tonight!" Shelly said with a big smile, linking arms with me.

"He always does well." I laughed at her. "That's why he's one of the captains."

"Oh, I know," she sighed. "It's just ... he's always much more fun after winning a game than losing one."

"I'm sure most athletes are the same way," I reminded her, moving to take a place at the end of the line.

We waited our turn and ordered sodas, but when we turned to walk back someone called Shelly's name and motioned for her to come over.

"Hang on a sec," she said to me and turned to throng her way through the thick crowd.

I walked over toward the fence to wait for her, but stopped short when I saw Vance was leaning up against it casually watching me, his arms folded across his chest.

I stood still for a brief moment before having a second of bravery, and I walked up to him.

"Hey. Thanks for the ride again," I said, feeling extremely stupid. What was I doing talking to him like I knew him?

"Any time," he replied, his gaze flickering over me.

"Really?" I blurted out before thinking. I felt the crimson color of my blood flooding my face as the heat crept into it.

"Why not?" He gave a half grin. "I kind of enjoyed running in to you."

I met his piercing eyes—stare for stare—trying to

see if he was just messing with me, before breaking contact with him and becoming suddenly interested in the ground beneath my shoes. I toed a crack in the sidewalk.

"Do you like football?" I asked, not knowing what to say and glancing at him out of the corner of my eye. I'd never noticed him at a game before.

He looked over toward the field and shrugged slightly. "It's okay, I guess." His eyes moved back to capture mine once again.

I laughed out loud. "Don't let the fans hear you talk like that. You might get mauled. People around here love high school football," I said, wondering why I couldn't stop babbling on like an idiot when I was around him.

He laughed a little at my response but didn't reply, instead just quirking an eyebrow at me like he was puzzled by something.

I stood there awkwardly for a few more moments before I heard Shelly call my name.

"I need to go," I said, still feeling stupid. Why did I need to explain myself to him?

He didn't reply, so I turned to walk away. I stopped after a few steps and looked back. "Hey, I'm having a birthday party tonight. You're welcome to come." I found myself holding my breath while I waited for his reply.

He seemed to ponder this for a few seconds before he answered.

"Maybe," was all he said, continuing to stare at me with that unreadable expression of his.

I returned his look for a couple of moments, wondering what he was thinking of my invitation, before turning to walk off to join Shelly.

"Were you talking to Vance Mangum?" Shelly asked with a disbelieving look on her face.

"Yeah," I replied, my head still swimming over the

interaction with him.

"Wow! Twice in one day!" she exclaimed. "I think he likes you. He never talks to anyone."

"Whatever!" I laughed, nudging her with my elbow. "Let's go sit down before the second half starts again."

She linked her arm with mine, hurrying me toward the stands. I couldn't resist one more glance over my shoulder, toward Vance. But when my eyes rested on the fence, I discovered he'd already gone.

Chapter 3

My party was going dismally and it was all the fault of those stupid Snowflake Lobos. I don't know what their coach said to them at halftime, but they came roaring out onto the field for the second half and proceeded to slaughter our team like a well-oiled machine. The final score of the game ended up being forty-two to twenty-one.

Several of the Sedona football players were here now, drowning their sorrows in my pink lemonade, while girlfriends hung on their shoulders trying to cheer them up.

Shelly was sitting on Brad's lap over at the picnic table, her arms draped around him as she tried to give him a pep talk.

The group of girls clustered around the stereo kept playing melancholy songs one right after another, serving to only enhance the gloomy mood.

I sighed and jumped off the small half wall surrounding Grandma's well-groomed backyard. I walked under all the hanging Chinese lanterns into the kitchen, letting the screen door bang shut behind me.

"Having fun?" Grandma asked, pulling a pan of her steaming enchiladas out of the oven, filling the air with wonderful aromas.

I let out a pitiful harrumph. Grandma cast a quick glance at me.

"Don't worry, Lollipop. It'll get better I'm sure."

"We should've planned this party for tomorrow." I descended with a sigh into a chair at her small dining table, laying my forehead on it.

I heard Grandma place the enchiladas on the stovetop. She came to sit next to me, sliding her hand over to cover mine.

"Everything will be all right. Let's get the food served and open presents. That always makes everyone feel more festive." When I didn't move she told me to go outside and put on some livelier music.

I pushed away from the table and meandered back out the door to go across the porch to where the stereo was. I picked through the selections before pulling the slow playing mood music out and put in my favorite pop artist.

As the strong beat poured through the air, Grandma began bringing the food to the table. Shelly hopped up to help, and I snagged a classmate named Wes, recruiting him to keep the fast music playing, and followed after her.

We quickly had the table loaded with the most delicious looking meal of red and green enchiladas with Spanish rice. The chips and salsa, along with a mouthwatering seven layer dip, soon had everyone looking a little bit peppier.

Grandma had several folding tables she'd placed end to end, to make one giant table decorated in bright fiesta colors. In the middle of each of the tables were sombrero hats that had the brims filled with chips, with a bowl of salsa or dip sitting in the top of the hat. Just as she predicted, my guests were soon sitting around the array, talking and laughing while the late night meal was going on.

We had a good time visiting and joking with one another, and when everyone looked like they were finished eating, Grandma surprised me by bringing out a giant piñata in the shape of a donkey. A couple of the guys helped her string it up from the large tree in the middle of her yard.

Since I was the birthday girl, I got nominated to go first. After I was blindfolded, I made a few feeble attempts to hit the swinging cardboard animal, but only managed to connect with it once, and that was just a slight brush. I eagerly pulled off the blindfold and passed it on to someone else before I made myself look any more foolish.

As it turned out, the piñata was just what the guys from the football team needed to get them going. They started to eagerly take turns, each one trying to outdo the next while their girlfriends laughed and cheered them on.

I suddenly realized we were all having a great time, and my eyes sought out my grandma who was watching the whole game play out with a large smile on her face. She snuck a quick wink at me. I smiled back at her, then moved back toward the rear of the group since some of the guys were getting pretty aggressive with the baseball bat.

Finally, the piñata gave a great crack when Brad whacked it with a super hard hit. Candy flew everywhere. Shelly ran over with a squeal to pull Brad's blindfold off and gave him a little kiss on the lips, while all the other kids scrambled at their feet gathering up candy. I laughed to myself at the funny picture they all made and wished I had a camera to capture the moment.

"Time for presents!" Grandma called over the din. She grabbed my arm, shuttling me over to a seat near a table where several gift bags were piled.

She placed a funny looking bow on my head and handed me a gift bag to open.

"This one is from Maggie Pratt," she said, reading the tag.

I shot Maggie a smile and began removing the tissue paper from the bag. Maggie and I had chemistry together, and she was a really sweet girl.

I opened presents for about ten minutes while Grandma wrote everything down on a list so I could send out thank you notes later. When we were all done, I was sitting next to a nice stack of gifts and feeling a little overwhelmed at everyone's generosity toward me. Grandma went back into the house and proceeded to bring out my birthday cake.

I had to admit the cake was pretty impressive. It was in the shape of a star with three tiered layers. There was one candle in the points of each of the stars and one in the very center of the cake on the top layer, making a total of sixteen. It was decorated in pink frosting with little white beaded accents around the sides.

My friends broke into singing the happy birthday song while Grandma lit the candles.

"Make a wish!" someone yelled, as I leaned over to blow the candles out. I was amazed to find an unbidden picture of Vance Mangum raced into my mind. I closed my eyes and savored the image for a moment before taking a large breath and blowing out all the candles.

The group cheered at my success and began lining up for a piece of cake. When Grandma was done cutting it for everyone, I went over and wrapped my arms around her in a giant hug.

"Thank you, Grandma. For everything you've done."

She laughed and hugged me back. "It was the least I could do. I'm just sorry your mom couldn't get off work so she could join us."

I nodded. "I do have another surprise for you, though." She smiled slyly.

"Really?" I looked at her expectantly, wondering what it could possibly be.

"Come with me," she added, stepping away and gesturing with her index finger for me to follow. She led me back into the house, through the kitchen and out into the family room.

"Dad!" I cried out when I saw the debonair looking man sitting in the armchair, reading the newspaper.

"Hey, Pumpkin!" He dropped the paper to the floor, jumping up to greet me.

We enveloped each other in a deep embrace.

"I thought you were in Denver!" I nuzzled my head against his shoulder, realizing how much I missed him.

"It's my little girl's sixteenth birthday! I couldn't miss it!" he replied, tightening his bear hug hold on me. "I'm sorry I couldn't get here sooner, but I came on the earliest flight I could get."

"I'm just glad you're here." I hugged him even tighter. "Mom will be so happy to see you. Did she know you were coming?"

"Yes, she did."

"And she didn't tell me?" I asked, wondering why she would keep such a secret from me.

"It was a surprise!" He laughed and wrapped an arm around my shoulders while we walked back toward the kitchen. "Plus I didn't want her to get your hopes up in case my flight was delayed for some reason."

"It's midnight now, Lollipop," Grandma broke into our conversation. "It's probably time for your guests to be getting home. Why don't you go say goodbye to everyone and get them moving in the right direction? Then you can visit some more with your dad."

"All right. Be back in a minute!" I bounded out the backdoor with a happy spring in my step.

I said goodnight to all my friends and thanked them for coming, opening the side gate to the yard so they could get out easier. I walked them out to the street and waved to them while they loudly piled into their different vehicles and drove away.

I went back into the yard, through the gate so I could close it and secure it tightly. Then I proceeded to go about picking up plates and cups that hadn't made it into the garbage can.

Soon Grandma was at my side helping me clean up. We visited while we made quick work of restoring the place to its normal order. We left the Chinese lanterns hanging though, because Grandma said she wanted to enjoy them for a little longer.

After we were done carrying the last of the dishes into the kitchen, I turned to start loading the dishwasher, but Grandma stopped me.

"I can do those later. Come sit at the table for a minute. I want to talk to you about something."

"Okay," I said walking over to the table and sitting down. "Where did Dad go?" I added, looking around and not seeing him anywhere.

"He's doing something for me," Grandma said, picking up a flat rectangular black box off the counter. It was tied with a purple ribbon. She came and sat down at the table and pushed the box across the surface toward me.

Even though I knew what was in the box, it still took my breath away when I opened it. My beautiful purple pendant on its silver chain lay stretched out across the black velvet lining. I gently lifted it out.

"Thank you, Grandma," I said, and she helped me to fasten it around my neck. I fingered the smooth purple stone once again. "I can't stop looking at it. I don't know why," I whispered. "It feels special already, almost ... magical." I laughed out loud at my stupid statement.

Grandma sat back down next to me and reached out to take my hand.

"I told you there was more, remember?"

I nodded, wondering what else she could possibly have in store.

"I'm going to tell you something you'll probably find a bit unbelievable. All I ask is that you listen to me openly, without judgment, and try to understand."

"Okay," I said, feeling a little bit apprehensive at her sudden seriousness.

Grandma squeezed my hand. "I am a witch," she said with a sudden twinkle in her eye.

I looked at her, scrutinizing carefully, before I burst out laughing.

"Yeah right." I rolled my eyes, looking round the room. "So is this some kind of candid camera joke you and Dad are trying to pull on me? Nice try. I know you two have a wonderful sense of humor, but sorry, I'm not buying it."

Grandma patted my hand, stood up, and went over to pick up a candle off the counter. She brought it back to the table and set it squarely between us. She cupped her hand around the unlit wick and blew on it slightly. It immediately burst into flame.

I jumped up, knocking my chair over in the process, and stood for a moment just staring at the flame. After a minute Grandma reached over and pinched it out.

"Oh, I get it," I said, the pieces of the joke clicking into place for me. "It's a trick candle! Anyone can do it."

I leaned over the candle and cupped my hand the same way she did and blew gently on the wick. Though it was slow, the candle sputtered to life once again.

"See!" I gestured proudly. "A trick candle!"

"Well, actually Portia, you're a witch too." She smiled gently.

"What?" I stammered, wondering what she was hoping to accomplish with this line of play. Had she lost her ever-loving mind? What was going on?

"You're a descendant from a long line of witches and warlocks," Grandma said, fixing me with her gaze.

"I thought warlocks are supposed to be evil." I blurted out the first thing that popped into my head.

"Some are. Just like some witches too. As with all things, it's a matter of choice," she replied, watching me carefully. "I happen to be the High Priestess for a very good coven, though."

"A coven?" My mind was spinning like it was on a roller coaster. I took a step away. "You're the leader of a coven."

She nodded, maintaining eye contact with me. I could see no hint of teasing on her face.

"No offense, Grandma, but I'm having a bit of trouble believing any of this. I still think you're trying to pull some big joke over on me, though I don't know what you'd hope to accomplish by that." I stared at her. "I really hope you're trying to pull a joke on me." I added the last part slightly under my breath.

"That's to be expected. Will you allow me to show you something?"

"Be my guest," I said, waving my hand through the air, wondering what she could possibly be up to.

"Follow me then," she replied.

We left the room and walked down the hall, stopping at her linen closet which she opened.

"Sheets? That's what you wanted to show me?" I said sardonically, beginning to feel a little irritated at this continued charade.

Grandma reached into the closet and pressed on something. To my surprise the whole set of shelves slid to the left, revealing a slim door behind them, the same color as the walls. She opened the door, and I could see a small set of stairs leading down into the earth.

"Now you're starting to scare me," I mumbled, suddenly aware there was definitely something serious going on here—much more than a practical joke.

Grandma stepped ahead of me and began to make her way down. As we neared the bottom of the steps, we entered an earthen room that had many shelves covered with bags and jars of different mixtures.

"This is my supply room where I keep most of my herbs and things I need for rituals," she explained.

I looked around, still not too convinced, because I knew she used herbs for her shop. This could just be a storage area, couldn't it? My mind was grasping at straws.

"Come along." She waved her hand for me to follow, and I did so, curious to see what else was down here in this place I'd never known existed. We turned the corner into a narrow hallway and followed it to where a dark cloaked figure was standing near a closed door.

"Here's your robe, Mother," the figure spoke, holding out a dark garment in his arms.

"Dad?" I croaked out. The figure tipped his hood back so I could see his face.

"Well, Pumpkin, what do you think of all this?" He smiled widely at me.

I sputtered and choked before I could speak. "But

you're an encyclopedia salesman!" I blurted out. It was all I could say as both he and Grandma laughed.

"That's just a cover for his real work. Right son?" Grandma patted his hand affectionately, taking the garment from him.

"Which is what? Super warlock?" I exclaimed, feeling as if my whole world just tipped upside down.

"I know it's a lot to take in, Pumpkin. Just try to be patient." Dad continued smiling. "We'll explain everything to you."

"Actually, your dad's the High Priest of our coven," Grandma interjected, and I could hear the proud note that rang in her voice.

"This is unbelievable." I drug a hand over my face while my brain tried desperately to process all this new information. My whole life suddenly felt like a sham.

Grandma donned her robe. "We're taking you to meet the rest of them, so please be respectful. I'll answer your questions later when we're finished."

"I'm meeting who? The coven? Now?" I asked incredulously, still wondering if there was some way this could all be some sort of giant prank.

Grandma and Dad both nodded simultaneously. Dad opened the door. Grandma walked in first, and he followed. I took a deep breath and stepped through the entryway wondering what I would find.

This room was also made of earth and lit by candles sitting on large ornate candelabras in each corner. In the center of the space was a round table covered with a red cloth. On it were purple crystals in the shape of a star, with a pillar candle lit in the middle. But what really caught my eye were the cloaked and hooded figures surrounding the table. There were ten other people in the room besides myself, Grandma, and Dad.

Dad spoke first, extending a hand out toward me. "This is my daughter, Portia."

"Blessed be, Portia," came the unified reply of both male and female voices.

I didn't know what to say, so I didn't say anything. I was sure the shock was apparent on my face. This did not appear to be a gag.

Grandma came and took my other arm, and the two of them led me together up to the first hooded member of the group.

"This is Portia," she said to the cloaked individual.

A man's hands reached out and took both of mine. He brought my knuckles to his lips and kissed them slightly.

"Welcome, Portia. Blessed be," he said. He dropped my hands and removed the hood of his cloak. "My name is Hal," he added with a smile.

Grandma led me to the next individual in line, this time a woman.

"This is Portia," she repeated again.

"Welcome, Portia. Blessed be," the woman repeated, kissing my knuckles in the same fashion as the man before her and then removing her hood.

I was shocked to see Babs, the massage therapist who worked at Grandma's store. She smiled softly at me.

Grandma continued to lead me around the circle, introducing me to each individual. Each one extended a welcome before they removed their hoods. I was amazed to find several people I knew.

Bruce was a local restaurant owner I'd seen around town and when our family had eaten dinner at his place on several occasions. Alice was a Pilates instructor at The Fountains at Fontane, and a good friend of Shelly's parents. A couple of my neighbors were there also, Sharon and her brother Fred, who lived across the street from each other, a couple of houses down from ours. The rest were new to me though, and I noticed then we had reached the last individual in the circle.

"This is Portia," Grandma said once again.

"Welcome, Portia. Blessed be."

My heart stopped beating at the sound of his voice, and the light kiss that brushed my knuckles sent static shock through my entire being.

The figure removed his hood, and I stared straight into the bright blue eyes of Vance Mangum.

Chapter 4

It was two o'clock in the morning. The members of the coven had all gone, and I was sitting at Grandma's kitchen table with her and dad.

"Do you have any questions?" she asked me sweetly, as if nothing was even amiss.

"Oh, I have questions," I replied a bit loudly, my irritation getting the better of me. "A lot of them!"

"Well, start asking," Dad said, patiently. "That's what we're here for."

"I thought we were Christians, for one thing," I stated, pulling the first thought that came to me out of my head. Even though our family had never been what people would consider super religious, my whole upbringing and belief system were being challenged. "Or were all the times we went to church just part of this illusion the two of you created?"

"We are Christian, Portia. All of that is true. We've never tried to lead you astray in that regard," Dad stated calmly. "Being a witch is just part of who we are, our genetic makeup, if you will. It doesn't take away our belief system. We've always believed in God and Jesus."

"I thought witches worshipped some goddess or something." I realized I knew absolutely nothing about witchcraft other than what I'd seen in stories, movies, or heard in history class.

"Some covens do," Grandma explained with a nod of her head. "It's the same as any belief system anywhere. The people choose what religion they believe and what they're comfortable with. Ours just happens to be full of Christian people and we choose to believe in God as our higher power. But we also believe that magic can come from many different elements and directions—even some involving other religious beliefs."

"Okay." I let that sink in for a moment. I guess that made sense, sort of.

"What else do you want to know?" my dad asked, and I knew I had to find out about the next thing or my curiosity would kill me.

"Vance Mangum," I said, not a question but a statement.

My dad sighed and sat back in his chair, shaking his head slightly.

"Vance has been a member of the coven for the past two years since he came here," Grandma said, when my dad didn't answer. "His aunt's in our coven also. You met her tonight, the woman named Marsha. Only she isn't exactly his aunt."

"What do you mean?" I was totally curious.

"Vance is under the protection of our coven," Dad spoke up.

"For what reason?"

"We're hiding him." He hesitated for a second before continuing, "From his father."

"What? Why?" I demanded to know.

"It's Vance's story to tell," Grandma interrupted. "But please trust us, Portia. His father is a very bad man."

"Is Vance a ... a," I faltered for the right word, "a warlock then or not?"

"He's one of the most powerful warlocks I've ever seen at his age," Dad answered truthfully. "I've never encountered powers like his in someone so young, or even in most adults."

I grabbed my head between my hands and rubbed my temples, resting my elbows on the table. My mind was throbbing with unanswered questions, but there was just too much to comprehend all at once.

"Why don't we all go to bed?" Grandma suggested, reaching out to squeeze my shoulder. "We can talk more about this tomorrow. Let's get some rest for now. The two of you are welcome to stay here tonight."

My dad shook his head, pushing away from the table to stand up.

"I can't, Mom. Stacey will be home from the hospital soon, so I'll go home to sleep. Portia can stay here, though," he offered. "That way you can show her some more things in the morning. Is that okay with you, Pumpkin?" he asked me, and I nodded my head wearily.

"All right then. Drive safe and have a good night, Sean," Grandma replied, giving my dad a peck on the cheek.

Dad gave her a quick hug, turned and hugged me. "Get some sleep. It'll all be better in the morning, I promise."

I nodded numbly as I returned his embrace.

After Grandma shuttled him out the door, she locked it and led me down the hall to the guest bedroom.

I'd always loved spending the night in this room. It was decorated in beautiful sky blue and white colors. The white four poster bed was covered in a thick down comforter, and the mattress was one of those comfy beds made with tempered foam stuff astronauts used on the space shuttle.

Grandma removed the throw pillows from the bed and turned the covers back.

"I think you still have some tank tops and shorts in the drawer over there from the last time you stayed," she said, nodding toward the dresser.

I went to check and found one of my white tops with a pair of tan plaid boxers.

"Yeah, they're still here." I pulled them from the drawer.

"Good. Get some rest," she said as I sat on the bed.

She bent over and kissed my forehead before she walked out the door, closing it behind her.

I changed my clothes and climbed into bed, pulling the comforter up to my chin. I closed my eyes, but I couldn't fall asleep. Too many things were racing madly through my mind as I replayed my entire life, looking for discrepancies in my personal history.

Of course my mind kept flitting back to the things I'd learned about Vance tonight too. Suddenly a whole lot of things about him were beginning to make more sense, and I couldn't help but wonder what all the kids at school would think if they actually knew the truth about him—not that they would ever find out.

Oh, my head hurt. I reached up to rub my temples wondering if anything would ever feel normal again.

I'd been lying there for several long minutes, contemplating the possible advantage of going to rummage through Grandma's medicine cabinet for something to help my impending migraine, when I heard a sound at the window. I jumped and looked over at it, but didn't see anything unusual. I sighed thinking my overactive imagination must be getting the better of me, so I closed my eyes.

No, there it was again. There was definitely something tapping on the window. I got out of bed and stood there for a minute. I took a deep breath, sucking in some bravery, and pulled the curtain back quickly. I saw nothing but the hedge.

I sighed, rolling my eyes at my self-induced paranoia. I quietly eased the window sill up, thinking perhaps a branch or something from the bush may be hitting the pane. I leaned out to look for the offender.

A large hand clamped over my mouth. I opened it to scream, but the voice that cut through the still night stopped me.

"Don't be scared. It's just me," Vance whispered into the air, and he removed his hand.

"Are you trying to give me a heart attack?" I asked, more than a bit irritated, my breath coming in quick little gasps. I placed a hand over my heart, which was pounding out of my chest, in a futile attempt to calm it.

"Not really." He laughed quietly, his gaze skimming over my scantily clad form in the moonlight. "Though I can understand how you might have come to that conclusion."

"What're you doing here, Vance?" I asked impatiently, even though my skin still thrummed where his hands had touched me.

"I came to see if you'd like to go for a ride," he replied, as if that were obvious.

I looked him over, considering the new information I'd learned about him, but only pondering his request for about half a second. If there was one thing I was absolutely certain of tonight, it was that I wanted to spend more time with Vance. I was completely intrigued by him.

"Yes, I would. But I need to get some pants on real quick." I glanced down at my attire, biting at my lip.

"That might be beneficial," he said with another sultry look over me, followed by an appreciative smile. "I'll wait here." He turned to lean up against the wall, folding his arms over his chest.

Hurrying over to where I left my clothes lying carelessly on the floor earlier, I pulled my jeans on over the boxers, buttoning them while slipping my feet back into my shoes.

I wondered if the incessant pounding in my heart would ever go away, but I didn't delude myself that it was due to the shock I'd just had. He was the one causing this reaction in me. I smiled before I headed back to the window.

I swung my legs up onto the sill, and Vance helped me slide out to the ground. He grabbed my hand, and I felt that current shoot through me once again. I wondered if he could feel it too or if my imagination was running overtime. He led me down the street past a couple of houses to where he had parked his bike on the corner.

I shivered a little and rubbed my sleeveless arms.

"Maybe I should've grabbed a sweater," I chattered, realizing in my hurry to join him I'd forgotten the cooler weather.

Vance immediately took off his leather jacket and placed it onto my bare shoulders.

"Thanks, but what about you?" I slipped my arms into the soft worn leather, noticing the scent of his aftershave which clung to it.

"I'll be fine." He smiled at me, giving me a wink. "If I get cold, you can keep me warm."

I blushed, unable to speak as I wondered what he expected me to do exactly.

"I'm just kidding, Portia," he chuckled. He swung his leg over the seat of the motorcycle and handed me his helmet.

"You remember the drill?"

I nodded and placed the helmet over my head. He had to help me with the strap, but soon I was on the seat behind him, ready to go.

Vance jump-started the engine, and it roared to life. I brazenly wrapped my arms all the way around him, laying my bulky helmeted head against his back as he took off.

We raced through the night air up to the stop sign on the main highway. Vance turned to the right and we proceeded up the road toward Oak Creek Canyon.

We'd traveled a few miles when Vance slowed down and made a left turn onto a small dirt lane. We crossed over a small bridge that spanned the creek and drove up the steep narrow road on the canyon wall. We only went a short way before the road ended.

Vance parked the bike behind a stand of trees. He helped me off, removed my helmet, placing it on the motorcycle seat.

"Where are we going?" I whispered.

"I'm taking you to a little place I like to go when I need to be alone." I silently pondered the reason he would bring me to his private sanctuary.

He reached over and grabbed my hand, leading me through the trees and brush. We climbed our way upward for several minutes before we stopped, and I looked around in amazement.

We were on a large stone slab that jutted out over the edge of the cliff. Below us were the tops of the trees, and here and there we could see Oak Creek glittering in the moonlight through them. Above us were some of the sheer rock cliff faces that dotted the valley, and above them was the beautiful bright moon and stars.

"This is breathtaking," I said, listening to the sound of the river below us.

"I thought so," Vance agreed. He sat down on the rock, letting his legs and feet dangle over the edge and leaned backwards onto his hands.

"Have a seat," he said, nodding to the space next to him.

I sat down, opting to cross my legs and rest my hands in my lap. After a few minutes of easy silence Vance spoke up.

"So you've had a busy day," he commented, flashing me one of those dimpled grins, making my heart do flip flops all over again.

I nodded.

"Still taking it all in?" he asked.

"Yeah," I replied and then let out tiny laugh. "Well, I would be if I knew where to begin."

"Well, I figured you'd have questions you wanted to ask me after tonight."

"I do," I said honestly. "If you don't mind."

"That's why we're here." He seemed completely relaxed with the subject. "So go ahead."

"Are you really a warlock?" I jumped straight to the point, realizing I really needed someone to talk to about all this.

He looked directly at me and nodded once.

"And what does that mean exactly?" I asked, still feeling more than a little baffled over everything, but comfortable with him for some reason.

"It means, like you, I can do magic."

"But I don't do magic," I replied quickly.

"But you can," he responded. "That's the difference."

He sat up straighter and lifted his closed fist toward me. He suddenly flung his fingers out, and a small ball of flame danced in the center of his palm. I could feel the heat generating from it.

"It's hot," I said, my eyes wide in amazement. "Why isn't it burning you?"

"Because I generated it," he explained, the light of the flames flickering over his chiseled face. "Hold out your hand now."

I held out my open palm and he placed the ball of burning fire into it, and it was so hot I could hardly stand it. Before I could drop it a cooling wave shot through my fingertips, and suddenly the fire was frozen, locked inside a piece of ice.

Vance's quiet laughter rumbled in his chest.

"How'd you do that?" I exclaimed, lifting my hand to examine the peculiarity.

"I didn't. You did." He smiled at me. "The magic's inside you. You just need to learn how to consciously use it."

He took the ice-encased flame and threw it onto the rock. It shattered into a million pieces and disappeared.

"Other than no one telling me about it, why didn't I know about my powers until now?" I asked him, truly curious about what he was telling me.

"It seems to manifest itself around the age of sixteen for most people."

"Is that when you got yours?"

He shook his head. "No. For some reason I started manifesting around the age of five."

"Is that good or bad?"

He shrugged. "No one really knows. My mom and dad were excited since they were both magical.

"My dad was the leader of their coven. Of course, that was before he got involved in some heavy, dark magic. My mom started to notice the signs, though at first she was in denial. It wasn't until she started observing that I was taking on some of his dark traits she became really scared. She thought he was molding me to become like him. I was ten by then."

"What did she do?" I asked captivated by his story, wondering what kind of dark traits he actually referred to.

"She ran with me at first, but he was always able to find us. Finally, she met this witch in another coven. Her name is Marsha—you met her tonight. She explained the situation to her and begged for her help. Marsha agreed. She got someone to fake some documents so Marsha looks like my aunt, and she took legal custody of me. We've been running ever since."

"What about your mom?" I asked, my heart feeling a twinge of guilt for pushing him to divulge things which were difficult.

"I don't know what happened to her." I heard a touch of longing enter his voice. "That was part of the agreement. We were never to contact her again."

"That must've been horrible for you both," I replied, knowing how I would've felt if I'd have been in his place.

"It is for me. I just want to know she's all right." He stared out wistfully into the night sky.

"So what brought you here?" I tried to gently steer the subject in a different direction.

"Marsha heard of your family and their coven. She came here and explained our situation, and they agreed to offer us protection. That's part of what your dad is doing when he's gone. He's scouting things out, making sure we're still safe."

"Wow," I said in surprise, thinking about all the times my dad had been gone from home recently. Could he have been out helping Vance? "I'm starting to see my dad in a whole new light."

"He's a very good man," Vance said sincerely.

"Oh, I know that," I replied. "I just mean ... encyclopedia salesman? Really?"

Vance laughed with me.

"So why all the mystery and everything at school?" I asked, changing the subject to a slightly easier topic for him.

"I figured if I stayed aloof, people wouldn't get too close." He shrugged. "It's easier to stay hidden that way."

I mulled that over in my head for a few moments. "Then why are you here with me?"

He sighed, sounding a little frustrated. He stood up placing his hands in his pockets and began walking back and forth in a line.

"Well, for one thing, you'll be the thirteenth member of our coven, which will make us the strongest we can be. That's a good thing."

"Oh," I replied, almost feeling a little sad but not really sure why. "Is that the only reason?"

"Well." He paused, looking slightly uncomfortable. "No, not exactly." He hesitated again.

"It's okay. You can trust me," I said, trying to offer him some kind of encouragement to continue.

He stared at me for several seconds. "You've been calling for me," he finally blurted out.

"I've been ... what?" I said, confused. When had I ever called for him?

"You've been calling for me," he said again. "Maybe you don't realize it, but it's happening a lot lately—mostly when you're asleep. But you did it consciously today when you were blowing out the candles on your birthday cake."

My face flushed crimson. "How can you know

about that?" I asked in amazement.

He walked back over to me reaching a hand down. I slipped mine into his, and he pulled me to my feet. We were standing toe to toe, and a breeze stirred up slightly, swirling around us. He reached to tuck a stray hair blowing across my face back behind my ear.

"We're linked for some reason, you and I," he said, his eyes searching mine intently.

"Linked?" I whispered, my throat dry.

"It doesn't happen very often," he explained. "But when it does it's usually something very special. I hate to use the word, but it's kind of like," he hesitated again, "like we're soul mates. Connected in a way that's extremely unique."

"But we barely know each other," I said, my heart beginning to beat rapidly at what he was telling me.

"I understand why you feel that way, Portia, but try not to be afraid when I tell you I know you better than you think I do. I've been watching you for a long, long time—a couple of years, in fact. I just couldn't say anything to you until you found out about your magic. I promised your dad I'd stay away from you until then."

He seemed almost relieved to share this with me. I knew his words should've struck me as being odd; however, something in the depths of my spirit began to sing. I knew he was speaking the truth. My eyes began to water as the emotions flooded my body with no place to go.

"What does all this mean?"

He shook his head. "I don't know. But I'm betting we'll find out," he whispered back. He reached down and took both of my hands into his, interlocking our fingers together, resting his forehead against mine.

We stood that way for a while looking deeply at each other for the first time, and I felt like we were reading, without words, into one another's souls.

"I'd better get you back to your grandma's," he said, finally breaking the silence.

I nodded, unsure of what to say.

He led me back through the woods to the motorcycle, and a short time later I was safely back through the window, into the guest bedroom.

"Goodnight, Vance," I whispered through the opening.

"Blessed be, Portia," he said back quietly, running a finger down my cheek, and then he was gone.

I thought it would be even more difficult to go to sleep this time, but I'd been awake almost the whole night. I fell asleep quickly, but my dreams soon turned to tortured nightmares. I was running from something, trying desperately to get away, but I couldn't see through the mist that was following me. I only knew whatever was in there was bad, evil, and I couldn't let it get me.

"Vance!" I called his name out into the darkness as the fog threatened to overcome me, and suddenly he was standing there before me. He grabbed me with both arms, pulling me to him.

"Portia," he said, and I reveled in the heat and close contact of him. I buried my head in his chest. "Portia, it's only a dream. You're safe at your grandma's house, remember?"

I suddenly sat straight up. I was wide awake and trembling in my grandma's guest bed. The dream had seemed so real. Vance had seemed so real.

I calmed my breathing and lay back on the pillow, wiping the sweat from my brow.

My mind was buzzing with remnant thoughts, but I tried to latch onto something safe and comfortable to ease my mind.

Soul mates. The word kept ringing over and over again. What did it really mean to be someone's soul mate? Was it even a real thing? I wasn't sure of what was happening between us, but I could think of a lot worse things in life than being the soul mate of Vance Mangum. I found myself hoping he was right.

After several moments of dwelling on the possibility, I finally drifted to sleep once again.

Chapter 5

Something was tickling my nose, and there was a loud motor-like sound ringing in my ear, but I couldn't quite place what it was. I rolled over in bed and buried my face into the pillow.

There, that was better.

No. Now something wet was licking my ear.

What?

I instantly made the jump to full awareness, bolting up in bed. I snatched the covers up protectively, looking around for the intruder.

I didn't see it at first since its white fur blended in with the down comforter, but a large, fluffy cat climbed up the blanket and nuzzled itself under my chin.

"Well, hello," I said, amazed to find my unexpected visitor. "Where'd you come from?"

As if in answer to my question the cat looked over toward the window and I could see I'd left it open.

"Oh. Well whose kitty are you?" I stroked the long white fur.

The cat jumped up and placed both paws on either side of my neck nuzzling against me as if it were hugging me. I laughed while I checked the cat, looking for a collar or identification. There was none.

"Well, I'm sure someone is missing you. Maybe I

should advertise I've found you. Are you male or female?"

The white ball of fur then proceeded to drop down to my lap and rolled onto its back. I reached over to scratch its belly.

"I see you're a female," I said, laughing.

It was almost like this cat could understand everything I was saying. I picked up the ball of fluff and proceeded to pad out into the hall, toward the kitchen where breakfast smells were coming from.

"You're up early," Grandma said without turning from the stove.

"I was awakened by a visitor," I replied, laughing. Grandma turned to look at me then, noticing the giant cat in my arms.

"Oh!" She removed the pan from the heat and came to stroke the animal. "Well, that happened fast!"

"What did?" I asked, not following.

"This cat is your familiar," she said knowingly.

"My what?"

"Your familiar," she said again happily while scratching its ear. "A familiar is a spiritual helper to a witch."

"I left the window open," I explained. "She just wandered in."

Grandma smiled. "A familiar will choose the witch, not the other way around."

"How do we know she's not just someone's lost cat?"

"Ask her to do something for you. If she does it, you'll have your answer."

I thought for a minute, thinking this task was harder than it sounded. I'd never asked a cat to do something for me before.

"Cat," I said, feeling a more than a little dumb not knowing what to ask for. I looked around and spied several leaves on the grass outside. "Bring me a leaf." I wondered what in the world I was doing.

The cat jumped out of my arms, pushed the screen door open with her nose and ran out into the yard. A few moments later she was back at the door meowing to get in. I opened it, and the cat bowed its head to pick something up and trotted into the room. It dropped a leaf at my feet.

"Well, paint me purple and call me stupid," I muttered in complete amazement.

"Don't talk like that! You might jinx yourself someday," Grandma said sternly.

"Jinx myself? Is that really possible?"

"You have to be careful how you say things now. Your words will have extra meaning," she explained. "By the way, what're you going to name your cat?"

I thought about it for just a few seconds.

"Jinx," I said, and we both laughed. "Is that name okay with you?" I looked at the fur ball. The cat purred loudly, rubbing between my ankles.

"Welcome to the family then, Jinx." I bent to pick up the beautiful animal. I nuzzled her fur, while Grandma stroked her again.

"Come eat some breakfast," Grandma said, straightening to go wash her hands in the sink. She pulled a saucer out of the cupboard and set it on the counter.

I sat dutifully at the table, while Grandma poured milk in the saucer for Jinx and placed it on the floor. Jinx hopped out of my lap and ran straight to it.

Grandma dished us up some eggs, sausage and toast, along with a large glass of orange juice. Then she sat down to join me.

"So how was your night out with Vance?" she asked casually just as I was putting a forkful of eggs into my mouth. I choked.

"You know about that?" I said coughing. I reached for my juice and downed a big swallow.

"Of course I do. I'm a witch too, remember?" She laughed. "Next time you two can feel free to use the front door. It's easier than the window. That's why I was surprised you were up so early this morning. You've only had a few hours of sleep."

"You aren't mad?" I was surprised she seemed to be going so easy about this.

"No. Vance is a good kid. He needs someone to talk his troubles over with, and I think he'll be good for you too. I noticed last night there's a strange energy between the two of you, but I think it's a good one."

We continued eating in silence for a few more moments, and the things Vance had told me during our visit drifted through my mind.

"What did his dad do?" I finally asked her, but my grandma shook her head, unwilling to answer the question.

"We won't discuss his deeds here. I prefer to do it in a circle of protection. It's safer that way."

"What's a circle of protection?" I would never feel comfortable with all this witch stuff.

"Finish your breakfast," Grandma replied. "Then I'll take you down into the basement. We'll get started on your training, and I'll teach you about some of this stuff."

We finished our food, and cleaned up after ourselves. Then we made our way to the linen closet, and Grandma showed me exactly where to press on the third shelf from the top to activate the hidden spring mechanism. Soon the narrow door was revealed again, and we made our way down the stairs and into the first room we'd entered on the previous night.

Grandma walked over to the wall where a wooden table

stood with a bench scooted up underneath it. She pulled the bench out, sat down and invited me to sit next to her.

"So the first thing you need to know is the Earth will provide you with pretty much everything you'll ever need for your magic.

"Here you can see we have all kinds of herbs. Some of them I've grown fresh, others I have ordered from unique places.

"There are herbs in their natural forms, some have been pressed into oils, and some have been placed in capsules, or powder forms. It's a bit of a pharmacy of sorts. These things can all be used in rituals and healings."

She stood and walked over to an aisle that ran between the sets of shelves and motioned for me to follow. We walked back through a few rows of the herbs before she turned down one with different articles.

My eyes widened when I saw gems, crystals and stones of every color imaginable. They were all lying in velvet-lined boxes, each stone labeled in its spot.

"There are so many," I whispered, continuing to follow her down the aisle.

"These are all amulets used in our rituals or to make talismans." She turned to finger the smooth purple stone hanging at my neck. "This is your talisman. It's why you were drawn to this particular stone. It'll help to protect you from harm, and it has been charged with magic from our coven. You should always wear it."

I reverently touched the gem at my neck, having a whole new appreciation for it.

"Is that why you said the jewelry picked me?" I asked curiously, and she nodded.

"The energy from the necklace was attracted to your energy," she said, and beckoned me to follow her again.

We rounded the next aisle, and I was surprised once more. This row contained all sorts of objects. There were sharp double-edged knives, silver goblets, incense burners, sticks, swords, silk cloths of many different colors, and even a large black pot.

Grandma went over and picked up one of the double-edged knives.

"This is called an athame," she said. "It's a witch's personal knife, used in rituals and spell casting." She placed the knife back and touched one of the silver goblets.

"This is a chalice, also used in rituals. There are a lot of all these items here since the whole coven meets here often. In fact, most of the things you see here are used in our rituals."

She pointed out the swords, telling me they were used in casting circles, censors for the burning of herbs to keep unwanted energies away, and the Hazelwood sticks were actually wands of some sort, used to channel magic through, though not very often.

The large black iron pot was a cauldron, and I found myself having to press back a giggle at the image of my grandma stirring over it. Next to it were smaller bowls which were used for grinding herbs.

There was a narrow wooden door at the end of this aisle, and we stepped through it into a very tiny, but organized, wine cellar. Most of the wine was in bottles lying on curved wooden wine racks, but there were a couple of small barrels that were stacked up on each other in the corner.

"This is our wine cellar. We often use wine in our rituals, but sometimes we just like to have a drink too." Grandma laughed, giving me a wink. "But we try not to indulge too much. Everything in moderation, you know." She turned to walk back out of the room. "Any questions?"

"Thousands," I replied, not even knowing where to start.

"Don't worry, dear. It'll become natural to you over time. The more you use it, the more comfortable it'll become until it's second nature to you." She paused for a moment. "So there's something delicate I need to ask you."

"Go ahead."

"Are you willing to become a member of the coven?"

"I thought that was a given," I replied, not realizing I had any say in the matter. I'd thought it was already a done deal. Wasn't that why she was telling me all this stuff?

"It must be of your own free will and choice," she stated. "It's the only way your magic will truly bind with the rest of ours."

"Then, yes. I'm willing," I answered without hesitation. I knew she and my dad would never purposely lead me into something harmful.

"Very good," she replied, smiling. "We'll hold the initiation ceremony with the others tomorrow then."

"There's an initiation?" A sudden case of nerves fluttered through me. I wondered what that would entail.

"Yes. You have to be officially accepted by the coven. That'll be what binds our magic together."

"I see," I said, even though I really didn't. "Is there anything special I need to know for this ceremony?"

"No. Just wear this." She handed me a black hooded robe.

We walked back through the rows of shelves, and she had me place the robe on the table. Then she took me to the ritual room from last night.

"We hold all of our meetings in here. Those candelabras in each corner hold specific candles to call the four elements. The elements are Water, Air, Fire and Earth. The blue pillar is for water. The yellow one is for air. The crimson one is for fire, and the brown one is for earth," she said, pointing to each candle individually.

"Here on the table is where we place the specific things we'd need when casting a circle. You'll see that done in our meeting tomorrow."

She walked over to a small cupboard and pulled out a medium-sized book.

The volume looked worn with age, sort of antiqued. I was surprised, however, to find it was full of crisp white pages on the inside which had been trimmed in brown to give the pages an older look.

"This will be your Book of Shadows," Grandma explained, handing the book over to me. "It's a journal of your craft and experiences. You'll write down important rituals and spells, as well as things you've learned. It'll serve as a guide for you to help you remember things in the future."

"Do you have a Book of Shadows?" I asked curiously.

"I do, and you're welcome to look through it if you'd like to."

I nodded. "I would."

"The book is up in my bedroom. Let's head up there." She led the way out of the ritual room and back down the hallway to the storage room.

I followed her up the stairs, where I found Jinx waiting patiently for me. She rubbed through my legs before following me down the hallway and into Grandma's bedroom.

Grandma went over to a drawer in her nightstand and pulled out a book that was clearly much older and thicker than mine. She handed it to me.

"All I ask is that you please don't leave the house with it. It's very sacred to me since it contains details of much of my life. And please feel free to ask me any questions you may have about it."

I thanked her, and we headed into the living room, where I plopped into an overstuffed armchair and began slowly flipping through the pages of her book.

She'd begun writing in this journal on her sixteenth birthday. It explained her own disbelief when her mother told her about the family powers that had been passed on for generations.

It talked of the very first spell she'd ever tried. In a moment of anger she had commanded a wart to appear on her brother's nose. The book explained in great detail the sorrow she received from that command when she woke up the next morning with three warts on her own nose which lasted for three hours longer than her brother's one hour. This was her first lesson in the Rule of Three, or the Laws of Return. What one gives out will come back to them threefold. She cried when her mother explained to her that the Law of Three didn't always work so precisely, but there were always consequences to magic even though those consequences might not readily be seen.

I was deeply immersed in her book when the front door opened and my mom walked in.

"There you are," she said, bending to give me a hug. Then she caught sight of grandma's book. "Ah. I see you're reading Milly's Book of Shadows."

"You know about all this too?" I asked, feeling

surprised for some reason. She had never alluded to anything magical.

She nodded. "I try to stay out of the way though and leave the magic to the experts." She smiled. "So are you coming home today or what?"

"Sorry, Stacey," Grandma said, entering the room. "I've been giving her the tour." She winked over at me.

"No problem," Mom said. "I was just wondering if she was ever going to come home and open her birthday present from her dad and me."

That got my attention. "I have another present?" I asked, jumping out of the chair and handing my grandma her book.

"Yes, silly. You didn't think we wouldn't get you something, did you? Go grab your things and load them in the car."

After I had dressed, Grandma helped me gather up the presents I'd received from my party the night before and carry them out.

"Thanks for everything yesterday," my mom said to grandma. "I was hoping I could get off early, but the hospital was crazy last night."

"No problem. We missed you though. It was great fun, wasn't it, Lollipop?" Grandma replied with a grin.

"It was the best, Grandma." I gave her a hug and a kiss and told her I would come by later, then hopped into the car with my mom.

The drive to our house only took a couple of minutes, and soon we pulled up in front of the garage door. Mom hit the button to open it, and I was amazed to see my dad standing in there with a sign that said "surprise" in big letters. He was standing next to a motorized scooter in one of the brightest shades of green I'd ever seen, with a wire basket on the back. There was a large purple bow on the seat.

Mom clapped her hands together in excitement. "Isn't it great?" she said, smiling.

I wasn't sure if my facial expression was giving anything away as I nodded in horror, trying to keep my fake grin in place. Should I be excited about a granny motorcycle?

"We know how much you wanted a car, but this was something we could really afford, and they're so easy to drive," my mom prattled on gushingly. "As soon as you get your license, you can start driving it to school every day!"

I couldn't deflate her excitement. "Mom, words could not possibly express to you what I'm feeling at this moment."

"Oh! I knew you'd like it!" She threw her arms around me in a giant bear hug. "She likes it, Sean!" she called out the window to my dad.

A lovely picture flew into my head of Vance Mangum on his massive beast of a motorcycle, and then suddenly there I was next to him on my little green moped.

I laughed so hard I cried.

Chapter 6

I hung my head over my book, pretending to read Shakespeare's *Hamlet*, in my English Lit class. My thoughts, however, kept drifting back to the previous night.

I had been inducted into the coven. I'd watched with amazement as Grandma cast a circle, and the whole group called the elements. Then a candle representing unity was lit on the center of the table.

After that I was presented to the entire group again, only this time I called them by name back and kissed their knuckles, while whispering the Blessed Be incantation. Then I was placed in a spot next to Vance, and a chalice was passed around and everyone took a sip of the wine inside.

When that was done, my Dad explained how God created the Earth and we're to respect the things on it, both spiritually as well as physically. He said when we use the things the Earth provides for us in a proper manner, we surround ourselves with the powers of creation and goodness. If we misuse the things we've been given, it calls forth a dark magic that can overtake us.

Grandma then explained the Law of Three, saying

how we're blessed when we use good magic. She also explained how sometimes the consequences of our magic may not show up immediately, so we should always be careful in what we do because the results of our magic can be far-reaching.

When they were done explaining things to me, the group began discussing Vance and his father.

Grandma filled me in on how Vance had been raised by a powerful warlock. They did not speak the name of his father, because they did not want to call his dark energy to them.

My dad said he'd been observing Vance's dad from a distance. He felt that he was still desperately looking for Vance but hadn't found his location.

Grandma explained to me in detail the story of how Vance had begun to manifest his magic at an early age. His father was delighted and had begun using him in their rituals.

Vance's mother noticed through the next few years his dad would often disappear with Vance for long periods of time, several times a week. She started to wonder what was going on and began to watch them closer.

She began to question Vance about what the pair of them were doing when they disappeared together. He would tell her about going to get ice cream, or going to movies and such, and it seemed like father and son were having a great time bonding with one another. But his mother just couldn't shake the bad feelings she was having, so she decided to follow them on their next outing.

She tailed them to a wooded area on the outskirts of town, staying quite a distance behind them to avoid detection as they walked through the trees to a small clearing.

His mom watched as his father cast a circle and called

dark elements in around him. She was horrified when she saw him put Vance into a trace. Then he took his athame and sliced into the young boy at the wrist. He filled a chalice with Vance's blood before sealing the wound over again. Then he drank the blood.

Vance's mother ran back through the woods. She jumped into her car and raced back home. She ran inside, throwing some of her and Vance's belongings into a suitcase, carrying it out and placing it in the trunk of the car. Then she waited for them to come back home, pretending she'd been busy cleaning while they were gone.

His mom called out happily to them from the sink full of dishes she was washing when they returned. Vance bounded up to her, telling her about the great excursion they'd gone on to the zoo. His mother laughed at his stories and told him she was glad they had a good time.

Vance's dad told his mother he would be away at a meeting for work that evening. She smiled and said that was fine telling him she would try to have dinner ready for him when he got home.

As soon as Vance's dad was gone, his mom asked him if he'd like to go out to eat with her. He excitedly went out and hopped into the car. His mother stopped at their favorite fast food drive-through and picked up some burgers for them. Next they stopped at the bank where she cleared out her bank accounts. Then she started driving.

When Vance awoke the next morning they were in a different city far from their home. His mother had driven all night long. She checked them into a hotel with cash, trying not to leave a trail. She used her magic to show Vance what his father had really been doing to him.

After that they kept moving from city to city trying to avoid being caught by his dad. His father came close to capturing them a couple of times, but they managed to get away. Finally, his mother met Marsha and begged her to take her son.

Grandma explained to me that Vance was a very powerful warlock, and by drinking his blood his father was adding to his own strength. She also explained as this exchange was happening, it was beginning to link Vance to the dark arts as well. She told me how they'd done a lot of blessings over him, trying to remove the unwanted attraction, and it was very important for him to be surrounded by good energy. If he were to be overwhelmed by bad energy, it could turn him in a less than desirable direction.

The whole time the story was being told Vance stared at me watching my reaction to everything.

I looked into his deep blue eyes. "I'm so sorry," I whispered, not knowing what else to say.

He didn't reply, but he did reach out to briefly squeeze my hand.

After the meeting ended, I walked with Vance out to his motorcycle. He leaned up against his bike while I stood looking at the stars overhead.

"So how do you feel now that you know I'm the coven's big dark secret? That I'm the bad guy, so to speak?" he asked, folding his arms.

I looked hard at him. "None of this is your fault," I said, wanting to reassure him.

"That isn't the point," he replied. "The fact is I'm the dangerous one. I'm the person who could be turned and destroy everything good about you and your family."

I walked up to him and placed both of my hands on

either side of his face. "I don't believe you'd ever hurt me or any of us for that matter," I searched his gaze. "The very fact you're worried about us tells me the kind of character you have."

He looked at me for several long moments before he reached out, mirroring my move, and placed his hands on the sides of my face, pulling me even closer.

"I hope you're right, Portia." He held me there for a few seconds before placing a light kiss on my forehead. He dropped his hands from me, hopped onto his motorcycle, and started the engine.

"See you tomorrow," he said.

I stepped back from the curb. I gave a little smile and a small wave after him as he drove off down the street.

He wasn't at the school when I'd arrived with Shelly in the morning. I waited by the door for him, but he hadn't shown before the warning bell rang. I brooded about him all day long. I hadn't seen him in any of the halls between classes either, but that didn't mean he wasn't here. We just didn't have any classes close together.

I finally decided to try to find him, trying to tell myself I was just checking on him to see if he was okay. I wasn't quite ready to admit I needed to see him to make myself feel better.

I went into the front office between classes and stood at the counter giving a sigh of relief when I saw Mrs. Parker was working today. She liked me, and I'd earned a few brownie points with her after helping her with a school project recently.

"Hi, Portia! Can I help you with something?" she asked, looking up at me from her desk with a smile.

"I hope so," I said, smiling sweetly. "My friend

brought my books to school for me in his backpack this morning, and I accidentally left my assignment for next period in there. I was wondering if you could tell me what his next class is so I can go get it. I can't find him, and I don't want Mr. Perkins to drop my grade because it's late."

"Sure, no problem," Mrs. Parker said, turning to the computer at her desk. "What's your friend's name?"

"Vance Mangum," I said, trying to seem casual about it.

Mrs. Parker smiled while she tapped his name into the computer.

"I wasn't aware you knew Vance," she said casually. "He's a cute kid. I've worried that he was a loner. Glad to hear he's making some friends."

"He's a nice guy." My heart was beating rapidly at my charade.

"Hmmm ... I'm not finding him," she said, staring at her computer with a frown, and I suddenly had visions of him fleeing into the night without a trace, his evil father chasing after him. "Oh, wait! Here he is! I forgot we had to transfer him into a new class this morning."

"A new class?" Had something happened to him after all?

"Yes," she answered while she wrote some information on a piece of paper. "We just realized his transcript didn't have enough of the required physical education courses on it for him to graduate this year. We had to drop him from one of his electives and put him in P.E. instead."

"So he's in P.E. now?"

"Yes, he should be." She stood and came over to the counter. "They're out on the baseball field today, though, which will make you late for your class, so I wrote a note to excuse your tardy too." She handed me a slip of paper.

I flashed a warm smile at her. "Thanks so much, Mrs. Parker! I appreciate your help!"

"Any time," she replied with a grin.

I quickly left the office and began making my way across the campus, down toward the baseball field. As I approached, it occurred to me that I didn't want anyone to see me since I didn't actually have a real excuse to be there, so I snuck stealthily up behind one of the dugouts. I peered around the corner and began looking through the uniform-clad boys who were out on the field, but I didn't see Vance anywhere.

I saw Shelly's boyfriend, Brad, standing in front of the dugout with a group of guys, but Vance wasn't there either. I was about to give up and walk away when I caught one of their voices.

"Dude, he didn't even dress out," the guy said, and I recognized him as Kurt, Brad's friend.

I followed their gazes up the hill and saw Vance approaching. Massive relief flooded my heart and I found myself releasing a breath I didn't know I'd been holding. I continued to watch Vance walk onto the field over to the coach, handing him a slip of paper.

"Coach isn't even saying anything about it," Kurt continued to complain.

"Maybe he hasn't had time to buy any from the bookstore yet," Brad replied with a shrug.

"I'm just sick of listening to all the girls rave about him," a guy named Jeff piped up. "I went to see Sara after school yesterday, and she went on and on about him like he was God's gift to women. I finally just left and told her to go date him instead. I don't see what the big deal is."

"Take the field, boys!" the coach's voice called out. "Brad, you and Vance here can bat first. Ten pitches each. Try to work the field."

"No problem, coach!" Brad called back to him, and I

saw Vance shrug out of his leather jacket and toss it over the fence, revealing his sculpted arms with their well-formed biceps.

"Now's our chance to show him what the guys at this school are really made of," Kurt said with a grin, smacking his mitt against Brad's arm before running out to take his spot on the pitcher's mound. I could see he was planning on setting Vance up, and it made me kind of angry to think they all would gang up on him like that.

Brad went over to the chain link fence where there were several bats of various sizes and weights hooked into it. Vance walked up beside him to look at them too, and I had to step back a little farther behind the dugout so they wouldn't see me standing there.

"Play much baseball?" Brad asked Vance casually.

"Haven't really had the time," Vance replied, reaching out to turn one of the bats.

"Well, pick a weight and length that feels good to you," Brad said, picking up a bat which was long and looked a little heavier weighted. "Then you can go stand over there and warm up while I hit. Just watch your stance, keep your eye on the ball, and do the best you can."

"I think I'll just use the bat you're using," Vance said, turning to lean casually up against the fence, folding his arms over his chest, and I couldn't help noticing that it caused his arms to flex even more.

"Whatever floats your boat, man," Brad said, shaking his blond head slightly at him. Stepping up to the plate, Brad dug his cleats into the dirt, got into his batter's stance and nodded to Kurt who stood waiting. "Bring it," I heard him say.

Kurt smiled and wound up. He threw a good pitch, and Brad swung, connecting easily with it. The ball soared far out into left field where the fielder ran back and caught it near the fence.

Kurt pitched again, and Brad got another good hit out toward center, which was also caught. The process was repeated over and over, and he hit every single ball with ease, giving the fielders a very good workout.

"Batter up," he said turning to Vance and handing him the bat when he was finished taking his ten pitches.

Vance moved away from the fence, taking the bat from Brad with a sigh and stepped into the batter's box.

"Just do the best you can, son," coach called out to him.

"Okay," I heard Vance mutter under his breath.

Brad stepped back from him to look at Kurt who was positively grinning with anticipation. I knew Kurt was going to give him a bad pitch.

Having watched a lot of baseball with my dad, I recognized when Kurt threw a sinker, and I rolled my eyes thinking Vance wasn't going to stand a chance. I heard the crack of the bat against the ball.

I watched in amazement as the ball soared out over the far field fence. Homerun! I found myself stifling a giggle with my hand, my heart pounding excitedly when all the guys turned to look at Vance incredulously.

Kurt's face slipped to one of angered determination as he bent to pick up another ball. He threw a curve ball this time. Vance hit the pitch with ease, the ball soaring over the fence once again.

Coach and fielders alike stood and watched in amazement as Kurt fed him everything he had in his arsenal, while Vance ate him up like he was candy, knocking every single one out of the park. On the last pitch, I heard the wooden bat crack, and it split into two pieces as the ball left the field once again.

Vance walked out of the batter's box toward Brad.

"Sorry, bro," he said handing the bat back to Brad. "I guess I broke your bat."

Brad just stared at him in amazement, looking completely dumbfounded.

"I said I hadn't had time to play. I didn't say I couldn't," Vance added, cocking an eyebrow at him before he turned to walk over to the fence where he had left his jacket.

"How about going out for the team, son?" the coach called out after Vance.

"Not a chance," Vance replied, and he walked out the field gates while we all just stood there watching him.

My teacher didn't complain at all about my extreme tardiness when I handed him the note Mrs. Parker had given me. I slid silently into my seat and dutifully did my classwork, but I was happy when the bell rang, signaling the end of the class period and that it was time for lunch. I met Shelly out in the corridor next to her locker.

"What do you want to eat today?" she asked me, completely unaware of my current infatuation who refused to leave my thoughts.

That was when I saw him leaning casually against my locker farther down the hall. He gave me a nod of invitation, casting his eyes toward the door.

"Um, Shelly?" I said, not able to take my eyes off him. "Would you mind horribly if I skipped lunch with you and Brad today?"

Shelly looked at me puzzled for a second before turning to follow my gaze.

"Oh," she said, and then the realization hit her. "Oh! No. Not at all. You go have fun!" she said with the emphasis on the "you." "And you better call me later," she added under her breath.

"Thanks, Shelly," I replied laughing. "You're the

greatest."

I walked up to Vance and was amazed when he popped my locker open, took my books from me, and placed them inside.

"How'd you do that?" I said, my eyes wide.

He leaned down to whisper in my ear. "Magic, remember?" His soft breath caressed the side of my face.

"Oh, yeah," I said, unable to keep myself from smiling up at him.

He reached down to grab my hand, interlocking our fingers together, and I felt that ever-present tingling at his touch. We began walking down the hallway. This action caused quite a stir among our classmates, and many of them stopped to stare, some even pointed. I could hear the whispers behind our backs as we passed.

"Silly, isn't it?" I said when we stepped out of the door into the bright sunshine.

"Not at all," he replied. "Now the whole school knows you're my girl."

My heart started pounding in my chest, and I stopped dead on the sidewalk, squinting up into his face through the sunlight.

"Is that what I am?"

He turned to look at me, moving so we were standing face to face. "That's what you are," he replied. His voice was husky with some sort of emotion, his eyes holding mine with a meaningful look. He lifted my face to his with both of his hands and proceeded to kiss me full on the lips, claiming me as his own right there for the whole world to see.

In retrospect, I thought I should've been mad at him for declaring me as his instead of asking me if I wanted to belong to him first. But I couldn't bring myself to care much as I sat across from him in the booth at one of the local fast food joints. He was holding my hand across the tabletop, stroking the back of my fingers with his thumb while we waited for our order. Ever since we'd shared that kiss on the sidewalk, we hadn't been able to stop touching each other.

I sighed again, unable to keep my thoughts from drifting back to that moment. I'd kissed my fair share of boys, and some of those had been good kisses, but nothing had ever been like what I'd experienced with Vance. I couldn't decide if he kissed like a god or the devil, or maybe even a bit of both. It was sweet and sensual, soft at first and then deeper, tender and then rougher, heavenly and more than slightly carnal too. There was most definitely something between us, and I for one was eager to find out what it was.

My thoughts drifted once again to his comment about it being like we were soul mates, and I began to truly wonder if there was some validity to his statement. I was drawn to him like a magnet, and I could already feel my heart strings reaching out to wrap around him. It was both scary and exhilarating. I'd never felt so easily attached to someone before. Suddenly, everything about him was so important to me—his welfare, his happiness, and his safety.

He sat here now staring at our clasped hands. Watching where his thumb rubbed over my skin, I wondered if he were maybe pondering the same things I was. He lifted his head casting me a meaningful look, and my breath caught and I tried to read what he was communicating to me.

Then a slow, sly smile crept across his face breaking my train of thought.

"What?" I asked with a confused grin.

"Did you enjoy the show this morning?" His eyes were twinkling in amusement.

"What show?" I was totally bewildered.

"I knew you were there, you know, hiding behind the dugout. What a sneaky little girl you are." He laughed, and I felt my face flush a crimson red.

"You knew?" I was completely mortified he'd caught me spying on him. "Oh, this is so embarrassing," I groaned, lifting my other hand to cover my face.

He continued chuckling at me. "Why don't you tell me what you were doing there?"

I sighed deeply, seeing no way to get out of this gracefully except to tell him the truth. I dropped my hand but couldn't manage to lift my gaze enough to look in his eyes, so I settled it somewhere in the general vicinity of his chin instead.

"I was worried about you," I confessed.

"Worried?" he said, seeming puzzled by my reply. "Why?"

"Well, you seemed so melancholy when you left last night. I couldn't get you or your story out of my head. I had all these nauseating thoughts of what would happen if your ...," I dropped my voice to a whisper, glancing up to make sure no one was listening to us, " ... if your dad were to suddenly find you. It terrified me to think I could wake up one morning and you would just be gone—poof—like you'd never even been here. Then I got to school this morning and you weren't here. I couldn't find you after class either and ..."

He cut me off. "And you thought the worst happened, so you came looking for me. Oh, Portia. I'm so sorry for worrying you. I had to help Marsha get her car to the shop, and it didn't open until right when school started. Then when I did finally get here I had to go to a meeting and do some schedule changes with the counselor. I didn't even think you might be alarmed about it."

I rolled my eyes. "Well, I feel completely foolish about it now," I said, mentally kicking myself for being such a busy body.

"Don't be." He clasped my hand with both of his. "You have no idea how much it means to me to know you cared enough to do something like that." He got really quiet, looking down at our hands. "I haven't had anyone do something that sweet for me in a long time." He lifted his eyes back to me, and I could see something completely unmasked in them.

Love, I thought. *Really?* I was shocked. But it couldn't be, could it? Not this soon.

The moment was shattered when our order number was called and he released me, standing to go get it, and I was left wondering if what I thought I'd seen had really been there, or if I just imagined it.

Chapter 7

I walked in the front door after school and was surprised to find my mom home.

"I got someone to change shifts with me at work," she explained excitedly. "Let's go take your driver's test!"

Normally, I would've been ecstatic at this idea, but now I knew having my license meant I would soon have to debut my granny motorcycle.

"Oh, Mom," I complained. "I'm really tired right now."

"Nonsense," she replied. "You've been excited about this for months! Now go get in the car."

I tossed my backpack on the nearest chair and rummaged through it for my wallet, checking to make sure I had all the proper I.D. I might need. Then I followed her dutifully out to the car. I looked at our silver Toyota Camry with its dark tinted windows and sighed. I guessed I wouldn't be driving it much like I'd previously envisioned.

We took the drive up through Oak Creek Canyon into Flagstaff, to the Department of Motor Vehicles. Mom got me signed in, and soon I was sitting at a computer taking the written test.

I finished it in about twenty minutes, and it was

graded. I'd missed only a couple of questions, and the lady at the window explained the appropriate answers to me. Then I was introduced to a man who took me out to a driver course that had been set up with orange cones in a paved parking lot.

I got into our car, did all the safety checks, and drove through the course with ease. When I was finished, the man joined me in the vehicle with his clipboard in hand. We left the lot to drive down the street and around the block before coming back to the building.

Soon, I was the proud owner of a new driver's license. After running a few errands, Mom and I headed back toward Sedona. Of course, she insisted on me being the one to drive us home, and I had to admit I was a little bit excited. After all, getting a driver's license is a certain rite of passage for a teenager.

My excitement was nearly extinguished, however, when my mom preached to me about how to drive all the way home. Apparently, she'd conveniently forgotten I'd passed my Driver's Ed class with an A plus, as well as getting a note of commendation from my teacher about my attention to safety. Instead she gasped at every corner we took and hung onto the door handle like she was about to die, or she was repeatedly running her fingers through her dark hair nervously. She kept telling me to slow down even though I wasn't going anywhere near the speed limit.

I tried to be patient with her and chalk it up to mothering nerves, but by the time we got home I bounded out of the car, running into the house and up the stairs to my room.

"Don't you want to practice riding your scooter now?" she called up to me from the ground floor.

"Later, Mom," I replied over my shoulder. "I really am tired now."

It wasn't even a lie. I was completely exhausted mentally. I flopped myself onto my polished oak bed and rolled up into the puffy purple patchwork quilt. I didn't even know I'd fallen asleep, until I felt Jinx nuzzling my face trying to alert me that someone was coming up the stairs.

The door opened quietly, and Shelly crept into my room, shutting the door softly behind her.

"Hey," I said groggily, pushing myself to sit up a little more against the pillow behind me.

"Oh! You're awake!" she said, and happily climbed onto the bed where she sat cross-legged next to me. "Your mom said you were probably still asleep. I was going to leave you a note on your desk."

"I was asleep until a minute ago." I reached out to scratch Jinx behind the ear. "Jinx woke me up."

"All right, so start dishing," Shelly said, petting Jinx also. "I feel like we haven't talked in ages, and I like your new cat, by the way."

"She adopted me," I said as a way of explanation. "I just woke up one morning, and there she was. She seemed content to stay awhile, so I figured why not?"

"How sweet. Now tell me about Vance Mangum." Shelly jumped right into what she was really interested in knowing.

I shrugged, pretending indifference just to make her suffer, even though the sound of his name made my heart begin to race.

"What do you want to know?" I asked innocently.

"Everything, duh!" she said, grabbing a pillow and hitting me with it. I lifted my hands to ward off her attack.

"I don't know what to say. We just sort of seemed interested in each other, and now we seem to be hitting it off pretty good."

"I'll say!" Shelly exclaimed, her eyes wide. "The whole school was buzzing about him kissing you this afternoon!"

I couldn't help smiling at the memory. "That was our first kiss," I said, a little dreamily, as I thought back to it.

"Apparently it was pretty hot. Girls were swooning just from watching it."

"Yeah, and I imagine a few of them hate me for it too," I said, suddenly feeling a spark of jealousy at all of them who had a thing for Vance. "I know several of them had set their sights on Vance a long time ago."

"So how did all this get started?" Shelly asked, digging for more details.

My mind scrambled to make a coherent answer since I knew I couldn't tell her the whole truth. I told her he'd come by and asked me to go for a ride with him after my party. He'd helped me sneak out and had taken me on a moonlit drive to Oak Creek Canyon. Of course, I edited all the magic parts that occurred. I told her he came by my Grandma's on Sunday to see me also, leaving out that it had been for a ritual to induct me into the magical coven my family happened to be the leaders of. This was all becoming a bit bizarre.

"I can't believe it!" she crooned, completely unaware of my omissions. "Vance Mangum! You realize you've just landed the hottest guy in school, don't you? Now we both have boyfriends!"

"Yes, boyfriends who are basically polar opposites of each other," I reminded her. Somehow I just couldn't imagine Vance being too big on the double dating scene.

"We'll make it work out somehow," Shelly said, her optimist personality coming right to the surface.

"Portia!" my mom's voice floated up the stairs. "Dinner's ready."

"Be right down," I shouted back.

"I guess I'd better go too," Shelly said, and she hopped off the bed. "My mom and dad should be on their way home from Phoenix right now. They were supposed to fly in from their trip to Italy this afternoon."

"I'm glad you came by to visit, even if it was only for a minute." I got up and gave her a hug.

"So, I'll pick you up in the morning then?"

"About that," I replied, "I got my license today."

"You did?" she squealed in delight, before looking puzzled at me. "Why don't you seem excited? You've been talking about this for months."

"Follow me." I walked out the door, heading down the stairs toward the garage.

"I'm showing Shelly my present," I called out to my mom, who was in the dining room as I passed the kitchen.

"Did they get you a car?" Shelly whispered excitedly while tugging on my sleeve.

We stepped into the dark garage, and I waited for the door to close fully before I flipped on the light switch.

"Tada," I said flatly, gesturing with my arm over to my new ride.

Shelly's smile faded a little as her eyes perused the neon green scooter. Then she burst out laughing. She walked over to it and fingered the wire basket, laughing so hard she nearly doubled over.

"It's great!" she choked out as the tears ran down her face. "I can't wait to see you drive it to school tomorrow."

"Uh huh." I folded my arms across my chest and tapped my foot against the concrete. "Are you finished yet?"

She held up one finger. "Just give me a minute," she said, trying to calm herself down.

At that moment my mom came out the door into the garage.

"Portia," she said. "I forgot to give you this the other day in all the excitement." She handed me a purple helmet with bright little green daisies all over it, smiling happily at me.

"Oh. Thanks, Mom," I replied, knowing my shame was now complete.

Shelly was positively flushed from trying to hold back the laughter. She managed to keep it in until my mom walked back into the house, before she fell into a nearby lawn chair and howled.

I helped my mom clean up after dinner and went back up to my room to do my homework I'd been procrastinating. I'd just finished my English assignment when my cell phone started buzzing. I reached out and absently answered it, knowing it would be Shelly since she was the only one who ever called me.

"Hey, Shell," I said with a sigh. "What's up?"

"I'm going to have to try a whole lot harder if you're starting to confuse me with a girl," a sexy, baritone voice spoke into my ear. "I'm starting to doubt my kissing skills. Perhaps I need a tutor?"

I couldn't hold back my laughter. "You so don't need a tutor, trust me," I replied, wondering if he could hear the increase in tempo my heart was currently pounding out into my ears.

"So you're speaking from experience then?" Vance asked. "Or am I to assume you're just guessing at my level of skill."

"I'm speaking from experience, of course," I replied, and he grew quiet for several seconds.

"I'm not sure how I feel about that," he said finally. "Just how many boys have you kissed before me?"

"How many girls have you kissed, Vance?" I responded, answering his question with a question.

"Point taken," he said, chuckling after a moment.

"Yeah, that's what I thought." I continued to goad him. "You don't get that good without a lot of practice."

"So you're saying you've kissed lots of guys then, because I think I felt the earth move when you kissed me back."

"Whatever!" I said, deciding it was time to move on to safer subjects. "How'd you get my phone number?"

"I have my ways."

"Are you going to share those ways with me?" I asked after I realized he wasn't going to continue.

"Nope." He laughed.

"Hmm, a secretive stalker. Maybe I should reconsider going out with you. It might not be safe." I regretted my teasing words the instant they left my mouth, considering the things in his life I knew he was worried about.

There was a moment of silence that seemed like an eternity before he spoke again.

"You'd probably be wise to reconsider," he said softly. "And I got your number from your grandma."

"I'm sorry, Vance. I was just kidding, and I spoke without thinking." I was terrified I'd offended him. "There's nothing for me to reconsider either. I'm right where I want to be," I added.

"No harm, no foul," he said smoothly. "So what're you up to tonight?"

"Homework." I gave a miserable sigh. "Do you want to come rescue me?"

"I'd love to, but I happen to be up to my eyeballs in the same stuff myself. If I have to research anything more about the fall of Rome, I may actually fall myself." He laughed and I joined him.

"So was there a specific reason you called?" I asked. "Did you need something?"

"Yes. I needed to hear your voice."

My heart melted into a puddle instantly and was replaced with the giddy knowledge that he missed me.

"Too sappy?" he asked when I didn't reply.

"What? No! I mean ... I mean I miss you too." I laughed nervously. "You just caught me off-guard. That was really sweet, and unexpected."

"I'm going to have to work on my game then, if it's unexpected." He chuckled. "Apparently, I need to try a little harder to let you know exactly how I feel."

"What do you mean?" I asked, feeling nervous butterflies in my stomach at his teasing words.

"I mean if I didn't think your dad would shoot me, I'd drop everything I was doing right now and come over there. Then I would pound on your door until you opened it up and let me kiss you senseless."

My breath caught in my throat. "My dad's not home tonight," I whispered, and I closed my eyes, trying to imagine the picture he'd just painted.

"Hey, Portia, can you hang on for a sec? I'll be right back."

"Sure," I said, wondering what he was up to now.

I waited for several moments and when he didn't come back right away I started working on my math problems. After I'd done about five problems, I glanced over at the clock, wondering what had happened to him. He'd been gone for several minutes.

A thought suddenly struck me, and I jumped up off the bed.

He wouldn't, would he? I glanced in the mirror running my fingers through my hair and rubbed at some mascara smudged under my eyelashes. That was when I heard a motorcycle engine roaring down the street, and laughter started bubbling up from my chest.

He had!

I bounded down the stairs and over to the front door, flinging it open just in time for me to catch him lifting his hand to knock.

He grinned dragging me out onto the step and into his arms, while reaching behind me to pull the door shut.

"Hey, baby," he said, stepping forward and pressing me against the door.

"Hey," I replied breathlessly, grinning up at him.

He dropped his lips to mine, kissing me hotly. His hands ran up into my hair and held my head tightly to his.

I couldn't even move, my knees were shaking so badly. I could feel his kiss like it was running through my whole body, sending little sparks everywhere. I lifted my hands to grip his shoulders, trying to balance myself.

He seemed to sense my need and moved one of his arms around my waist, pulling our bodies into full contact with one another.

I started to slip my arms up around his neck when suddenly he broke the kiss, stepping away.

"I think that's enough kissing for tonight," he said, backing slowly away from me.

"Really?" I asked, unable to contain the

disappointment that wove through my voice, and he laughed lifting his finger to shake it back and forth at me.

"Now, now. We'll have none of that tonight!" He scolded.

"None of what?" I asked, completely confused, watching him as he continued to back away toward his bike.

"No more looking so ... kissable!" He grinned and turned to straddle his motorcycle. "Go finish your homework!" he added, not leaving me time to reply before he jump-started the loud engine.

He backed out of my driveway, his eyes never leaving me until he turned and zoomed away.

I watched him drive all the way down the street, and then stumbled back into the house, trying to collect my senses.

"Who was at the door, Portia?" my mom called out to me.

"It was Vance," I answered back, continuing toward the stairs.

"What did he want?"

Me, I thought, and a huge smile spread across my face wondering how she would react if I actually said that.

"He was taking a quick break from his homework and dropped by to say hey," I answered truthfully.

"Well, that was nice of him," she called back.

"Yes it was." I lifted my fingers to brush my kiss-swollen lips before adding under my breath, "You have no idea how nice."

I showed up at school very early the next morning trying to avoid the most amount of fellow students as possible. I parked at the farthest, most secluded end of the parking lot, and I was just undoing the chin strap on my helmet when Vance roared into the space next to me. I was mortified.

"Nice wheels," he said, with a nod toward the scooter.

"Ha, ha. Very funny." I ripped the helmet from my head, hanging it by the chin strap on the handlebar.

"I'm serious," Vance said, getting off his motorcycle. He sauntered over to pick up my backpack out of the wire basket. He slung it over his shoulder. "You make anything you wear look good."

He snaked an arm around my waist and pulled me to him. We were soon having a repeat of the kiss he'd given me last night. Only this time, I succeeded in wrapping my arms around his neck and pulling him closer to me—really kissing him back.

I couldn't even begin to describe the feeling this gave me. Heat went streaking through my veins, racing through my body, and it was as if the entire world melted away and this was what I was meant to do.

Vance pulled away abruptly, his breathing a little bit ragged.

"Wow," was all he said, but he stared at me hotly.

I didn't say anything. I was too busy trying to breathe.

"I'm beginning to think kissing you might be dangerous," he finally added seriously, his gaze focused on my mouth.

"I think maybe you're right." I felt a little dazed at all the emotions rushing through me.

Vance grabbed my hand, and we started slowly walking toward the school, not wanting to rush our time together.

"So your dreams have been better the last few nights," he stated casually, and I could see he was determined to change the subject.

"What? How do you know that?" I asked, surprised.

"You haven't called to me in your sleep anymore," he replied, as if having me call to him in my sleep was totally normal.

"I dreamed you came to wake me one night," I told him.

"I know, and I did."

"But I woke up and you weren't there," I replied, trying to understand what he was saying.

"I didn't come to you physically. I came to you mentally," he explained.

"You were really there?" I asked, astonished.

"In a sense." He shrugged, nonchalantly.

I sighed. "I have a lot to learn."

He chuckled slightly. "Yes, you do. But I keep telling you there's something special between you and me. I've never experienced a bond like this before. So it's okay if you feel a little confused. This is all new to me too." He opened the door to the school, and we walked into the hall.

We went to my locker first and deposited my backpack, after drawing out the books I needed. Then I followed him to his. We didn't speak much since there were other students and teachers roaming the halls, all giving us stares.

"Walk with me," he said, quietly.

I followed him to a small, out of the way corner. He guided me into it, while shielding me from view with his back.

"When do you start learning more about your powers?"

"Today, actually," I replied. "Babs is going to cover the store for Grandma so she can work with me this evening at her house."

"Cool," he said. "Do you think she'd mind if I came with you?"

"I don't see why she would. You're part of everything that's going on."

"Why don't you give her a call real quick just to make

sure?"

Now I knew why he was hiding me in the corner. Cell phones at school were an absolute no-no, even though nearly every student was hiding one somewhere on their person.

I quickly dialed the store, and Grandma picked up on the second ring. I proceeded to ask her about Vance coming over. I'd just finished the call and snapped the phone shut when Mr. Percival rounded the corner. Vance leaned in to make it look like we were kissing.

"No making out in the halls!" Mr. Percival called out loudly while I stealthily slid the phone into my back pocket.

"Um, sorry, Mr. Percival," Vance said, stepping away from me with a grin. He grabbed my hand, and we headed off together.

I spoke when we were finally out of earshot.

"She says come on over. She'd love to have you there."

"And what about you? Will it bother you?"

I laughed and didn't even bother to respond as we walked up to the door of my first class.

"I'll see you at lunch," I said with a smile.

"It's a date," he responded, gradually releasing my hand as he stepped away.

Chapter 8

Vance met me at Grandma's right when I was pulling up on my scooter. He waited for me to park and get off, before coming over to drape his arm around my shoulders as we walked up the front steps.

Grandma swung the door open before we could even knock.

"Hello, kids!" she called out, stepping to give me a hug, then patting Vance on the back. She ushered us into the living room.

Soon the three of us were in the cellar, where she pulled the wooden table out from the wall. She already had some items sitting on it.

"Have a seat." She gestured toward the benches. Vance and I dutifully sat down together, while Grandma remained standing.

"All right. The first thing I want to start with is a concentration exercise," she said, jumping right into things. "Your magic is already a strong current flowing through you. You'll not always use it in a circle of protection but out in the open if need requires it.

"Since you'll need to be able to call upon your powers at any given point in time, I want you to learn to recognize the energy.

"Just close your eyes now and clear your mind. I

want you to try and think of nothing. Use deep breaths to help calm you, like we use in the meditation rituals at the store."

I did as I was instructed letting my mind drift peacefully, and soon began to feel deeply relaxed.

"Very good," Grandma's voice said softly after several minutes had passed. "Now keep your eyes closed and listen carefully. I'm going to start saying random words, and I want you to think about them like you normally would, visualizing them mentally. Do you understand?"

I nodded.

"Tree," she said.

Instantly, my mind was flooded with the image of a beautiful oak tree in its full green leaves of spring. I could see the gnarled twisted branches as the sunlight filtered through the flittering foliage. I could even smell the tree, and I reached out to touch it.

"Cat," Grandma's voice cut through to me.

Immediately, I was nuzzling Jinx as she rubbed herself up under my chin. I could hear her purr and feel the tickle of her whiskers, and it brought a smile to my face.

"Flower," her voice came again, and I was leaning over the most beautiful red rose. It hadn't completely opened yet, but it was still round and full with the most delicious scent coming from it. I reached out to grab it and felt one of its thorns sink into my finger.

"Ouch!" I said, and I snapped back to reality. I looked at my finger and could see the blood oozing to the surface. "How in the world ...," my voice trailed off as I questioned what I was seeing. I glanced at Grandma and Vance, holding my finger up for them to see too.

"You were manifesting," Grandma said, smiling a look of approval at me.

"Okay. What does that mean?" I asked.

"It means your powers are much more advanced than we originally thought. Normally, only you would experience the things you were seeing."

"You mean you could see them too?" I asked, surprised.

"We experienced it just like you did." Vance held up his pricked finger.

"Amazing!" I said, truly meaning it.

"Your finger is bleeding?" Grandma asked him. "Mine isn't." She showed us her hand. "What did you see exactly?"

"I saw myself reaching out to grab the rose, and it poked me," he said. "Didn't you?"

"No," she replied, shaking her head. "I saw hazy images of Portia trying to pick a flower projected in front of me. I find this very interesting that you experienced it from her perspective. I knew there was something different between you two."

She stared at him for a moment, and I wondered if he would tell her his suspicions about us, but he didn't volunteer any information.

"Hmm. I'll try to do a little research on this later to see if anyone else has kept a record of such a reaction. Let's try another exercise for now though." Grandma picked a wooden bowl up off the table. She placed it squarely in the middle. "Portia, see if you can make this levitate."

She didn't give me any further instructions, so I just concentrated on the feelings I had previously and tried to direct those emotions toward the bowl while thinking of the word "up" in my mind.

It took a few seconds, but I began to distinctly notice the bowl starting to wobble a bit from side to side. I concentrated harder trying to focus all of my energy into that dish. Instantly it lifted off the table, floating several inches above it.

"Wonderful!" Grandma said, clapping her hands. "I can't believe it!"

"Is that good?" I asked her, not knowing.

"It's unheard of on your first attempt. You've much better control of your emotions than one normally does."

She bounded around the table and gave me a hug, while I smiled at Vance over her shoulder.

"Look at the bowl, Milly," Vance said, redirecting her attention. Grandma and I both turned to look at the bowl, which was still floating in the air.

"Are you still doing that?" Grandma asked, her eyes widening.

I shrugged. "I guess so. No one told me to put it down."

"This is amazing," Grandma said, looking at Vance.

"I know," he agreed with an appreciative look.

"What's the big deal?" I asked, not understanding what was so wonderful.

"You kept the bowl in the air all this time even with us distracting you. That's usually the sign of a very accomplished witch."

"Oh." I stared at the levitating object.

"You can put it down now, show-off," Vance said teasingly, with a gentle elbow to my ribs.

I concentrated on lowering the bowl to the table until it softly touched the hard surface once again without making a sound.

"I'm going to suggest something a little unorthodox," Grandma said, tapping her lips with her fingers.

"All right." I was a little apprehensive, wondering what she had in store for me now.

"I want you to wander around the house, and yard, or wherever. Try to use your magic for whatever crosses your mind. Don't hold yourself back, just do anything you feel like doing."

"But what about the Law of Three?" I asked, worried about upsetting some sort of balance and being punished for it later.

"As long as you're not hurting anyone or anything in a bad way, you'll be fine. The Law of Three is there as a guideline. It doesn't necessarily mean something bad will happen to you or a consequence will be immediate."

"Then how come you got warts after casting against your brother?" I asked, not understanding how it all worked.

She laughed at me. "Apparently, you didn't read the part about my mother being the magic behind that. She was trying to teach me a lesson, and it's a lesson for everyone whether they're magical or not. You get back what you put out there. So if you're doing good works, the chances are you'll reap good works in return. But if the things you sow are evil, then that's what you'll harvest as well."

"So it's basically a metaphor?" I said, trying to wrap my head around this pearl of wisdom she was trying to teach me. "It doesn't necessarily apply to magic?"

"It is a metaphor, and it can apply to magic depending on the things you're doing," she replied.

"I'm confused," I said, my head starting to hurt again.

"I'm saying it's not absolute, but you should always try to be aware of what you're doing."

"So, better safe than sorry?" I asked.

"Exactly, but don't be afraid to use your magic either."

"Okay," I said, thinking I kind of understood what

she meant.

The three of us headed upstairs and I began my wandering, not really knowing what to do. I tried to concentrate on the energy flowing through me.

I spotted a glass vase on the mantle. I focused on it and raised my hand slightly into the air, flicking it. The vase swept off the mantle and landed with a loud crash onto the wooden floor, shattering into a million pieces.

Instantly, I felt sorry for breaking Grandma's vase. "Oh no," I cried out, and I leaned over to pick the broken pieces up wishing I could put it back together. I think I was just as shocked as everyone else when the vase reassembled itself in front of me. I carefully reached down, picked it up, and gently placed it on the shelf.

"That was impressive," Vance said and my grandma agreed.

"Can you do that?" I asked both of them.

"Yes," Vance replied. "But it took me a few days to master it."

"Days?" Grandma chuckled, shaking her head slightly. "It took me months."

Not willing to risk damaging the house anymore, I ventured out into the yard and walked over to her flower beds, where the flowers were showing some signs of wilting with the cooler fall air approaching.

I slowly ran my finger over one of the plants, and it immediately began turning greener, standing up straight as the flower burst back into full bloom. I made my way down the entire flower bed until it was completely brought back to life.

"I've seen enough," Grandma said. "It's clear she has good control over her powers."

"But I don't really know what I'm doing or how I'm doing it," I complained.

"Maybe not consciously," Vance pointed out. "But you do in here." He pointed to my head. "That's what matters. The rest will follow."

"You two are the experts," I said, slumping into a lawn chair. "Now what?"

"I think you just need to practice things on your own and see what you can find out about yourself. Each witch's magic is different from the next one. Just like people have different physical features, witches and warlocks all have unique powers that are individual to them. You'll need to experiment and find out what yours are. I'll continue to tutor you on the different herbs we have and what we can use them for. They'll help to supplement your natural magic." Grandma paused a second. "I also think I'll give you a little homework assignment. I want you to write your own spell for something in your Book of Shadows."

"But I don't know anything about writing spells," I reminded her.

"Spells are all individual to the witch or the warlock too. It can be anything you want it to be. Just think about it carefully and then follow your heart and your instincts," she explained. "I just want to see what you'll come up with."

"All right," I said, both a little nervous and excited.

"You two had better get going. It's almost supper time," Grandma said, looking at her watch.

We followed her back in to the house and through to the front door.

"Thanks for everything, Grandma." I gave her a hug.

"It's my pleasure." She squeezed me tightly.

"Thanks for letting me come too," Vance added as we stepped out the door.

"Anytime, Vance," she replied with a smile.

Grandma stood on the porch watching us while we both walked out to our bikes.

"Guess I'll see you tomorrow," Vance said, casting a quick glance at Grandma, and I knew he wanted to kiss me goodbye but having her watching was making him nervous.

I reached up and gave him a quick peck on the lips, even though she was there, lingering for just a moment to enjoy the feel of his lips pressing back against mine.

"I'm glad you came," I said as the breeze stirred up my hair and blew it across my face.

Vance reached out tenderly and tucked the wayward strands behind my ear.

"Me too." He moved away to get onto his motorcycle.

He waited for me to get my helmet on and start my scooter. Then he gestured for me to go first. I was surprised when he followed me home, waving to me as he continued on past our driveway.

I parked in the garage and then went into the house. My mom was working again this evening, and Dad had gone off to another "sales meeting," whatever that meant.

I popped a bag of popcorn, poured it into a bowl, and carried it up to my room.

Jinx was snoozing happily on the bed when I entered. I tried to be quiet, but she still woke up and did her lazy cat stretch before coming over to greet me with a soft meow and a nuzzle.

I told her all about my afternoon, and she listened with rapt attention to me. I thought I could almost sense she was proud of me, which seemed ridiculous when I thought about it.

I settled cross-legged on the bed and decided to work on the spell assignment Grandma had given me. I calmed my emotions for a few seconds before looking over to my desk, seeing my Book of Shadows lying there. I reached out toward the book with my palms open and mentally commanded the book to come to me. It lifted easily and settled into my outstretched hands.

Next, I managed to conjure up a pencil I couldn't see, but I knew was in my book bag. That was exciting for me. Everything else I'd done previously revolved around things I could physically see.

I wrote all these things down in the book, and then sat pondering for a few minutes on what I'd want my first spell to be for. It didn't take me long to figure out exactly what I wanted to do. I would write a protection spell for Vance.

I thought long and hard about it. I was just writing the spell for now, and I wouldn't actually put it into use until Grandma had approved it, so there was nothing to fear. After about thirty minutes I felt like I finally had it down.

A Spell of Protection for Vance.

Items needed:

1 large White Pillar Candle

1 Aloe Plant

Sword

Lock of Vance's Hair

Instructions:

Cast a Circle under a Waxing Moon. Place the pillar candle in the center of the circle and light it. Cut a piece of the aloe plant off and squeeze out the juice letting it drip while walking around the candle in a circle clockwise and repeating these words:

Oh moon, tonight I call on thee
To help me set a spirit free.
Give thy protection on this night,
Ever surround him with the light.
Let no evil near him get.

May only goodness now be met.

Squeeze the remainder of aloe back onto the original plant, and place the bits of hair into the dirt. Give the plant as a gift to be kept near the entrance of the house for protection.

I closed the book with a satisfied feeling, anxious to show it to Grandma and see what she thought about it.

I wasn't surprised one bit when my phone started vibrating, and this time I was positive I knew who it was.

"Hey, gorgeous," I said when I answered.

"Please tell me you knew it was me this time and not Shelly," Vance teased.

I laughed at his joke. "What's up?"

"Well, I'm having withdrawals. You see, I didn't get to kiss you goodnight properly," he complained.

"You could've stopped when you followed me home, you know?"

"I thought I had more homework than I did," he replied. "And I didn't want to interrupt your homework either. I'm trying to be supportive right now."

I snorted. "For your information I don't have any homework tonight. I got it all done at school today."

"Really?" he drawled out. "Well, how would your mom feel about me taking you out on a last-minute date then?"

"My mom is at work tonight, and my dad's out of town," I told him. "How would you like to come over here?"

"Be there in five minutes." He chuckled.

"Sounds great!" I said, my face breaking into a wide smile, and I hung up the phone.

I headed downstairs to the kitchen to rummage for some food, wondering if Vance had eaten anything yet. I pulled some items out of the fridge to make hamburgers and placed a pan on the stove to heat.

There was a soft knock on the door, and I heard Vance

call out. "Hey, it's just me."

"I'm in the kitchen," I answered, continuing to pat out the hamburger patties.

He entered the room, coming to a dead stop, clasping a hand to his chest. "And she cooks too," he said with an exaggerated sigh. "Can this relationship get any better?" He came up behind me and moved my hair away from my neck, leaning down to place a kiss there.

I tried to ignore the immediate goose bumps that raised, and I laughed.

"You might want to hold your remarks until you've actually tasted it," I said, tipping my head to the right when he dipped in to kiss my neck again.

"I have faith in you," he said against my skin. I savored his touch for a moment before shoving him away with my elbow.

"Stop it. You're distracting me, and you're not going to get the chance to find out if I can cook or not."

"I'm okay with that too," he said, stepping toward me again.

"Vance! I mean it!" I held up my greasy hands. "If you come near me again I'm going to wipe this all over that pretty leather jacket of yours."

That turned out to be the trick. Vance held his hands up in defense and backed away from me.

"You wouldn't dare desecrate the jacket, would you?" He grinned.

"Try me and find out," I threatened, taking a step toward him, though I knew I would never do anything to hurt that wonderful coat of his. He looked amazing in it.

He shrugged out of it and placed it on the back of one of the kitchen chairs.

"I think I'd better put this baby out of the line of

fire," he said, and I laughed at him, turning back to wash my hands at the sink. "What can I do to help?" he asked.

"There's some plates and cups in that cupboard up there, and bags of chips in the pantry around the corner if you want to get those out."

He helped me prepare the rest of dinner, and soon we were sitting down together, enjoying our food.

"I was right," he complimented after finishing his first bite. "You're a good cook."

I couldn't help my smile.

When we were finished, we went into the family room and turned on the television snuggling on the couch together.

"This is so much better than homework," Vance said, running his hand through my hair absently.

"I agree," I replied, looking up at him.

He winked at me, and I smiled.

"Tell me something about you I don't know," I said, suddenly wanting to hear everything I could about him.

"Like what?" he asked, light laughter rumbling in his chest.

"I don't care. It can be anything. I just want to learn more about you." I bit at my lip in anticipation.

"Hmmm." He pondered my request for a moment. "How about this? I really, really, love sugar cookies."

"Sugar cookies?" I asked, giving him a questioning look and wondering if he was messing around with me.

His face grew wistful then. "My mom used to make them for me when I was little." He stared into my eyes while he continued to stroke my hair. "I remember coming home from school and the whole house would be filled with the most wonderful smell. I'd run into the kitchen and she'd just be pulling a tray out of the oven." He chuckled lightly, caught up in the memory. "I think she timed it that way.

She'd always let me eat one warm while the others cooled, and then we frosted them together while I told her about my day. I've loved sugar cookies ever since."

He smiled softly at me, and I felt my eyes tearing up for him, knowing he'd lost so much that was precious to him in his life.

"Sorry. You probably think that's a little too corny. Am I going to need to give you my 'man card' now? Did I just lose all of my masculine allure?"

I silenced his depreciating remarks by leaning over to kiss him on the lips, surprising him for a second. But then he pulled me up onto his lap, wrapping his arms around me, and kissed me back. I threaded my arms around his neck, hugging him to me even closer, letting him freely explore my mouth for several long moments until I finally pulled away from him. I rested my forehead against his, looking into his eyes.

"That was a wonderful memory, Vance. Thank you for sharing it with me."

"Now it's your turn," he said back to me, placing his hand against my face and running his thumb over my bottom lip.

"My turn?"

"To tell me something I don't know." He smiled, moving to gently place a soft kiss near my chin.

I took a big breath and prepared to spill my guts. "I've had a crush on you for two years, since your first day of school here." I held my breath waiting for his reaction, but he only smiled and leaned in to kiss me on the cheek this time.

"That doesn't count. Pick something else," he said.

"What do you mean it doesn't count?" I asked, pulling back from him a bit, giving him a confused scowl.

"It has to be something I don't already know." He

grinned slyly.

"What?" I asked him skeptically. "What're you saying?"

His self-assured smirk grew even bigger. "I'm saying I'm aware of your crush and have been ... since my first day of school here." He laughed now, his eyes full of mischief.

"How's that even possible?" I said in shock.

"I can't tell you." He smiled widely.

I got up off his lap and stood over him with my hands on my hips.

"Why not?"

He stood up taking a step toward me, so I stepped away from him trying to keep some distance between us.

"Because then I'll have told you two things about myself, and you still haven't told me one thing about you," he said, stalking toward me again.

I moved backward until I hit the wall with my back, and he continued walking until he had me trapped there with his body.

"Come on. Let's hear it," he said, running his hands up my arms, leaving a trail of goose bumps in their wake before he stopped and rested them on my shoulders.

"When I was younger I wanted to be a fashion designer. I played with Barbie dolls until I was thirteen, mixing and matching all their outfits so I could have runway shows with them," I blurted out, the heat of my humiliation spreading quickly through my body.

He let out a soft laugh at that, sliding his hands up my neck and into my hair. I knew he was trying to distract me, and he was succeeding.

"See, that wasn't so hard."

"Tell me how you know about the crush," I prodded, trying to keep my head. "I never told anybody about it."

He leaned in closer to me, his lips brushing against my ear when he spoke.

"I can hear your thoughts," he whispered seductively. "I've wanted to tell you but …." His reply was cut short when his phone started buzzing, and he dug it out of his pocket so he could answer it.

"Hey, Marsha. What's up?" he asked.

I could hear Marsha speaking rapidly about something through the phone, and Vance gave a sigh while he listened.

"No problem," he said. "I'll be right there." He ended the call, sliding the phone back into his pocket. "I'm sorry, Portia, but I'm gonna have to run now." He gave me a look filled with true regret.

"Is everything okay?" I asked him, suddenly worried something had happened with his dad.

"Everything's fine," he assured me. He gathered me into his arms and gave me a sweet kiss. "Thanks for having me over. I had a wonderful time, and I promise I'll answer all of your questions later."

"Okay," I replied, sad that he had to leave already. I slipped my hand into his while I walked him to the door. He stopped to kiss me hungrily one more time before he stepped outside.

"See you tomorrow, baby," he called over his shoulder. In another second, he'd started his motorcycle, and then he was gone.

Chapter 9

The next day after school I went to Grandma's shop and I brought my Book of Shadows with me so she could read through it.

There were no customers when I entered the store, and Grandma was sitting in a wooden chair near the register reading an ancient-looking tome.

"Hi, Lollipop!" she said, getting up and coming over to give me a hug. "How was your day?"

"It was good," I replied, following her back behind the counter.

I reached into my bag and pulled out my book, handing it to her.

"Wonderful! Did you already write your spell?"

I nodded.

Grandma flipped open the book and began perusing through the pages, while I wandered around the store feeling a bit self-conscious.

"I can't believe this," I heard her say.

"What?" I asked, wondering instantly what I'd done wrong.

"How did you know the correct ingredients for your spell and the proper moon phase?"

"I don't know. It just seemed like the thing to do," I explained to her, feeling a little moment of glee that I'd done something right. "A white candle seemed pure, and aloe is known for its healing. As far as the moon goes, I have no idea where that came from," I added, laughing.

"Well, it's a very good spell," Grandma said. "Simple, yet to the point. I also find it very enlightening that you wrote it specifically for Vance."

"He's very important to me."

"I've noticed the connection. He's a good kid, and the two of you have good karma together," she replied with a smile.

"Well, he still worries about the negative energy attached to him. He's afraid he'll do something to hurt me, or my family."

"I wouldn't brush off his worries. It's a legitimate concern," Grandma agreed. "There'll probably always be some sort of attraction to the dark side of things for him. I guess the important thing is he doesn't want it to be that way. As long as he's fighting it, then he's progressing." She paused then, giving another glance at my book. "I think you should give him a call and tell him to come down here."

"Okay," I said, all of a sudden wanting to test his proclamation that I called to him mentally.

Grandma handed me the phone, but I denied it.

"I want to try something else," I said. I closed my eyes for a few seconds and centered the energies running inside me before speaking.

"Vance, come," I said, though I felt extremely foolish doing it. I opened my eyes and looked at Grandma.

"Has that worked before?" she asked, seeming a little skeptical.

"I've never tried it before," I said, laughing. "Vance is always claiming I subconsciously call to him. I just want to see if there's any validity to his claims."

"He says you call him?"

"I guess, when I have bad dreams and stuff he says he can hear me calling him," I explained. "And he said something yesterday about being able to hear my thoughts, but we were interrupted before I had the chance to ask him anything further about it."

"Was this before or after you joined the coven?" she asked.

"Before," I replied. "I've slept like a baby ever since my initiation."

"That's interesting. What were your dreams like?"

"I never really could tell. I was always surrounded by this thick intense fog, but I could feel a dark presence lurking there, like something was chasing me. I would run from it and then I would wake up, except for one time. Vance showed up in my dream and told me to wake up."

"I think I'll talk to your dad about this," Grandma said, looking a little bit concerned.

"Why?"

"Well, it could possibly have some significance to what has been going on with Vance and his father. You weren't protected by the magic from the coven at that time. Perhaps you were sensing something."

"Oh." The bells to the door chimed and Vance entered the store.

"Vance, come?" he asked, shaking his head at me. "Am I like your loyal dog now or something?" He grinned his sardonic grin at me.

"Sorry," I said apologetically. "I just wanted to see if it would work. Apparently it does." I walked over and wrapped my arms around his neck, reaching up to peck him on the lips.

"You're forgiven," he said with a smile, wrapping his arms around me and pulling me closer. "I was driving toward your house anyway. So why did you need me?"

"Actually, I wanted to show you something," Grandma spoke up. "Come here."

Vance released his grip on me and put his arm around my shoulder. We casually walked over to where she was holding my book.

"Take a look at this." She handed it to him.

He dropped his arm from me and took the book leaning up against the counter. After a few seconds, he lowered it to look at me.

"You wrote your first spell to protect me?" he asked, looking completely amazed.

I nodded, a little embarrassed now.

"It's a good spell," he said, placing the book down and walking back behind the counter. He soon emerged with a pair of scissors. "Here." He handed them to me.

"I don't want to mess it up," I replied, suddenly nervous about cutting it. I loved his hair.

"You'll only need a little bit," Grandma said. "Just cut some off the very end."

I carefully selected a spot where my cutting wouldn't be too noticeable and snipped some of his fine wavy locks, being careful to keep my hand cupped to collect the trimmings.

"Wait just a minute," Grandma said, going into the back and emerging again in a couple of seconds. She was holding a small silver locket on a chain. "Put his hair in this."

I took the locket, gently placed the cuts inside and then snapped it closed. Vance lifted the locket from my fingers and placed it around my neck next to my talisman.

"Wearing this will help to charge it for your ritual. The more you touch something, the more you charge it with your magic," he explained to me, his fingers lightly brushing my skin in a gentle caress when he was finished.

"The same goes for your candle," Grandma added, not noticing the interaction that had set my heart racing. "Go pick out the white pillar you want, thinking of the purpose you're going to use it for. Use it only for the purpose you intended it for—otherwise, you'll waste the magic you put into it."

I went over to the candles, selected one and carried it over to the register to pay for it, but Grandma shook her head at me.

"These are my gifts to you," she said, "in celebration of your first spell."

"Thanks, Grandma," I said giving her a hug.

"I just have one request," she added. "May I come to watch you work it? There's a lovely waxing moon right now."

"Of course you can come. Then I'll know if I'm doing it right." I turned to Vance. "Will you come too?"

"I wouldn't miss it," he replied.

We picked a pretty, little, secluded spot Grandma knew about, out under one of the giant red cliffs which dotted the land. We'd been able to drive most of the way, but had to set out on foot to get exactly where we wanted to be.

Grandma led us in a mediation ritual while we waited for the sun to set completely and for the moon to begin its ascent into the night sky.

It was very serene up here, and we could see the bright stars shining above and the lights of Sedona twinkling below. There was only the softest of breezes every now and then, which rustled the leaves of the foliage. It was the only sound other than our breathing.

We sat that way together, not moving, until

suddenly I felt the urge that now was the time to perform the ritual.

I got up without speaking, walked over to where I'd placed the candle next to the aloe plant, and lit it. I picked up the sword and used it to draw a circle in the dirt around myself, the candle, and the plant. When it was complete, I lifted the sword and pointed it in each direction—North, South, East, and West—acknowledging the presence of the elements. Then I broke the piece of the aloe plant and squeezed out the juices around the circle while reciting my chant.

When I was done, I knelt on the ground next to the plant and opened the locket, gently shaking the small pieces of Vance's hair into the soil surrounding the aloe. I mixed the hair into the dirt until I couldn't see any of it anymore. I stood and raised my sword once again thanking any listening deity, the moon, the earth and her elements, and I released my circle. I blew out the candle and picked up the potted plant. I carried it over to Vance, placing it in his hands.

"Blessed be, Vance," I said, leaning forward to give him a kiss on the forehead.

"Blessed be, Portia. Thank you," he replied, pulling me back toward him and placing a soft kiss against my cheek.

I laid awake for several hours into the night thinking of all the things that happened in my life over the last few days. I also pondered over the energy I'd felt flowing through me during my first solo ritual tonight.

Jinx suddenly lifted her head and nudged me under the chin with a soft meow. That was when I heard the tapping at the window. I went over and opened it, finding Vance standing on the trellis outside.

"What're you doing here?" I whispered with a smile, surprised to see him.

"I couldn't sleep," he explained. "You have too many things running through your head."

"I'm keeping you awake?" I said, wide-eyed.

He nodded. "Can I come in?"

"Of course," I said, moving to the side. He easily boosted himself in through the window, walked over to the bed and patted the sheets.

"Come get in," he said with a nod.

I lifted an eyebrow at him questioningly, but he'd never given me a reason not to trust him, so I complied with the request.

He quickly covered me up and hopped up next to me, but on top of the quilt. He laid his head on the pillow next to mine and wrapped his arms around my shoulders, so that one arm rested beneath my neck and the other rested over the top of the blankets. My heart raced a little more at him here on my bed with me.

"You need to get some sleep," he whispered into my hair, his breath giving me goose bumps as it blew softly against me.

"I know. My mind won't stop racing though." I didn't have any hope his presence was going to fix that either. Him being here like this caused a whole new set of thoughts to rush through my head.

Vance placed the palm of his hand against my forehead and began whispering words I couldn't quite understand. I suddenly felt very tired and relaxed. My eyes slowly drifted shut while I listened to his quiet mutterings.

I wouldn't have known I'd fallen asleep, except for the fact I was now standing in a large beautiful meadow full of little purple and yellow wildflowers. The clearing was surrounded by cedar and pine trees, and I could see the tops of red rock cliffs in the distance. A breeze passed over me, ruffling my hair, and I could feel the golden sun washing over my skin heating my body.

"There. This is better," Vance's voice came from behind me as he joined me in my dream, wrapping his arms around my waist. I leaned my head back into his shoulder.

"It's so beautiful here," I said, looking around to take in the soothing sight.

"You created it. It's your dream." He nuzzled his face in my hair.

"I've been wondering something."

"What's that?" he muttered, placing a small kiss at the edge of my jaw.

"How come you can always hear my thoughts, or when I'm calling to you, but I can't ever hear yours?"

He stopped to ponder this for a moment and shrugged. "I guess I've been blocking you."

I turned to give him a quizzical stare, and he laughed.

"Don't worry. I haven't been doing it intentionally. I've just become so tuned in to keeping my mind closed to protect myself I'm doing it now without realizing. You're so new at this, and your mind is so fresh and unfettered it's easy to read you."

"Can anyone read my thoughts then?"

"No, it's part of the special connection between the two of us. This is rare," he said, waving his hand to the scene in front of us.

"So I could read your thoughts, if you'd let me?"

He turned me so I was facing him and lifted my arms up around his neck. Then he wrapped his arms around my waist and gazed deeply into my eyes.

"Read away," he said softly.

I felt a shock go through my system, and suddenly I was connected to him. His emotions flooded over me in great waves, and I started to tremble.

"Don't scare her." The words weren't spoken, but thought to himself. I could feel him begin to pull back a little.

"Stop," I said out loud to him. "I want to see everything."

The wave washed over me once more. Everything came rushing at me. I could see scenes from his life complete with all the emotions, thoughts and feelings that accompanied them.

He started with some of his childhood memories. I saw and felt the joy of the sugar cookie secret he'd shared with me, as well as some other happy family moments. Then the images in my head changed. His father's abuse, his mother running away with him all ran through my mind. I wanted to cry over the sorrow and hurt I could feel emanating from him.

The memories changed again.

I experienced his magic with him as he became familiar with the workings of things. I could completely comprehend everything he did and why he did it. It was like having a life's worth of lessons handed to me all at once, only from another person's perspective. After viewing several things from this part of his life, things shifted once more.

I saw the first time he'd ever laid eyes on me and felt the shock he experienced when he felt my emotions run through him. I saw how he watched me every day from that moment on, but doing it discreetly to not draw attention to himself. I felt how he began longing for the day when I would get my powers, and he could share his secrets with me, making me realize he was terribly lonely.

I could feel a slight hesitation before the next set of scenes started coming.

"Please don't stop," I whispered, staring deep into those blue eyes. "I want to know."

He let loose honoring my request, and I felt the most powerful feelings coming from him yet.

Visions of him tossing and turning at night as he would dream about me filled my mind before moving on to dreams of my own I'd forgotten. I saw him sitting many nights outside my house, or even my bedroom window, giving into temptation once or twice to climb the trellis so he could watch me sleep. He was always watching over me, consumed with making sure I was safe, yearning to make a connection with me but unable to do so because he'd promised my dad he would stay away until I knew I was a witch.

I felt an overwhelming sensation then. One I'd never experienced in my life, but I recognized instantly. He was in love with me ... deeply in love. The attachment was so powerful it threatened to devour him at times, and he was certain we were meant for each other—destined to be together forever.

It was at that moment my own emotions mingled with his, and I realized I totally reciprocated his feelings. He just shared every ounce of his being with me, unfettered and laid out for me to accept or reject. It was a tremendous gift to be given.

I wrapped my arms tighter around his neck, pulling him to me and kissing him with everything I had inside.

It was intense.

His fingers tangled in my hair, slipping up behind my head to push my mouth harder to his. I could feel my lips bruising as we tried to convey our feelings to one another through the contact. My lungs were on fire and felt like they were about to burst from lack of air, but I didn't want to stop. I just wanted to keep on kissing him like this forever.

Soon, however, we both had to step back, gasping.

We stood that way staring at each other for several moments while we tried to catch our breath, lips swollen and chests heaving. Then we both started laughing.

The tension broke, and he pulled me into his embrace once again. I could hear the rumbling in his chest while he continued to chuckle.

"I've never experienced anything like that in my life," he said, stroking his hands softly up and down my back.

"Neither have I. Are you sure this is just a dream?" I tilted my head up to smile at him.

"Yes, but we'll need to be careful. When I kiss you I don't ever want to stop, and that could end up being dangerous." I could see the fire was still lit in his eyes. "But I won't ever try to do anything that would harm you. You know that, right?"

"I trust you with everything I am." I hugged him tightly.

"I'll do my best to earn that trust," he said, brushing my forehead with his lips. He suddenly cocked his head as if listening for something.

"Your mom is coming to wake you up for school," he said, starting to back away from me. "It's time for me to go."

Instantly, I was standing alone in the meadow of flowers, and I could acutely feel his absence.

"Portia, wake up, sweetheart," my mom's voice called softly.

I opened my eyes, turning to automatically search for Vance, but he was already gone. I thought maybe the whole thing had been some really amazing dream. But then I noticed the indentation still left in the pillow next to mine, and I knew he had really been there.

Chapter 10

I wasn't surprised to find Vance waiting for me on his motorcycle when I walked out the door to go to school. I gave him a happy smile when he handed me a spare helmet he had with him. I placed it on with ease this time and climbed on behind him. He kicked into gear, and we raced off down the road.

We parked when we arrived, and he helped me off the bike. "Sleep well?" he asked.

"The best ever!" I replied, laughing. He grabbed my hand, and we started walking toward the school. "Was it real?"

"Every second of it," he said, giving my hand a squeeze.

He walked me to my first hour again, dropping me off at the door with a kiss goodbye on my forehead.

"Catch you later, baby," he said with a wink.

I went and slung myself into the desk and reached into my backpack for my books.

"Hey. You want to go out tonight?" Vance's voice caught me off guard, and I sat up abruptly, looking around before hearing his laughter in my head.

"This is weird," I said back to him mentally. "It's definitely going to take some getting used to."

"I like it," he replied, and I could almost hear the smile in his voice. "Just think of it as a phone call but without the phone."

"Yeah, but a phone rings to let someone know when they're calling," I said wryly.

Instantly I heard a ringing sound in my head, and I jumped at the harsh noise tempted to cover my ears with my hands but knowing it wouldn't help.

"Is that better?" he asked with a chuckle.

"No," I said, amused. "Your way is much better. Let's stick with that."

"You didn't answer my question."

"Yes. I'd love to go out with you tonight, or any night for that matter. What do you want to do?"

"It'll be a surprise," he said, turning suddenly mysterious on me. "It's my turn to treat you with something."

"That sounds great."

"Cool," he answered. "Now listen to your teacher. I believe he's about to call your name."

"Portia Mullins?" Mr. Shanks called out.

"Present," I said, and he flicked his pencil to check me on the role card.

I was surprised when Vance agreed to go to lunch with Shelly and Brad. I didn't think that would be his type of scene. We all ordered a burger and fries, then sat at a table together while we waited. Brad kept asking Vance questions about his motorcycle and telling him how he had always wanted to get one, and Vance told him how he had restored this motorcycle and customized it to his taste. The two of them launched into all this mechanics stuff, and soon Shelly and I were completely lost from the conversation.

"So do you want to go out and do something tonight?" Shelly said to me while the boys continued their own discussion, after we got our food.

"I'd love to, but Vance has some surprise planned for this evening," I replied with a smile, but Shelly made a pout-lipped face at my remark.

"We never do anything together anymore," she complained, dipping a French fry into some ketchup.

"I'm sorry. How about going tomorrow night?"

"Yeah," Vance said, suddenly breaking into our conversation. "Why don't the four of us catch a movie or something?"

"Sounds good to me," Brad said with a nod. "What do you think, Shelly?"

"Only if the girls get to pick the movie," she said quickly, and Vance and Brad eyed each other.

"Chick flick," they both said in unison, and Shelly and I laughed.

"So we'll pick you girls up at seven. Would that be okay?" Brad asked.

"That'll be great," I replied, while Shelly nodded sipping on her straw. The four of us left the restaurant and headed back toward the school.

The rest of the day passed quickly. I silently laughed over the few mental conversations I was able to have with Vance as we passed the boring times in class. I had to cover myself after laughing out loud a couple of times over things he said to me, pretending to have a little coughing fit until two of my teachers had asked me if I needed to go and see the nurse.

Vance, of course, found all this quite entertaining, and I was almost certain he'd made it his secret mission to see how often he could trip me up. He was all innocent smiles when he met me at my locker after last period. I sent him a scathing glare but couldn't hold it, and we both started laughing again.

I enjoyed the ride back to my house, my body tucked tightly up against the back of his, but as usual it was over too soon. I got off the motorcycle and handed Vance his spare helmet, which he secured to the seat behind him.

"So can I come pick you up at seven tonight?"

"I'll count the minutes until then," I said with a somewhat cheesy smile.

"Good," he replied, before leaning over to give me a quick kiss on the lips. "See you then."

As it turned out I did count the minutes until his arrival. I didn't realize how excited I was to see what his surprise was going to be. I even tried to sneak a mental peek into his mind here and there—finding nothing but a solid wall to greet me. I did get enough of a connection to him at least once to get a small chuckle out of him. He made some comment about patience being a virtue, so I busied myself getting ready for our date, wanting to look really special for him.

I found that being magical did wonders with my unruly hair. I managed to twist it up into a slightly messy up-do that had soft wispy tendrils falling around the sides of my face and neck. I had to basically command the hairs to cooperate, but they did.

After my hair was done I carefully applied my makeup. I used very soft pastel colors in my attempt to avoid looking like a call girl, but I was a little bit brazen by adding soft, black eyeliner around my eyes with black mascara. It looked all right though with the pale pink lip gloss and blush.

I went to my closet and pulled out a purple V-neck shirt that had a short vest over the top of it that tied in the back. I put it on with leggings, a cute black denim mini-skirt, and a pair of flats. Then I checked my jewelry in the mirror.

The purple shirt brought out the beautiful color of my amulet. I touched it as it shimmered in the light from my dressing table, admiring it before deciding to also add a small black ribbon like a choker at my neck.

I stepped over to my full-length mirror to get the full effect, and I was surprised to see myself. Shelly would be so proud of me. I actually felt pretty.

I heard Vance's motorcycle coming down the street, so I turned the light out and headed down the stairs. My parents were both gone again, so I was the one who answered his knock at the door.

"Hi," I said with a soft smile when he came into view.

He didn't say anything. He just stared at me and let his eyes run up and down me, and I felt a flaming flush arising in my cheeks.

"You look great!" he said, reaching out his hand toward me, and I placed my hand in his. He pulled me toward him to kiss me thoroughly, and soon we were both breathless once again. He stepped back from me then, looking a little uncomfortable all of a sudden.

"Sorry," he said, raking his fingers through his hair.

"No apology needed," I replied with a smile. "I enjoyed it."

"Me too," he said. "A little too much I think. Kissing you is like a drug to me. One I can't get enough of," he added seriously. "Sometimes it scares me," he added, surprising me.

"Why?" I asked, trying to understand.

He took a step closer to me, lifting a hand to my face.

"Because I could allow myself to lose control with you so easily."

We sat staring at each other for a moment. The weight of his words sinking in between us, he turned and briskly walked to his motorcycle, towing me along behind him.

He handed me a helmet questioningly, and I shook my head in denial.

"It'll mess up my hair," I complained.

"Better messy hair than a broken head," he replied, pushing the helmet toward me again.

I grumbled while I complied with his request, before I climbed onto the back of his motorcycle, wrapping my arms tightly around him.

I soon realized, after we had been driving for a few minutes, that he must be taking me to his favorite spot in Oak Creek Canyon again. I relaxed and enjoyed the ride as he smoothly made his way through the bends and curves, until we turned off on the small dirt road. Shortly after, we stopped and parked the bike.

Vance helped me off the motorcycle and to remove my helmet. A quick glance in the rearview mirror revealed that, amazingly, the helmet hadn't done much damage to my hairdo.

"Let's go," Vance said, grabbing my hand impatiently.

We made our little trek through the dense foliage without much difficulty, and when we arrived at the smooth rock, I found that the entire area had been transformed.

Pillar candles of all sizes and varieties were lit in a large circle surrounding a small table. Some of the candles were actually floating at different heights in the air, while others rested on the ground. There were several magical items on the small table in the middle.

"This is beautiful!" I said, feeling a little breathless at this surprise, wondering what he could possibly have in store for me.

"I need to ask you something important," Vance said, turning toward me, his handsome face aglow in the candlelight.

"Okay." I was a little nervous now, and suddenly he seemed very nervous also.

He took both of my hands in his. "Portia, I love you," he said solemnly, his eyes searching mine, and my heart soared at his verbal declaration of it.

I nodded. "I know you do." I lay my hand on his chest over his heart. "I can feel it."

"I've loved you for a long time, even though you didn't know it. During that time I've become very good at reading you and your emotions, so I'm aware of your feelings toward me also," he stated.

I nodded once again. "You know I love you with every fiber of my being," I said quietly.

"Yes, I do." He ran his cupped hand down the side of my cheek. "And I can't stop being awed by it."

I leaned my head into it, closing my eyes for a moment, savoring his touch.

"This is happening really fast," he said, and my eyes popped opened, my mouth ready to protest.

"Not too fast for me. I may be new to all of this, but it doesn't mean my feelings are any less real." I wanted to reassure him, and he chuckled before placing one of his fingers over my lips to stop me.

"Don't worry, baby. I'm not asking you to slow things down. I'm asking you to speed things up."

"Speed things up?"

"Portia, I know all these things are new to you—magic, covens, and even me—but I've been waiting for you for a long time. Two years to be exact. I've known from the beginning, since the first day I connected with your feelings, you were the one for me. I started viewing you as my friend, my partner, even my soul mate, for lack of a better term. It may seem strange for me to say that I loved you before you knew me. I understand how crazy all this must seem to you, but I need to know … do you feel the same way?"

"I do," I replied honestly, a little awed I didn't even need to think about my answer. "There's something that feels complete when I'm with you."

He smiled at me. "I know, huh?" He caressed my lips with his fingers. "It's amazing, and it's what brings me to this moment. My desire is to be with you for—well, forever. Under normal circumstances two people would just get married. However, as you're just sixteen and I'm eighteen already, I think most of society, including your parents, would probably frown on such a union between the two of us right now."

"I agree," I said, although I took a dreamy moment just to think about how wonderful it would be to be married to him.

"I guess I thought this would be the next best thing." He gestured to the candlelit scene behind him. "It's a binding ceremony, which is a very special ritual that'll seal two souls together."

I was shocked into silence. I couldn't comprehend that this wonderful Adonis-like creature before me could possibly want to be with me forever. I didn't know what to say.

"If I'm misreading you or moving too fast just tell me, we can table this discussion for later." I saw doubt creep into his expression as he misread my hesitation. "I'm more than a little neurotic when it comes to loved ones, I'm afraid. Having lost my family, it tends to make me feel a little desperate about wanting to tie you to me. Having you in my life is the closest thing I've had to real family in a long time. I want you to be my family."

This time it was me who reached out and grabbed him in a crushing hug.

"We don't need to table this for later, Vance," I said,

feeling a little teary at his words. "I would be honored to be included in your family."

He placed his hands on my arms and gently pushed me back so he could see my face.

"Then answer me this," he said. "Do you Portia Mullins consent of your own free will to join with me in a binding ceremony that will hold our hearts together from this time forward? And will you do it with the intent that when the time is appropriate we'll be married, bound together by the laws of both God and man?"

I blushed from my head to my toes, and I answered without hesitation. "Yes, Vance. I will consent to this binding."

He smiled widely, leading me over to the floating candle circle. With a small wave of his hand, a few of the candles parted and we entered the ritual space. He closed them behind us.

He positioned me on the right side of the waist-high table, and he stood on the left. Picking up two large red roses that were both in full bloom, he handed one to me while he kept the other. He began to carefully rip the petals from the rose, placing them in a crystal dish and motioned for me to do the same.

"These red rose petals signify the passion of our love," Vance said softly, and I knew instinctively this was part of the ritual. "As we mix these petals together, our hearts will become as one."

We layered them together until there were no more left on the stem.

Next he poured some wine into a silver chalice and took a large drink from it. He then turned the cup in a half turn and handed it to me to drink from the same spot he had. I drank a large swallow and handed the cup back to him. Instead of taking the chalice from me, he placed his hands over mine and together we poured the small amount of wine remaining onto the rose petals.

"This wine symbolizes our intent to keep our relationship in harmony."

He guided my hands and we set the chalice down, and the wicks of two candles on the table burst to life. He picked up one, and I the other. Together we lit the third candle on the table which was the largest. He picked it up and walked around the interior of the flaming circle three times.

"This flame represents the uniting of our souls together as one," he said, before coming back to place the candle on the table.

He lifted his athame then and pricked his finger until a single drop of blood fell into the crystal dish. He then handed the knife to me, and I did the same.

"We have sealed our desires with our blood," he stated.

Vance reached for my hands and guided me around the table until we were standing toe to toe. He took a small length of flaxen rope, wrapping one end of it around my wrist and the other end around his wrist as we clasped hands together. Then he began to recite his spell.

"Portia Mullins, Blessed Be.
I give now, my heart to thee.
My soul is yours to bind and take,
My love for you will never shake.
I promise to always keep you pure,
And never into evil lure.
Let Heaven be our destiny,
I love you, Portia, So Mote It Be."

My eyes watered at his beautiful vows. I knew I needed to repeat them back to him for the ritual to be complete. I didn't need his help since the words he'd just spoken were seared into my very being.

"Vance Mangum, Blessed Be.
I give now, my heart to thee.
My soul is yours to bind and take,
My love for you will never shake.
I promise to always keep you pure,
And never into evil lure.
Let Heaven be our destiny,
I love you, Vance, So Mote It Be."

Vance took the rope and tied it around the large pillar candle. He lifted a few of the rose petals out of the bowl and pressed them into the hot wax in the candle, sealing them there.

Suddenly the items in the crystal bowl swirled together, and the flower petals drifted upward until they were far over our heads. Then they slowly drifted back toward the earth, floating down around us.

Vance pulled me into his embrace and gave me a very long, very lingering kiss. I could feel our hearts beating together as one, in exactly the same rhythm. My blood was racing, singing through my body as his fingers tangled in my hair loosening it from the restraints. He kissed my cheeks, my eyes, my neck, and even the strands of hair running through his hands. He finally released me when I felt like I might possibly explode with desire.

"It's finished," he said, smiling, his eyes bright. "I love you, Portia."

"I love you too, Vance," I said, feeling as if light were pouring out from the very center of my soul.

Then he kissed me again.

Chapter 11

I wondered if everyone in love felt like this. Was this ever present, hot sizzling fire running through my veins normal? I'd never experienced anything like it in my life.

Every moment I was with Vance seemed wonderful, extraordinary, and magical, though we often felt like we were going crazy with need when we were together. And at the opposite end of the spectrum, every moment I was away from him seemed like torture, and I was filled with an aching I couldn't describe.

When we were apart we ended up spending a lot of time in each other's heads. It helped ease the separation a tiny bit, but Vance explained the feelings we were having were much greater than he'd ever heard of before. We finally decided to go talk to Grandma about it and get her opinion.

We entered the store and saw no one, so we headed into the back room and found Grandma there, working at her table. Her head popped up when we walked through the beaded curtain, and she looked at us for a second, concerned, and then got up to come over to greet us.

"Ah! A binding spell I see!" she said, looking carefully at us.

"Is it that obvious?" I asked, continuing to cling to Vance's arm.

"So obvious I wonder why I didn't feel it when you walked through the front door." She gave me a pointed look. "Here, come sit with me." She gestured toward the table. "It's a very strong spell. Did you work it, Vance?" she asked, continuing to observe us, and he nodded.

"I don't recall ever hearing of anyone experiencing a binding this strong," Vance said. "Did I do something wrong?"

"No, I doubt that," Grandma replied, shaking her head. "For some reason the two of you have an extremely strong connection. The power of your magic is intensifying it dramatically I would imagine."

"It isn't always a bad thing," I piped up trying to explain. "It's just when we're apart I feel like I'm going to die or something."

Grandma laughed. "Well, dear. What's done is done. That's the trouble with spells. Sometimes you don't really know what the end result will be. The two of you are going to have to find a way to make things work for yourselves. I imagine you'll eventually become used to the intensity of the feelings you're having, probably to the point they'll almost seem second nature to you. Your bodies should physically adjust to it, a new normal so to speak." She gave a slight shrug. "I wish I could help you more until then, but I have a feeling that you two are something special. Vance's magic manifesting at such a young age and you having an instant comprehension of your powers are unusual. Together you make a very powerful couple. This is uncharted water for me I'm afraid."

Vance squeezed my hand. "We'll be fine. I know it," he said, trying to reassure me.

"I know we will. I just wish you could always be with

me. The longing is driving me crazy!" I replied with an exasperated sigh at what we'd done to ourselves.

He leaned over and kissed me softly, but it quickly developed into something much bigger, with hands and arms tangling together as we pulled at one another, trying to get closer to each other. We completely forgot we had an audience and didn't stop until Grandma broke in.

"Okay! Enough! You two are making me blush!" She laughed, turning away from us to avoid our public display of affection, and we broke apart smiling.

"Sorry," Vance said apologetically, raking a hand through his already disheveled hair.

Grandma waved her hand in the air. "Don't worry about it," she said with a smile, before he grew pensive again. "On second thought, I do have one suggestion that may help you."

"Let's hear it," I said, knowing Vance and I were willing to try anything at this point.

"Do you still have the silver locket you kept Vance's hair in for the ritual you performed?" she asked, and I nodded.

Grandma went to a drawer and pulled out a similar silver locket, with a more masculine design, and handed it to Vance.

"I think you should clip a little bit of each other's hair and keep it in the lockets. Wear them all the time. This will keep something physical of the two of you together. It won't stop your feelings at all, but it may dampen things enough for you that those separations aren't quite as excruciating."

"We'll try it. Thanks for your help," Vance replied, sounding hopeful.

"Let me know if it works."

Vance and I went back to my house and found my locket. We pulled out a pair of scissors and proceeded to cut an inconspicuous lock for each of us, placing the trimming in the lockets. Then we each helped the other to place the chains around their necks.

"Shall we test it?" he asked, leaning in to kiss me softly on the cheek. I leaned my head so he could nuzzle against me better.

"No," I mumbled, lifting my hand to slide it up his face and into his hair. "Not until we have to."

His kisses soon trailed down my neck and feathered onto my exposed collarbone, before dipping a little lower.

"All right!" I said, shoving him playfully away from me knowing things were quickly getting out of control. "Let's go watch some TV with my mom. There's safety in numbers."

He let out a big sigh and followed dutifully behind me, close but not touching me. We entered the family room, and Mom patted the couch next to her, inviting us to come and sit down.

"How're you today, Vance?" she asked, politely.

"Very good, Mrs. Mullins," he replied back to her in kind. "Thank you."

"Call me Stacey," she said with a smile. "You're family now, Vance." I wondered if she knew just how much those words would mean to him.

We sat down on the opposite end of the couch, and I curled up in Vance's arms with Jinx on my lap. Soon we were laughing over a favorite old sitcom. I'd seen the reruns a thousand times, and it never got old, but I found my eyes starting to droop after a while. Operating at this level of emotion was exhausting.

"You need to go to bed, baby." Vance brushed his hand through my hair while I lay in his lap.

"I don't want you to leave," I mumbled softly, turning

into him so I could wrap my arms around his waist.

"You need your sleep," he responded.

"Go to bed, Portia," my mom broke in. "Let the poor boy go home. He looks exhausted!"

I slowly got up and walked with Vance to the front door. He opened it and turned to pull me into his arms once more.

He gave me a searing, passionate kiss, locking his arms around my body as he focused on my mouth. All too soon he was pulling away. "See you shortly," he said.

After he'd gone, I turned and padded up the stairs to my room where I waited for the crushing emptiness to overwhelm me just as it always did. When it came, it was not nearly as intense as it had been before. It looked like Grandma's idea was working. The longing was still great, but not so overpowering.

I crawled into bed and pulled the covers over my head, letting sleep claim me. I hadn't slept well since we had done the ritual. I was still vaguely aware when Vance climbed through my window a couple of hours later and snuggled up next to me, being careful to keep the thick quilt between us. Then, finally, we both slept deeply.

Grandma's trick seemed to work well, and over the next few weeks Vance and I became more acclimated to our new, intense set of feelings. We handled our day-to-day separations easier, though he still climbed into my window every night to sleep next to me.

I was pretty sure we weren't fooling anyone about that, except perhaps my mom. Grandma explained things to my dad and told him about the binding ritual. He hadn't appeared horribly worried. He was more concerned over our well-being. I was happy they didn't make a big fuss over it. To say they both trusted Vance implicitly would have been an understatement. I was glad they understood. I was sure my dad was not thrilled in the least about Vance being there every night, but it was so much easier when he was right next to me.

Life began to fall back into a routine, and things seemed to be going well for everyone, until the day my dad showed up looking somewhat frazzled and called an emergency meeting for the coven.

When the group had gathered and the circle had been cast, he began explaining what he was worried about.

"As you all know, I've been involved with laying a false trail that leads Vance's father farther away from here. Things seemed to be going pretty well. I had him searching in an area back East, and he'd been stationed there for quite a while. However, he seems to have vanished, and I can't find a trace of him anywhere. He had several followers working with him, and they're all gone too. I don't know if he has any idea we were leading him astray, or if they just left. They could be anywhere."

"We need everyone to be on their guard, watching for anything that might be suspicious," Grandma added.

I looked over at Vance in concern. He instinctively reached out and grabbed my hand.

"It's all right, baby. I'm okay," he whispered softly in my head, trying to reassure me. "Don't worry. I'm not going anywhere."

I squeezed his hand back. "Please be careful," I replied.

We spent the rest of the evening chanting several protection spells over the whole group before releasing the circle to head home. When we were walking out of the house, Vance turned to Marsha.

"Aunt Marsha, I'm going to spend the night at Portia's house tonight. I don't want to leave her alone," he said, inviting himself over.

Marsha just laughed. “So how’s that different from any other night of the week?”

“You knew?” he replied in surprise. “You never said anything.”

“I knew,” she said, smiling. “It’s my job to keep an eye on you. Don’t you think that would look bad, if I didn’t know where you were?”

Vance had the decency to look semi-repentant. “I’m sorry. I should’ve confided in you sooner about this.”

“It’s okay.” Marsha smiled. “I remember what being young and in love felt like. Go on, and please be safe.” She gave him a quick peck on the cheek.

He hugged her back and led me over to his motorcycle. He helped me on, and we were soon headed off down the road to my house.

Several minutes later we were lying next to each other on my bed, the ever-present quilt tucked carefully in between us once again.

“Why do you always do that?” I asked him curiously.

“Do what?”

“Sleep with the blankets in between us. It’s like you’re afraid to be next to me.”

“You know why. I’m protecting your virtue,” he said matter-of-factly, and I almost choked.

“My virtue?”

He chuckled softly. “I guess I’m protecting mine too.”

“You know, there are an awful lot of stories about you and all the girls you’ve deflowered in your lifetime floating around the school.” I watched him carefully for his reaction.

"And that's exactly what they are—stories," he replied, moving in to nuzzle my chin with his nose.

I pondered this for a moment. "So you're saying you've never been with a girl, like that, before?" My pulse raced because I was afraid of what his answer would be.

He stared at me, his expression soft. "That's what I'm saying," he answered, and I released the breath I'd been holding.

"Doesn't it bother you that people think things about you that aren't true?"

"Why should I care?" he asked, giving a shrug of his shoulder. "I know who I am. That's all that matters."

"Well, I'm sure people are thinking the same thing about the two of us."

"Let them think it." He propped up onto his elbow to look at me better. "Does it bother you?" His eyes drilled into mine.

"No," I said, considering my next words carefully. "I wish it were true, sometimes."

This time he sighed deeply and closed his eyes, as if searching for control. When he opened them again he looked at me for a long moment.

"You've got to know I want you more than anything in this world, Portia. Emotionally, physically, magically, mentally, I want it all—to possess every inch of your being," he answered honestly.

He caressed my face with his fingers, stroking them down the side of it, and instantly I was overcome with the feeling of his desire. His need washed completely through me. The force of it took me by complete surprise, and I gasped out loud at the connection, but he didn't stop. Instead he leaned over me and placed his lips softly on mine.

His touch only increased my reaction to him, and I reached out to pull him closer to me, enveloping him in a deep kiss, opening my mouth to his invasion.

I released everything I had pent up inside me back into him. He wrapped his arms tightly around me, answering my intensity, his hands sliding up to tangle in my hair. His mouth pressed even harder against my lips, and he continued to devour them.

My pulse was racing, on fire, and I could feel the same emanating from him. It was like someone had lit a match to gasoline, causing an explosion we had no control over, and I could think of only one thing. I wanted more.

I didn't even know how it had happened, but somehow that infernal quilt separating us finally got pushed out of the way, and he moved, laying his body over the top of mine. I welcomed his heated weight against me, and my hands found their way up under his shirt. I ran them feverishly over his hard muscled back, pressing him even closer.

His lips left my mouth, sliding over my face to the skin of my neck, and he bit me lightly, trailing little love bites down to my collarbone. I couldn't help letting out a soft moan, my body naturally arching up against him when his tongue flicked out, licking a sensitive spot there.

He pulled back then, and I heard him suck in a tortured breath.

"No," he said, but I reached out to bring him back to me, kissing his mouth.

He kissed me back, but he reached up to untangle my hands from him, pinning them back to the bed. He moved away to look at me again, breathing heavily, and I squirmed slightly beneath him, trying to maintain contact with his body.

"Portia! Stop!" He released me as he fell over to

his side, rolling off both me and the bed. He moved quickly to stand near the window.

I pushed up on my elbows, my chest heaving, and looked at him.

"What's the matter?" I asked, my body trembling, confused by his departure. I raked my gaze over his wrinkled shirt and at the hard body beneath.

"Don't look at me like that," he said, turning away from me toward the window, breathing hard. He lifted the sash and leaned out into the night air.

I sighed pitifully and looked away from him. That was when I caught my reflection in the dresser mirror.

I was completely disheveled. My hair in tangled masses and my pajama top had a little rip in the seam of my shoulder from where he'd pulled on it. My lips were swollen and bruised looking, and pink bite marks trailed brightly down my neck, proof that he'd been there. I looked like one of those sexy pin-up models in a magazine.

"Oh!" I said softly, running my fingers through my hair while I looked at my flushed skin for a moment. I got up and walked over to the window to join him. I reached a hand out and place it on his shoulder.

"Don't touch me," he said brusquely, without turning and I felt a tinge of hurt course through me. He sighed heavily at that, and I could see his body was trembling slightly.

"Portia, I love you more than anything in the world, but if you know what's best for you, then I suggest you get back into the bed and cover up."

I just stood there staring at his back for a moment, feeling injured because he wouldn't look at me.

"Now!" he added, through gritted teeth, every muscle in his body tense.

I dutifully turned around and went back to the bed,

crawled in and covered up like he asked me to do. Jinx hopped up on the bed, nuzzling my chin, while I patiently waited for Vance to say something.

Several minutes passed by before he turned to face me. He leaned his hips back against the window sill, folding his arms across his chest over his wrinkled shirt.

"I'm sorry," he said, his expression somewhat guarded. "I didn't mean to lose control like that."

"I'm sorrier then. I wanted to lose control like that." I stared straight into his eyes. "I'm even more sorry you stopped."

"Portia, I'd like nothing better than to give you what you want. You don't understand." He shook his head, a tortured laugh escaping him.

"Then enlighten me please," I replied, wondering what I'd done wrong.

He stared hard at me, silent for what seemed like an hour, clenching and unclenching his jaw before he finally spoke.

"The reason's two-fold," he began, his eyes never leaving me. "The first one being I just pledged myself to you in a binding ceremony where I promised to keep you pure and never lure you into evil."

"You think making love to me would be evil?" I asked in amazement, unable to believe what I was hearing.

"No. Never." He left the window and came to sit on the edge of the bed, reaching out to take both of my hands in his. "I just want to do it right," he explained with a sigh. "I want to share something with you, okay?"

He didn't continue until I nodded.

"When I was on the run, I never knew from one moment to the next if I was even going to be in the same place at the same time the next day. I never had the time to cultivate real relationships with the people I met. But there was one time when we'd been able to stay put for a few months, and I started making some friends. I even had a steady girlfriend."

My body flared with jealousy at the mention of another girl, but I tried to rein it in so I could hear what he was trying to say.

"One night we were at a bonfire party on this beach. This girl and I, we snuck off together out into the dark. We made out with each other in the sand, for what seemed like hours, until my body was so on fire I thought I wouldn't be able to control myself a minute longer. I decided right then I was going to sleep with her. She was more than willing, and so was I."

The more he spoke, the more I wanted to cry. I couldn't stand hearing about him being with another girl. I kept trying to tell myself he hadn't cheated, but my heart wasn't listening very well.

"It was at that moment my phone rang," he said. "I don't even know what made me stop to answer it, but it was Marsha telling me my dad had found us again." I saw a pained emotion run through his eyes. "I got up off that girl and I ran, never even looking back at her once. I hopped on my motorcycle and followed the escape plan Marsha and I set up precisely for such an occasion."

He lifted one of his hands, dragging it through his hair, before he leaned forward, resting his elbows on his knees.

"Marsha and I didn't stop until the next night. And when I collapsed onto my bed in the hotel, I finally let myself think about what nearly happened. I was horrified."

He looked up at me then.

"Do you realize if Marsha would've called a few minutes later it would've been too late? I would've already been physically intimate with that girl and then got up off her and ran, never to see her again."

He shook his head, and I could see the self-loathing in his eyes.

"I didn't have any protection with me. I could've gotten her pregnant and left her alone with a child, to deal with the circumstances all by herself. And I could've ended up with a child I knew nothing about. Could you imagine if that had happened? My kid would've been growing up out there without me, magical blood flowing through its veins with a mom who doesn't have a clue about our kind. It would be a disaster waiting to happen."

"But it didn't happen, Vance," I reminded him, trying to help him feel better. "Everything turned out okay."

"No, Portia. It's not okay," he argued. "I abused that girl when I got up off her and left her without saying one word. I left her in the heat of passion wondering what she did wrong. I didn't stop when I heard her calling after me. I didn't give her any explanation. I just left. She probably wonders to this day what the heck happened that night because no one there has ever seen me again. I just disappeared."

I suddenly felt very sorry for this girl, whoever she was. My heart ached for her because I realized she'd actually lived my biggest fear, which was waking up one morning and finding Vance gone. I couldn't help the involuntary shudder that coursed through me while he continued to speak.

"I made up my mind in that moment I wasn't going to have sex until I was married. If I was married to someone, then it meant I'd be able to be in a real relationship with someone I really loved, not some poor one-night stand who happened to be an unfortunate victim of my circumstances.

"This is precisely why it's so hard for me to be with you. You're the person I want to have all that with. I realize now everything I've ever felt about anybody else in my past was just the result of meaningless hormones coursing through my adolescent male brain.

"It's different with you, though. I love you, and I want to be with you because I love you. But I'm still in the same turmoil too. Even now my dad is still threatening me, and I have to start worrying about the safety of everyone around me.

"I don't want to put you in any kind of position that could leave you in a bad place. And I don't want to have some cheap fling with you either. I want to give your first time at the right time, and I want it to be crazy special—not because we lost control for a moment. Call me old-fashioned if you want, but I can't think of a better time to celebrate the joining of our bodies than after the legal joining of our hearts. It's the most intimate gift I can give you."

He looked deeply into my eyes, searching for some type of reassurance from me, and I pulled him into a tender embrace.

"Thank you, Vance, for sharing this with me. I do understand better now that you're explaining it." My eyes got teary when I considered all the trauma this poor guy had been through in his past. He hugged me back, but we didn't hold each other for very long since there was still a strong undercurrent passing between us. It was hard to stop whatever this was.

"You said the reason was two-fold," I probed, letting go of him so he could continue to explain the things in his heart to me.

He sighed, getting up to pace the room.

"I'm not a good person, Portia. I'm naturally drawn toward things that aren't good for me to do. My connection with dark magic and its elements has never been completely removed, and it's an attraction I fight every minute to overcome. I think having a physical relationship with you, outside of marriage, is something I'm drawn to because it's considered a taboo thing to do. There's always this part of me that wants to do everything rough and wild. I want to be completely out of control, throwing all caution to the wind." He turned to look at me, making sure I could see the power of what he was trying to tell me in his eyes.

"I want this physical relationship with you, badly. It's to the point I feel consumed by it at times. But I worry if I were to give into it, bypassing the goal I've set for myself, it would start me down a path I've been trying very hard to avoid. And trust me, Portia, when I tell you … once I cross this line with you, there'll be no going back for me. I won't be able to stop."

The heat of his words began to sink in and I felt overwhelmed. He moved over next to me.

"I can't get past the fact that I'm the terrible one in this relationship. It's me that could destroy everything—everything I really love, and everything you love too. I'd never be able to forgive myself." He lifted his hand and ran his fingers through my hair.

"That's exactly why I believe in you," I replied. "You love us, and I think you'll honor your vows because of that."

"I hope you're right," he said, moving away from me to sit dejectedly on the end of the bed. I crawled up behind him, wrapping my arms around him and hugging tightly.

"What you did tonight was proof. You stopped something you didn't want to stop, and that takes a lot of control, Vance. Give yourself credit where credit is due."

He leaned his head against mine and patted my arm.

"Thanks for understanding." I could still feel the mental struggle he was having with everything. "It's so hard for me to stay away from you. You honestly have no idea what I've gone through over this."

I kicked myself for causing him more stress. "I'll try to be more helpful from now on too."

"Let's get some sleep," he replied suddenly, cutting the conversation off by standing up and walking over to the head of the bed. "Come get under the covers, my little vixen, so I can tuck you in properly."

I smiled a little, but did as he asked, and when he lay next to me this time, he stuck a pillow and the quilt in between us. He still reached over and grabbed my hand though.

"Sorry, but I think just a little hand holding will be more appropriate for the rest of the night," he said, smiling.

Jinx seemed to sense the tension also and settled on the pillow in between us. I laughed lightly at this before I rolled onto my side to face Vance. I closed my eyes as the pad of his thumb stroked repeatedly over my hand, lulling me into relaxation along with Jinx's purring. My body melted into the pillow and bedding, and I was right on the verge of sleep when I heard his last conscious thought run through his head.

"I almost didn't stop, Portia," he confessed. "I wanted it all."

Chapter 12

I took extreme care in the days following our little incident in how I conducted myself around Vance. I found myself dressing as modestly as possible, covering any exposed skin that could be construed as seductive, and I also paid special attention to how I touched or kissed him. I only held his hand now, instead of running my hand down his arms or over his chest, and when we kissed I was careful to keep it chaste and pure, pulling away before things could get too intense.

I assumed the things I was doing were helping him, since he didn't bring anything up with me about it, and life seemed to progress forward as usual.

On this particular evening we were sitting on my bed, working on some of our homework. I snapped my math book closed when I was finished, using a little magic to float it over and neatly placed it on my desk.

"Hey, I'm getting ready for bed now," I said, placing a tiny peck on his cheek. He hardly acknowledged me, giving a little grunt as he continued to work on his English homework.

I went to my dresser, lifting the shopping bag which contained the things I'd purchased today after school, and went into my adjoining bathroom to change. I took out the thick flannel pajamas that were a size too large for me, and covered in bunnies, looking at the childish design. They'd even come with a pair of bunny slippers.

After quickly dressing, I shoved my feet into the slippers, turning to check my reflection in the dressing mirror on the back of the door.

The image was totally what I was going for—completely unflattering and very unattractive. I couldn't even make out my shape underneath, so I figured it should be okay to wear around Vance.

I pulled all my hair back from my face, twisting it into a tousled bun on the top of my head, before I washed off what little make up I was wearing and brushed my teeth.

Checking the mirror one more time, I assured myself I looked positively retched, and then I opened the door to step out.

Vance had apparently finished his homework during my absence and was lying stretched out on my bed. He was resting with his arms behind his head, his legs drawn out with his feet crossed at the ankles, and he was staring up at the ceiling, looking completely lost in thought.

He glanced over in my direction momentarily when I walked out of the bathroom, before averting his gaze back to his study of the ceiling.

I smiled to myself. Success, I thought. He barely looked at me.

"It isn't working, you know?" his voice interrupted my thoughts.

"Hmmm?" I questioned, lifting my eyebrows and pursing my lips.

"The clothes—those horrible things you've been wearing. Shirts up to your chin, pants down to your ankles, the bad hairdos, the quick kisses and hugs, none of it's working."

"What do you mean?" I was trying to appear as

innocent as possible.

He sat up suddenly, getting off the bed and striding over to me. He grabbed both of my arms and yanked me roughly against him.

"I mean it isn't working," he said, his voice low and seductive. His face was so close to mine his lips brushed across my forehead when he spoke. "You're trying to help, and you're making it worse."

I was paralyzed. I couldn't have moved if I wanted to.

"When you wear your hair like this, I just want to rip it down so I can run my fingers through it." Without him moving a muscle I felt the magic emanating from him. Instantly my hair was released from its bonds, falling to cascade down around my face. He moved his hands up my body until he reached my face and then slid his fingers up to tangle into it. He grabbed a couple of fistfuls, pulling back on it, causing my face to angle up toward his.

"And your clothes," he continued, sighing in exasperation with a slight shake of his head. "Let's not even discuss what I'd like to do with those."

He closed his eyes for a minute, and I could feel him trying to regain his control. He took a deep breath, but when he opened his eyes I could still see the intensity burning through them.

"You just don't get it, do you? I could be blind, and you'd still attract me the same way. Your blood sings to me as it races through your veins. I feel every increase in the rhythm of your heart, every catch in your breath, and sometimes even every thought meandering through that silly little noggin of yours."

I was speechless, captivated, not knowing what to say, so I just stood there drowning in the blue pools of his eyes.

"Don't hold yourself back from me, Portia. It doesn't help. It only makes it worse because then I crave you even more." His eyes searched deep into mine. "Do you understand?"

I nodded a little woodenly, and bit the corner of my lip. "I'm sorry. I didn't realize. I thought I was help…."

"Enough talking," he growled, cutting me off. "Just kiss me already."

I wrapped my arms around his neck and reached up to his mouth. He met me halfway in a crushing grasp. He kissed me hotly, longingly, until neither of us could breathe properly anymore, and even then he didn't stop.

My lungs began to ache. They felt as if they were on fire, but I couldn't let go. My pulse was racing at a fevered pitch, matching his beat for beat until he finally released me all at once, taking a step back from me, and I fell to the floor.

I sat up, confused.

He reached a hand out to me, a look of concern passing briefly over his face. "Are you okay?"

"Were we … floating?" I asked, suddenly noticing his feet were a few inches off the floor.

"Sorry. I thought you knew," he said apologetically, stepping back onto the ground. "I wouldn't have let go so abruptly."

"We were actually levitating?" I asked again, my voice sounding uncertain.

"Haven't you ever heard witches can fly?" He chuckled, sounding a little bit like he was teasing me, but I couldn't tell for sure.

"Seriously? I thought that was like some broomstick legend," I replied, trying to grasp what he was telling me.

"Well, there's some truth to the rumors, although they

may not be completely accurate. Care to go do a little bit of experimentation with me?" He grinned.

"Sure." I glanced quickly down to my attire. "Do I need to change though?"

"Don't worry about it." He waved his hand in dismissal. "The bunnies are starting to grow on me."

He took me over to the window and jumped easily down to the ground before turning and gesturing for me to do the same.

"Think light on your feet," he called softly to me, keeping his voice low in the quiet night air.

I did think light and found I landed quite easily on my feet. Not at all the sort of impact I would've expected.

We went out to his motorcycle and hopped on. I cringed a bit at the loud sound it made when he started it up. He turned left when we reached the highway, and to my surprise he took me to the football field at the high school.

"We need some space to work with," he explained to me while he helped me off the bike.

"What if someone sees us?" I asked nervously.

"Don't worry. It's late and the lights are off, so we should be fine," he replied, after a quick glance around.

He took my hand and led me down through the gate at the top of the guest side stands, and out into the middle of the field.

"Okay. So using this power is more about levitation than flying really. Witches don't actually sore over the moon on their broomsticks. It sure would save on airfare if we could though." He laughed slightly, reaching his hand out and pulling me toward him once more.

"I want you to kiss me like you did before, only this

time I want you to think about feeling as light as air while you're doing it. Don't worry, I won't let go this time."

I happily did as he instructed. Kissing him was so easy. However, I soon found I was totally wrapped up in the kiss, forgetting about why he was doing this. He pulled away from me once again, only this time he continued to hold me around the waist.

I looked around curiously to find we were indeed floating about two feet in the air.

"Can you center your emotions on the feeling running through you right now?" he asked.

I searched for my center and then nodded.

"Okay then. I'm going to let go now," he warned. He loosened his grip, and he took a step back, releasing me. I continued to float in the air beside him.

"This is awesome!" I said in amazement, looking all around myself.

"All right, now I want you to take a step toward me."

I did, and he backed away a step, so I took another step toward him. He moved back again. I noticed we descended a little bit with each step we took, until finally we were back on the ground.

"Why did we lower?" I asked. "I didn't feel as though I was consciously doing it."

"We're still bound by the laws of gravity. I guess you can say we're bending the laws a little. That's why a witch can't actually fly away on a broomstick. You could make a broomstick levitate and you could hop onto it. But every movement you would take would bring you closer to the earth again, making it kind of a poor choice of transportation." He laughed, and so did I at the image he'd created.

"So what good is levitating then, other than being for fun?"

"Well, it's useful for standing outside someone's window," he said with a chuckle and a wink.

I laughed again.

"It's also good for combat maneuvers, if we needed to protect ourselves," he added.

"Show me," I said, settling down onto the field.

"For instance, running and jumping. You can do things higher, farther and faster. Hang on. I have an idea." He started to run off the field. "Be right back," he called over his shoulder.

He returned a couple of minutes later, holding a football in his hands.

"I'm going to go downfield," he said, tossing me the football. "I want you to throw this to me as hard as you can when I tell you to."

I nodded, and he ran off in the other direction.

"Any time," he yelled back to me.

I took the football and threw it hard, straight at him.

He ran toward the ball, and suddenly it was like he was climbing a staircase I couldn't see. He caught the ball easily in mid-air, flew into a somersault, and ran a few steps before descending back down to the ground.

"Why don't you go out for the team?" I asked, amazed at the stunt he'd just performed. "You'd fly by the competition every time!"

"It would be a little bit obvious, don't you think?" He grinned.

"No wonder you aren't impressed by sports." I laughed at him. "They must seem positively dull to you."

"Not always. A lot of those athletes have great natural ability. That's fun to watch. Come here," he said, changing the subject and grabbing my hand so he could lead me up toward the school. "I want to show you something else."

I followed him to a place where the sidewalk went narrow between two of the buildings.

"The same concept applies here," he said, gesturing between the walls.

He jumped up, stepping one foot on the side of the building, then bounced to the wall of the other building, repeating the processes until he had climbed to the roof in a matter of seconds.

"Now you try it," he called down to me. "Don't worry. I won't let you fall."

I took a second to suck up some bravery, then attempted to copy exactly what I'd seen him do. I wasn't quite as graceful as he was, but I made it easily to the top. I threw my arms out and wrapped them around his neck while he spun me around.

"Fun, isn't it?" he said, his eyes sparkling, alive with enjoyment.

"Yes," I agreed, totally wrapped up in the enjoyment of learning. "Show me some more."

We soon were scaling across the rooftops of the school, jumping from building to building, floating and flying across the gaps until we ran out of roof. We then descended back down to the ground beneath and crumpled on a grassy spot, laughing.

"That was great!" I said breathlessly, gazing at the twinkling stars overhead.

"Yeah, it was," Vance said, rolling over onto his stomach so he was the only thing in my vision now. He stared at me, his eyes taking on new meaning while he looked at me. "I love you," he added, brushing a wayward hair to the side.

"I love you too," I replied, reaching my hand up to his face.

"I wish I could show you what I really feel for you. Words don't ever seem like enough."

"I know, Vance. I feel it too."

"Sometimes it's like my life is just beginning. It's a new awakening for me. Even when I knew you were the one for me, I had no idea it would be this strong." He ran his fingers over my lips. "It's not just the physical part of it either. It's everything. I don't know, like I was only halfway living before now."

I placed my finger over his lips to quiet him.

"You don't need to try and explain," I said. "I feel it too, like my heart's always on the verge of overflowing, or about to burst."

"I wish I could marry you right now," he whispered seriously. "I want to show you everything."

"Someday, Vance," I replied. "Like you said before, it just isn't time yet."

"I know." He dipped his head toward mine.

This time he kissed me softly, almost reverently. It was a sweet, innocent kiss, but it still made my heart race. Then he kissed both of my eyelids, followed by my cheeks and the tip of my nose, before he settled on my mouth once more.

When the kiss was over he lay back on his side and pulled me up to spoon against him, and we stared up at the stars. He quietly stroked my hair and occasionally down my arm until I finally fell asleep.

When I woke up later, the first light of morning was starting to crest on the hills around town and Vance was staring at me.

"I didn't want to wake you," he whispered. "You're so pretty when you're sleeping."

I rolled over and wrapped my arms around his neck, giving him a long kiss. He pulled away from me much too soon for my taste though. I tried to pull him back for more, but he held firm.

"I need to get you home before it gets any lighter. How will it look to be riding through town at first light with you in your pajamas?"

"I don't care what people think," I said, not wanting to leave this moment.

"I know, but it's time to go just the same." He hopped up and pulled me to my feet after him.

"You're so beautiful," he said, kissing me lightly once more.

"Of course I am. With my messed up hair and bunny pajamas, I'm sure I look just peachy," I grumbled, rolling my eyes at him.

"Yes, you do." He smiled devilishly. "Like a peach I could eat over and over again, never getting tired of it."

"Oh hush!" I shoved him playfully and raced off toward his parked motorcycle.

He caught up with me easily, and I was "punished" with another breathless kiss before he pushed me away again.

"Come on. Let's get you home. We have school today!" He helped me onto the bike, and we were soon on our way down the deserted road.

Chapter 13

I forced myself to stay away from Vance for one evening so I could have a girl's night out date with Shelly. I noticed she was beginning to feel sorely neglected.

It wasn't like I could just break out and tell her all the things happening in my life. She wouldn't even come close to understanding. I wanted to tell her though. I missed having her as a confidant. It was hard keeping secrets from her.

Even now, Vance was out there, lurking somewhere on the grounds of The Fountains at Fontane. I couldn't stand to be too physically separated from him still. It was hard enough to drag my thoughts away from him, let alone my body.

I plopped in the middle of Shelly's four poster queen-sized bed, crossing my legs underneath me so I could look at pictures of her and Brad from their homecoming date.

Shelly had been upset with me when Vance and I had declined to go on the group date with them to the dance. Actually, the two of us avoided homecoming completely. It had been held during the early days of our binding spell, and there was no way we could've attended that party and not drawn attention to ourselves. We probably would have clawed the clothes right off each other in front of everyone.

Of course, there was no way for me to explain this to Shelly. She took it as a personal insult since she had been in charge of the decorations for the event. And to make things worse, in the weeks following, I'd only ever seen her at school and ditched her at every available opportunity to be with Vance. I had a lot of making up to do.

I turned my full attention to listen to Shelly explaining each picture in a tired, sort of dejected tone.

"It would've been way more fun if you'd actually been there," she said with a sigh, casting me a sideways glance. She gathered the photos and went to place them on her dresser.

"I don't know how else to apologize to you," I said softly. "I'm sorry I wasn't feeling well."

That at least was the truth. I just couldn't tell her I'd been going crazy with desire.

"I know," Shelly replied. "I'm trying to be understanding and adjust my way of thinking. I had all these ideas of how we were going to spend this year together, and then Vance came along, and well ...."

I intensely studied my fingernails, not knowing what to say.

"You really like him a lot, don't you?"

"No, I don't just like him a lot," I said with a short laugh before looking her straight in the eyes. "I'm in love with him. I couldn't imagine my life without him."

Shelly paused for second before she laughed and waved her hand to the side.

"You don't really mean that. Girls our age always think they're in love with someone. Then a week later they're mooning over someone else."

"That may be," I replied, feeling a bit hurt by her

dismissal of my feelings. “But it isn’t true in my case.”

She looked at me with skepticism on her face.

“I love him to the center of my being. No, he is the center of my being.” I let my stare bore into hers, even adding a little magical push to it for emphasis.

Shelly shrank back, as if nervous from the intensity of it.

“Oh, sorry.” She turned away from me. “You know, I don’t really feel up to the movie tonight after all. I kind of feel like I have a headache coming on. Besides, Angie Wilhelm told me it was dumb.”

I nodded in complete understanding. I didn’t need to remind her she’d been looking forward to seeing this movie for weeks, and nothing Angie said to her would’ve stopped her from going. She was trying to get rid of me politely.

Sadly, it was actually a relief to me because it meant I could get back to Vance. Still, I felt bad with the way things were, and I wished I could tell her what was really going on. I wanted her to understand.

I stood up and walked to the door before turning around to say goodbye. I waited there awkwardly for a moment, hoping for her to make eye contact with me, but she never did.

“Well, ‘bye,” I finally said, and I quietly slipped out the door.

Vance was at my side the instant I was out the front door.

“That didn’t go so well. Sorry things are rough because of me.” He put his arms around my shoulders, giving me a squeeze.

“It isn’t your fault,” I said, pausing for a second to look through the window as we passed it.

Shelly was on the phone, and I could hear her

clearly.

"Hi, Mrs. Anderson is Brad home?" she asked, and after a short second she began speaking again.

"Hey, Brad. My plans with Portia didn't work out. You want to go to the movie with me tonight?"

I turned away not wanting to hear anymore.

Vance and I walked down the hill to where he had parked his motorcycle. We climbed on, and I instinctively knew he wasn't taking me home. After a short drive we pulled up in front of his house. He helped me off the bike, and we went inside.

"This is surprise!" Marsha exclaimed, looking up from the movie she was watching on the television. "Come in, come in!" She jumped up and gave me a hug, acting like she'd never entertained company before.

"Portia's feeling a little blue this evening, and she needs to get away from everything for a while. I thought maybe we could entertain her," Vance said. He gave Marsha a peck on the cheek. "Sorry I didn't call first. It was sort of a last-minute decision," he explained, while I stood there feeling dumb for intruding.

"No need for an apology." Marsha smiled. "Why don't you two flip through the channels and see if there's something on you want to watch while I make some popcorn?"

"I don't want you to miss your movie," I said, still feeling overwhelmed by her warm welcome.

"I've seen it already," Marsha called back as she entered the kitchen. "No worries."

Vance checked the guide on the television, and we finally decided to order a comedy on pay-per-view none of us had seen yet.

Marsha soon reappeared with a steaming bowl of buttered popcorn, and a handful of napkins. We all settled in on the overstuffed sofa and began watching the movie.

Surprisingly, I began to feel better almost instantly. I didn't realize until sometime later I was actually feeling happy thoughts coming from Vance, subtly sent my way.

I didn't mind though. We snuggled up closer together, laughing over the funny situations the guy in the movie kept getting himself into. The time passed quickly, and soon the popcorn was gone and the movie was over.

"Boy, I'm tired!" Marsha suddenly exclaimed, a little too obviously, running her hand through her short blond curls. "I'm not used to staying up this late. I guess I'll leave the partying to the two of you and head for bed." She gave us a quick wave and she left the room with a smile.

"She's sweet," I said to Vance. "I like her."

"I do too. Marsha's like true family to me. She's always treated me well, and even though we aren't related, I'll always have a special place in my heart for her."

"She must be a spectacular person to take care of someone she didn't even know."

"That's true," he agreed, becoming quiet. "But let's not talk about that here, okay?"

I nodded in understanding, quickly thinking of something else I'd like to do.

"Can I see your room?" I bit at my lower lip in anticipation.

"My room?" He gave me a quizzical look.

"Yeah, your room. This is the first time you've ever brought me here." I nudged him with my elbow. "I want to see where you live."

"How have I managed to not bring you here in all these weeks we've been together?" He smiled at me with a slight shake of his head. "It must be because I always feel so at home at your house."

He led me down the narrow hallway to a plain, wood paneled door at the end. He opened it, reached inside to flip on the light switch, and stepped aside. He gestured for me to enter.

The room was of moderate size, and I was surprised to find it very clean as well. A twin-sized bed was pushed into one corner, under a large window that was covered in plastic mini-blinds. The bed was draped in a dark blue denim quilt with a pillow in a white case that matched the white sheets peeking out from beneath.

On the opposite wall sat a desk with several of his school books stacked on top of it, along with some motorcycle magazines. The Aloe Vera plant I had given him was sitting on it too. A matching chair held one of his leather jackets tossed over the back of it.

The door to his closet was open slightly, and I could see it was very well-organized. His Levis were hanging nicely in one section, t-shirts on the other side, and his shoes were thrown casually underneath on the floor.

A large wooden wardrobe stood at the opposite end of the room. I walked over and touched the handle of one of the doors.

"May I?"

"Help yourself," he replied, leaning up against the doorjamb and folding his arms.

I opened the cupboard and was surprised at what I found inside. It was an altar, of sorts, a shelf, covered in purple velvet, and it contained all of his magical belongings.

My fingers ran over the twisted black handle of his athame, which I had to admit was a bit wicked looking in its design. It had pointed gold embellishments around the hilt, and the metal on the blade looked dark and pitted, except for around the edges where it gleamed a bright, silver color. There were three strange curved notches with sharp points in one side of the blade. I'd never seen this on an athame before.

I lifted the knife, glancing over at him. "What are these for?"

"They're called gut hooks." He chuckled.

"Oh," I replied, a little taken by surprise. "That's kind of self-explanatory, isn't it?" I turned the knife in my hands wondering why he could possibly need these.

"They're just for show," he said, reading my mind. "That knife was custom made for me by a local craftsman I met. I happened to come across his store one day and was admiring his work. We struck up a conversation about how he made his knives and he showed me an old pitted chainsaw blade he'd found. I thought the pitted metal looked cool, so I commissioned him to make me an athame out of it."

"Really? That's awesome. It turned out very nice, though it does look a little lethal."

"It is," he replied. "So be careful."

I smiled at him, moving to replace it in its spot. I noticed a small chalice, a few crystals, and his Book of Shadows. I ran my fingers over the worn leather cover and it was as though I could feel his essence emanating from it when I touched it.

It was then I noticed the bent corner of an old photo hanging out of the book. Curiosity got the better of me and I pulled on it slightly, without removing it completely, so I could see what the image was.

There was a beautiful woman in the photo. She had brown curly hair, a soft pretty smile and was holding a toddler on her hip.

"That's me and my mom," Vance said from the doorway. "It's the only photo I have of her."

"She's very pretty," I said, continuing to look into the eyes of the woman who had given up her only child to protect him. My heart constricted tightly. "I hope she's all right." I slid the picture carefully back into the book.

"Me too," he replied, a hint of sorrow echoing in his voice.

I closed the doors quietly and turned to walk back toward him, but my eye caught something else, another book sticking out from under his bed. I went over and pulled it out, surprised to see last year's yearbook with bookmarks in several of the pages.

I opened the annual to the first place marked and found myself staring at a picture of me. It was the same for every page marked after that. Class pictures, candid shots, club photos, anywhere I appeared in the book had been flagged. I looked up at him expectantly.

"I'm sorry if it seems a bit stalkerish, but it's the only pictures I have of you. I couldn't very well follow you around with a camera snapping photos of you all the time." He shrugged. "I still look at them every day, but it used to be a lot more before you got your powers."

"I guess I'll have to see about getting hold of a camera and getting you some new ones then." I closed the book, sitting down on his bed, before sliding it back underneath where I found it. "Besides, I'd love to have a few pictures of you too."

Vance pushed away from the door and crossed the room to come sit next to me.

"You didn't find my biggest secret," he said with a sly grin, and he leaned over reaching farther back under the bed. When he sat back up, he was holding a guitar in his hands.

"You play?" I asked in amazement.

He nodded. "A little. My mom taught me while we were on the run. I think she thought it would help take my mind off things." He began strumming quietly on the strings, tuning them.

"Do you sing too?" I asked.

"Only to myself." He laughed before adding, "And usually very quietly. I wouldn't want to scare anyone."

"Play something for me," I said gleefully, delighted he would share this part of himself with me.

"What do you want me to play?"

"Anything," I replied, my smile wide.

Vance stared off into space for a moment and then began playing a soft melody I'd never heard before. It was a beautiful haunting sound, filled with longing. He'd grossly understated his talent. He was very accomplished.

I let his music and the mood he was creating wash over me as he played, leaning back onto his pillow and closing my eyes so all my senses were tuned into only him. Here and there he would quietly hum along with the tune. The sound was enchanting. After several minutes he stopped and placed the guitar on the floor next to the bed, before he moved to lie next to me.

"Why are you crying?" he asked in surprise, wiping a single tear from my face. "It wasn't that bad was it?" He smiled slightly.

I shook my head. "No. It was beautiful. I'm sad because I can't imagine how lonely you've been," I replied. "I've always been surrounded by friends and family. I was loved, nurtured, and cared for."

"I've had those things too—just not in the traditional sense. True, most of my memories of family come from my past, but Marsha has taken good care of me, and we have a healthy kinship that's been born out of the things we've faced together. It hasn't been all bad." He stroked his hand over my hair. "I'm sorry. I didn't mean to make you feel sad."

"No, I loved it. It was wonderful. It was you." I nuzzled my face into the space between his head and shoulder, loving the smell of him ... fresh air, leather, and some cool scented aftershave he wore. I inhaled deeply as he held me in his arms.

"Thank you for caring about me, Portia. It means a lot," he said softly.

"I love you." My eyes brimmed slightly with unshed tears. "I want to be part of your family."

"You already are my family," he corrected me. "More family than I've had in a long, long, time. I've missed having a really close connection with someone, the kind where you can share everything. You've given that back to me."

We didn't speak at all to each other after that. We just relished the feel of being in each other's arms, holding each other for the better part of an hour, and it was magical.

"Do you think your parents would mind if we just slept here tonight?" he whispered softly to me.

I shook my head. "Dad knows I'm with you, and I'm sure he's filled Mom in on everything by now. I'm positive they trust Marsha."

"Do you need to call them?"

"No, they're both gone again tonight, though maybe I'll leave a message on the machine, just in case my mom comes home from work early."

Vance pulled his cell phone out of his pocket and handed it to me. When I was finished making the call, he got up and pulled me up too. He reached down and turned the covers back, before he removed his shirt off and took off his belt. He sat down to unlace his boots.

I was wearing a loose flowing mini dress over leggings and a tank top, so I pulled the dress off and sat down on the edge of the bed, slipping out of my shoes. I took a few clips out of my hair and placed them on the nightstand next to the bed. When I was finished, I turned to place my feet under the covers.

Vance stood, walking across the room toward the light switch.

"Vance," I called softly, and he looked back at me. "Will you sleep with me tonight? Under the covers, I mean."

He stood still, staring at me for a mere moment before he came to join me. He slid into the bed and pulled the covers up over us both. He moved up against me, turning me so we were spooning.

"You forgot to turn out the light," I whispered, giggling slightly.

He reached one hand out from under the covers and with a snap of his fingers the light turned off, covering us in darkness except for a soft glow through the window. He put his arm back under the blanket and hugged me tightly.

"I love you," he whispered into my ear as he cradled me.

"I love you too. Thanks for bringing me here tonight." My hand searched out his under the covers and I laced our fingers together.

"Was it everything you imagined it to be?" he asked with a chuckle.

"No." I laughed. "Your room is much cleaner than I expected."

"I'm glad I can still surprise you."

"I'm surprised by you every day." I gave his arm a

squeeze.

"How so?" he asked, sounding curious.

"Every day I wake up to find you're still here and you still want me."

"That'll never change, but I don't see why it surprises you."

"I just feel so unworthy of your attention sometimes, let alone your love," I whispered.

"Don't ever talk like that." He hugged me tightly, his lips brushing my hair as he spoke. "You're worthy of so much more than me."

"Vance. I don't want anyone else but you." I tried to turn so I could kiss him, but he held me firmly in place, not allowing me to move.

"Don't, Portia, please. We're so close right now, and this feels so intimate. I don't think I could stop if you kissed me." He was silent for a moment, taking in a deep breath. "I've dreamed for a long time about when I would finally be able to hold you next to me in my own bed. Only I'm afraid my version wasn't quite as chaste as this."

"I understand," I said, laying my head back onto the pillow, facing the wall.

I really did understand him. I'd had my own dreams that were similar. They came instantly the moment I closed my eyes at night, drowning me in the promises of future pleasure, and I relished them. Even now I could easily picture myself tangled in his arms in the heat of passion. It was something I longed for, even though I really wanted to respect his wishes on the matter too.

"Portia," he growled at me through gritted teeth. "You can't even think about it. The temptation is too much for me." He started to move away. "I'm going to have to go sleep on the floor."

"Don't leave." I grabbed at his arms before they slipped

away from me. "I'll be good. I promise." I immediately pictured myself in my bunny pajamas.

"Nice try," he laughed, capturing the image of my thoughts. "But you're still in your pajamas. Think of something else."

I imagined bunnies romping through a field together.

"Got anything besides rabbits?" he asked.

Immediately, lions in a fierce fight jumped into my mind.

"Nope. Too carnal." He laughed. "Can't handle the bloodlust."

I sighed in exasperation and imagined my grandma making out with her mailman.

"Ugh, that's working. Please stop, though, you're killing me here," he said. "Now I need to have my mind wiped completely."

I laughed and tried my best to think of nothing, and I slowly drifted off to sleep.

Chapter 14

Vance and I noticed a serious decline in Shelly's mental attitude over the next few weeks, so I began making an extra special effort to incorporate her into my day-to-day activities. I sat by her at lunch and called her after school. Vance and I even went on a few double dates with her and Brad.

The puzzling thing about it was while Brad and Vance became ever closer as friends, Shelly and I drifted farther and farther apart. It wasn't just me who was experiencing the apparent cooling either.

Brad pulled me aside one day to tell me things between him and Shelly had been getting difficult also.

"I don't know what to do," he said in a frustrated voice. "She's totally despondent. I can't get her to be excited about anything. All the things she used to like she doesn't have any interest in anymore. She just wants to be alone all the time, and it worries me."

I'd promised him I'd try again to talk to her to see if I could find out what was going on. That led me to where I was today, sitting outside the school early in the morning, waiting for her to arrive.

I almost missed her when she came, not because I didn't see her, but because I didn't recognize her when she did. I wasn't prepared for her once pink mustang to now be painted pitch black with a funky little skull and crossbones air-brushed onto the back. As shocked as I was over that, it was nothing to what I experienced when she stepped out of the car.

Gone were the gorgeous blond curly locks. While it was still long, she had dyed her hair jet black except for a few platinum streaks. It had been flat ironed straight and had several small braids with little silver threads running through them.

Her makeup had been done a shade too pale, and she had lined her eyes thickly with coal black liner. She also wore a deep shade of red lipstick.

Her clothes were comprised of skin-tight leather pants and a form-fitting matching jacket, placed over a tight, white tank top. Around her neck was a long, thin leather cord which hung nearly to her stomach. It bore a round, silver skull and crossbones emblem on the bottom. Black heeled, knee-high boots graced her feet, which made her Barbie-like figure seem even taller.

Shelly reached into her car and pulled out a large leather bag with silver studs. She slung it over her shoulder and began walking toward the school.

"Shelly?" I asked when she approached my position, still wondering if it was actually her.

She paused for only a moment to give me an arched eyebrow as she glanced over my appearance. She gave me a not-so-nice sardonic grin, flipped her hair, and continued right on past me into the school.

I sat dazed for a moment, too shocked for words, before I turned to follow through the glass doors after her.

I was not the only one surprised, apparently.

The locker hall was lined with students who had gone completely silent. They were staring at Shelly as she made her way down the hall. In fact, the clacking of Shelly's boots was the only sound I could hear.

Shelly seemed completely oblivious to the silent stares as she made her way through the crowd toward her locker. She stopped, quickly twirling out her combination. She opened the door, grabbed out a book, and slammed it closed again. That was when I noticed Brad standing on the other side of her, a disbelieving stare of his own on his face.

"What the heck, Shelly?" he said, giving her the once over. "Are you all right?"

"Whatever could you possibly be referring to?" Shelly gave him the same arched eyebrow she'd just given me.

"What's all—this?" He gestured toward her hair and clothing with his hand.

The two stood there, staring at each other for several moments without speaking. Finally, Shelly broke the silence.

"Just let it go, Brad, okay? I have better things to deal with than you."

With that she shoved past him, knocking him up against the lockers as she went. She didn't apologize, or even look back, as she continued down the hall and into one of the classrooms.

Instantly everyone was abuzz, students talking and pointing at Brad, unable to believe what they just witnessed.

Brad turned, catching my eye, and began weaving through the throng of people toward me.

"Hey, Vance, Portia," he said, nodding to each of us.

I hadn't even realized Vance was standing behind me until Brad spoke.

"How long have you been there?" I asked,

wondering why I hadn't felt him before.

"Long enough to catch the show," he muttered.

"Yeah," Brad broke in. "What's up with that?"

"I have no idea." I shook my head. "She wouldn't even give me the time of day when I tried to talk to her outside."

"Well, I'm guessing the two of us are through," Brad replied, looking totally downcast. "She made it pretty clear I'm not too high on her list of importance."

"Sorry, guy." Vance reached out to clap Brad on the shoulder. "Hopefully it'll get better."

Brad shook his head. "I'm not holding my breath."

I felt bad as Brad turned and walked away from us. I wished I could've said something that would have made him feel better, but I was just as stunned as he was.

"Something isn't right with Shelly," Vance said, breaking into my thoughts.

"I thought that was obvious."

"No. I mean something besides the obvious. I'm sensing some sort of weird vibe around her."

"Weird vibe? You don't mean something magical, do you?"

He shrugged his shoulders slightly. "I'm not sure, maybe."

"Well, that'd definitely be a twist that I didn't see coming," I said, wondering what was going on. "Is there a way we can find out for sure?"

"I don't know. I'd need to watch her a little bit longer. Maybe even follow her around a bit."

"Do whatever you think you should. This is Shelly we're talking about. You have my complete support."

He nodded, leaning in to give me a kiss on the cheek. "I'll do what I can."

The next few weeks were a total testament to Shelly's

popularity at school. Dozens of girls were soon sporting her new gothic look, as well as more than a few of the guys too. Of course, their look was a little more masculine, but still, it was unreal to see.

I watched in amazement as Shelly routinely dropped each one of her previous friends from her list of associates. She steadily recruited new friends to replace each of those she had lost.

These new "friends" of hers were the kind of people we never really bothered to notice before—the druggies, partiers, and students who were generally always in trouble with some type of authority or another, whether it be the school administration or the local law enforcement.

I watched her closely, trying to find any resemblance to the girl who'd previously been my best friend. Occasionally, I noticed Vance shadowing her from a distance also, observing her actions.

I asked him a lot of questions about her, but he had few answers. He kept saying something wasn't right and he felt compelled to find out what it was. I found I was spending a lot less time with him as he followed her around. At the same time Vance was slipping out of my life more and more, Brad became a near-constant figure at my house.

Basketball season was drawing nearer and he would come over after practice to hang out. We watched television together a lot, or sometimes we'd just sit out on the porch swing wrapped in our coats, since the air was now very chilly. He never really said much. He seemed to desire being in my company. I hadn't realized until now how much he must've cared for Shelly. He was taking their break up very hard.

"I'd better get going," Brad said when we heard

Vance's motorcycle roar into the driveway one evening.

"Okay. Have a good night." I stood to wrap my arms around him, giving him a hug.

"I don't even know what that means anymore," he said with a small laugh, reaching his arms around me, holding me tightly. "Thanks for being here for me, Portia."

"Anytime." I stepped out of his embrace just as Vance walked into the courtyard.

"Hey, man," Vance said to Brad, and they gave each other some sort of guy fist-bump thing.

"I'm just heading out," Brad said, clapping him on the shoulder in a friendly gesture when he walked by. "Thanks for loaning me your girl. Have fun."

"Later," Vance answered.

Vance waited until Brad was gone, then he wrapped his arms around me and gave me a big kiss.

"You two shouldn't sit out here so long every night. You're freezing." He shuttled me back into the house.

"Sorry," I said. "Brad seems to enjoy it though, and I'm just trying to help him out."

"I know. I just want you to be careful. Your health is important too."

"I'm fine." I led him up the stairs, into my room. "So how's Shelly?" I asked, shutting the door behind us.

Vance shrugged, sitting on the end of the bed. "More of the same." He sighed, sounding exhausted himself.

"Still hanging out at that bar?"

"Yep. Every single night this week." He ran his fingers through his hair like he always did when he was frustrated. "The funny thing is no one seems to care. Her parents act like they don't even notice anything different. No one at the bar cares she's underage. They serve her whatever she wants. Even an officer doing a business patrol didn't blink an eye at her. It's so weird. I haven't seen any evidence of anything magical, but my gut keeps telling me something is different."

"That does seem strange. By all means keep listening to your instincts, though." I watched him shrug out of his jacket. "Would you like to use the shower?" I added, changing the subject. "You positively reek of cigarette smoke from that place."

"Sure." He got up and grabbed some of his clean clothes out of my dresser. He had started leaving some of his stuff here after I complained about him not smelling too great after his little spy outings to the bar. He went into the bathroom, and I heard him turn the shower on.

I used this time to change into my pajamas and crawled into bed. I must have fallen asleep quickly, because the next thing I knew he was lying on the top of the quilt, and he smelled wonderful.

"I love you," he whispered, placing a soft kiss against my cheek.

I didn't even know if my answer made it out of my lips before I fell asleep again.

Vance was gone in the morning when I woke. I hurriedly got ready for school and headed downstairs to eat breakfast.

"Hey, kiddo!" Dad called out. He stood up from the table to give me a kiss before settling back down to the morning newspaper.

My mom gave me a quick peck on the cheek too, before she placed a plate of hot eggs and toast in front of me.

"Isn't this nice?" she said, pouring orange juice. "It's been a long time since we've had a family breakfast together." She brought three glasses of juice back to the table and sat down to join us looking expectantly at my dad.

Dad folded his paper, and the three of us held each other's hands while he said grace over the meal.

When he was done, Dad asked casually, "What're everyone's plans today?"

"Just school and any homework I have," I replied and bit into a piece of toast.

"I'm off tonight," Mom added.

"Let's go do dinner and a movie in Flagstaff tonight then. It's been a while since we've been able to do anything as a family."

"That sounds fun," I said, really meaning it, but worrying about being away from Vance too.

Dad must have read my mind. "Vance can come too if you'd like." He smiled. "It'll be a double date." He winked at me.

"Thanks. I'll ask him when he gets here."

I'd just finished and was putting my plate in the dishwasher when I heard Vance pull up. I met him at the door.

"Hey, gorgeous," he said softly, bending to give me a kiss on the cheek.

I told him about the invitation for the evening from my parents, and he consented to go. I relayed the news to my parents and we left.

When we got to school, we saw Shelly and her brood hanging out in a secluded part of the parking lot. I noticed she sent a somewhat scalding look in our direction. I was really puzzled by this since we'd never done anything to her.

We went inside, and Vance walked me to my locker. He waited patiently for me to arrange my things and get what I needed. Then we went to his locker.

I was leaning against the wall, waiting for him, when

Shelly came into the hall with several of her flunkies following behind her. She stopped to glance around, then seemed to make a beeline straight for us. She walked up next to me, standing directly behind Vance.

"Hey, Vance," she said in a soft, sultry voice.

Vance turned around to face her, a somewhat quizzical look on his face.

I was horrified when she stepped forward, rubbing her body up against him like a cat. She wrapped her arms around his neck and proceeded to kiss him full on the mouth, moving her lips back and forth over his for several seconds.

Vance stood still, in complete shock until she stepped back away from him, her red lipstick smeared all over his mouth.

"I knew you'd be hot," she said, running a black polished nail down the side of her mouth as if she were wiping something away. She then reached over to trail the same finger back and forth across his chest, moving lower, down toward his flat stomach.

Vance regained his senses and reached out to snag her hand.

"What the heck are you doing, Shelly?" he asked, holding it out far away from his body.

I didn't wait for her to answer. I swung back and punched her square in the face.

Chapter 15

Shelly and I sat in chairs on the opposite sides of the hallway while we waited for the principal to call us into his office. She was still holding a large handful of tissue over her nose, pinching it, while the school nurse continued to give her instructions on how to stop the bleeding.

I didn't feel a bit sorry, even when Shelly kept glaring over at me. I knew she was trying to intimidate me, but I just folded my arms and stared back.

After warning the two of us to behave, the nurse finally left.

"Nice punch," Shelly sneered, her voice sounding muffled by all the tissue. "The nurse thinks you broke my nose."

"Good," I said, suddenly feeling very satisfied.

"I can't believe you hit me over some stupid boy," she whined.

"I thought I already explained how I feel about Vance to you."

"Whatever," she said. "He's not into you the way you think he is."

"Is that so?" I wondered what could possibly be running through her head.

"He's been following me around for weeks now."

Shelly lowered the tissues so she could glare at me better. "Everywhere I go, every time I turn around, there he is, watching me."

"Duh," I said flatly, looking at the raccoon bruises which were already forming under her eyes. "That's because we've been worried about you."

"Well, you should worry. I've never felt sparks like that flying off a guy. He was like butter and honey all rolled together, soft and delicious. I'm definitely going to need another taste." She licked her lips for added emphasis.

I was instantly on my feet ready to pound on her again, when the door to the principal's office swung open.

"Miss Mullins!" he called out loudly, stopping me in my tracks. "Please step inside."

I gave Shelly one last glare, clenching my fists at my sides, before I turned and headed into the room.

Mr. Holland closed the door behind me, motioning for me to have a seat in the chair at the front of his desk, while he walked around to the other side to seat himself.

"Miss Mullins, I have to say I'm surprised and frankly a little disappointed also," he began, folding his hands together in front of himself.

I did my best to hold my peace and listen to what he had to say.

"You've always been a model student here, and the teachers have good things to say about you too." He paused expectantly, as if waiting for me to say something. When I didn't, he gave a big sigh and continued on. "As you know we have a strict no fighting policy here at Sedona High School."

I nodded.

"I understand from several of the eyewitnesses you may have felt somewhat provoked in this incident."

I gave him a half shrug.

"Do you care to elaborate?"

"Nope," I replied, wishing he would just hurry and get on with the punishing part of this speech.

"Well, under the circumstances since you threw the only punch and did cause significant bodily harm to Miss Fontane, I'm going to have to suspend you for three days. I need to advise you also, pending a visit with Miss Fontane and her parents, a legal complaint may be filed against you."

"I understand." I wondered how bad this whole thing might actually get.

"In that case you need to go get your things and wait in my secretary's, office. I'll be calling your parents to come pick you up."

"I have my scooter here today. I can drive myself," I explained, wanting to delay the call to my parents as long as possible.

"School policy says a parent has to come get you. Sorry." He opened the door to his office and waited for me step out. "Miss Fontane," he called, beckoning to Shelly.

She stood and began walking toward me. "Sucker," she whispered as we passed each other.

I ignored her and continued back on to the locker hall to get my things. Vance was there waiting for me in the empty hall. I could see he'd scrubbed his face clean since it no longer had Shelly's lipstick smeared all over it.

"I'm sorry." He leaned up against the locker next to mine. "You okay?"

"Just peachy," I said, throwing a few things into my bag before slamming the door closed.

Vance grabbed me by the shoulders, turning me to face him.

"You know there's nothing going on there, right? I mean between me and Shelly." He stared into my eyes, and I saw the honesty radiating from them.

"She isn't going to stop, you know?" I pushed past him to walk down the hallway. "She made it pretty clear, now that she's had a taste she wants more."

He quickly caught up to me, grabbing my arm and spinning me around.

"I could care less what she wants." He placed his hands on both sides of my face. "I'm bound to you, and only you." His eyes searched mine and he gently kissed me.

"Go back to class, Mr. Mangum," Mrs. Bloomfield's shrill voice cut through the moment. "Miss Mullins, follow me please."

Vance's hands dropped to his sides. "I'll see you after school," he whispered, sounding frustrated, but not wanting to rock the boat anymore. "I love you."

"Love you too," I said and turned away to follow Mrs. Bloomfield back to her office.

Both of my parents came to the school to pick me up. After a brief visit with the principal, Mom drove me home in the car while Dad rode on my scooter behind us.

I normally would've laughed my head off at the image of my dad on a green moped with a purple flowered helmet on his head, but under the circumstances, no one was laughing. In fact, no one said anything until we were all settled in the living room.

"So what happened?" my mom asked me, looking mildly worried.

I began explaining the events which had been leading up to this over the past few weeks, and what had caused my reaction today.

"Well, I will say I can understand why you did what you did," my dad began, stroking his chin in thought. "However, it does give me some concerns over your control issues. You're a witch, Portia, and as a witch you should always be in control. Bad things can happen when you rule totally from emotion."

"I understand." I knew what I'd done was wrong, and I wasn't arguing that fact. "So what's my punishment?"

"No punishment," Mom said, with a shake of her head. "Just do your best to repair things with Shelly."

I nodded, thinking making up with Shelly would probably be near to impossible, but I would try.

"Well, is there any work you need me to do?" I asked glancing at both of them while I stood. "Looks like I'm going to be here for the next three days."

"No. Just the usual picking up," Mom replied.

"Sounds good. I'll be in my room if you need me."

"Don't forget about our plans for this evening," my dad called after me. "Unless you don't want to go now."

"No. I still want to." I headed up the stairs. I needed to do something, anything to get out of my own head for a while.

Jinx was waiting to pounce on me the minute I entered my room. I threw my belongings on my desk and plopped myself onto the bed, letting her nuzzle my face to her heart's content.

"I was a bad girl today," I mumbled while I stroked her soft white fur.

Her replied meow sounded like a denial. "Well, you're kind of biased." I laughed.

I rolled her over and tickled her belly. She purred loudly, batting at my hand playfully with her paws, and trying to nip at me with her teeth.

"I love you, Jinx," I said, scooping her up and

cuddling her. "You're a good little kitty."

She licked my nose before she jumped out of my arms, back onto the bed. I flopped over onto my pillow and closed my eyes.

"Get some rest," I heard Vance's voice whisper softly in my mind. "I'll be there at lunch."

"All right." My heart ached with his physical absence.

"Love you."

"Love you more," I replied.

"Not possible," he returned with a chuckle.

"Do your schoolwork!" I chastened.

"Okay." His laughter faded from my head.

I didn't know I had fallen asleep until I felt Vance's soft kiss on my forehead.

"Hey, sleepyhead."

I opened my eyes to his smiling face.

"Hi," I said, stretching. "Is it lunch time already?"

"Yep. You were out like a light." He laughed. "I couldn't even hear your dreams when I'd try to check in on you."

"This morning was a little bit emotional for me," I said with a slight pout.

"That's completely understandable. By the way, great right hook." He grinned. "And it didn't even have any magic in it!"

"Yeah, well I guess my baser instincts took over."

"I'm glad you're on my side!" He laughed. "I've never had girls fist fight over me before. Well, unless you count that time that ...," his voice trailed off, and he glanced over at me. "Never mind. We'll save that story for another day."

I gave him a small forced grin before I sobered up again.

"The next three days will be miserable without you here," I complained, pulling him down next to me.

"Don't worry," he said, wrapping his arms around me. "I'll be here every minute I can, and the rest of the time I'll only be a thought away."

"I know. But it still won't be the same."

There was a soft knock on the door, and my mom walked in holding a plate with two sandwiches. She had a bag of chips and two cold sodas in her other arm.

"I thought you two could use some lunch." She set the items down on the dresser.

"Thanks, Mom. You're the best."

"By the way, the school called while you were sleeping. Shelly and her family said they won't be pressing any charges," she told us as she left the room.

"Well, that's a relief," I said, turning to Vance. "The nurse said she thought Shelly's nose was broken."

"It is," Vance replied with an assured air.

"How do you know?"

"I have my ways." He held his hands over my head and wiggling his fingers while making a mysterious looking face and crazy eyes at me.

I started laughing out loud, and he started tickling me.

"Stop!" I gasped after several seconds of his assault. "You need to eat, or you'll be late to go back to school."

"Oh, all right." He moved away, picking up one of the sandwiches off the plate, and offered the other to me.

"Seriously, though, can you use your magic to diagnose people's injuries?" I asked.

"I can if I touch them. I held Shelly back after she charged at you, right before the teachers broke it up."

"Interesting." I carefully chewed a bite of my sandwich. "Can all witches and warlock's do that?"

"Not all. It's a special gift exclusive to healer witches."

"So you're a healer witch ... um, warlock?"

"Yes."

"Can you heal yourself if you get sick?"

"No. A healer witch besides me would have to do that."

"Why?"

"Because my powers could be affected by my illness, depending on what it type it was."

"Oh." I pondered this for a moment. "So how does one find out if they're a healer witch?"

"When they have the opportunity to heal someone and it works." He reached for the bag of chips.

"Who did you heal?" I asked out of curiosity.

"My mom." His eyes got a faraway look in them. "She accidentally cut her hand on a knife while doing dishes. I saw all the blood, ran over to place my hands on her cut and it healed."

"How old were you?"

"Five. It was my first manifestation of my power," he said, looking at me.

"Wow. No wonder everyone's impressed with you. How'd you even know what to do?"

He shrugged nonchalantly. "Just instinct, I guess."

"Can I ask you something else?"

"Sure. Ask away." He took a big swig of his soda.

"What's your mom's name?"

He sat there for a moment before signaling me to be quiet by placing a finger over his lips.

"Krista Leah Mangum," his voice whispered very softly in my mind.

"And your dad's?"

This time he shook his head.

"Not here. Not now. It isn't safe," he said out loud, and when I looked discouraged he added, "It's more of a precaution really, Portia. We're just trying to keep anything he might be doing to track us at bay."

"Sorry," I mumbled, looking down at my half-eaten sandwich, worried I'd crossed a line with him.

He hooked his finger under my chin and lifted it to meet his gaze. "You never have to be sorry around me. Not for any reason." He leaned forward and kissed my forehead.

"Vance! You're going to be late if you don't leave now!" my mom's voice interrupted, calling from downstairs.

"I'll be back after school," he promised, standing to leave.

"All right. I think I'll go spend the rest of the afternoon with my grandma at the store, though." I replied, getting up to give him a hug goodbye.

"Okay. I guess I'll meet you there then."

He ended our hug with a kiss, then he was off, running down the stairs. I followed him outside just so I could watch him drive away.

"He's a good kid," my mom said from behind my back.

"Yes, he is."

"He cares a lot about you. I find that unusual in a young man of his age."

"Vance is exceptional," I stated.

"You'll be careful, won't you?" Mom asked. "I know he's eighteen already and he's an adult, but you're still only sixteen. If he hadn't been on the run and gotten behind in school, he'd have been graduated and long gone by this time. It worries me he may be ready to move on with a part of his life you're not ready for."

I turned back toward her when he was out of sight.

"Mom, I'm not trying to be disrespectful, but I would happily go wherever, and do whatever, Vance wanted me to."

"That's what I'm afraid of," she said seriously. "You could end up on the run with him, out there alone and unprotected." She looked me over. "Or even pregnant."

I gave a half laugh. "Is that what this is really about? Sex?"

"Are you sleeping with him?" she asked me point blank.

"Yes, mother, I am. Every night. Emphasis on the sleep." I folded my arms over my chest. "And just for the record, I personally would love to be doing a whole lot more than that, but Vance has some other goals that are important to him. I'm doing my best to help him honor those."

"You two are playing with fire, you know, spending so much time together," she said, but I could see the apparent relief on her features.

"I know we are, and I'm not going to lie. It's been hard, Mom." I raked a hand through my hair, needing to talk to someone and feeling thankful my mom and I had always shared a close bond. "I almost feel obsessed with him at times. The whole view of the world changes for me when I'm with him. I love him a lot, and I want to be with him in every way possible," I replied honestly. "But I also realize it's not time for some things yet, so please know I'm not rushing into anything I'm not ready for."

She smiled softly at me, lifting her hand to my face. "You're growing up so fast," she said. "Where did the time go?"

"I don't know," I replied, giving her a hug. "But no matter how old I am, I'll always be your little girl."

"Thank you for trying to be responsible," she whispered into my ear, and I laughed out loud.

"You do remember I just got suspended for three days for beating up my best friend, right?"

"You know what I mean!" She joined in with my laugh, giving a playful spanking to my rear end. "Do you have any homework? I need to run to the store real quick."

"No, I don't, but do you care if I go over to Grandma's store for the rest of the afternoon?" I asked her.

"Not at all. She'd probably enjoy your help."

I followed her into the kitchen, watching while she gathered her purse and the grocery list.

"I'll be back by four so we can go to Flagstaff," I said, walking her to the garage.

"Okay. Do you want me to give you a ride to Milly's?"

"I'll take my scooter."

"All right, sweetheart. See you later then," she said and got into the car.

I went into the house, grabbed my coat and headed back to the garage. I thought better of it after a second, deciding instead to walk. I had a lot of pent-up energy and felt I could use the air right now. A brisk jaunt down the road seemed just the thing to clear my head and help me work out some of my emotions concerning Shelly. I wasn't alone in my thoughts for long though.

"You're amazing," Vance's voice whispered.

"What're you talking about?"

"That conversation with your mom. I was eavesdropping."

"Were you now?" I smiled to myself.

"Yes. And I think you're even more wonderful now than I did before, though I don't know why I'm surprised."

I laughed out loud, and a passing jogger gave me a funny look.

"I really don't know what you're going on about," I said back to him.

"You were so honest with her. I can't think of many girls who would tell their mom point blank how much they want to sleep with their boyfriend." He chuckled. "Unless of course you were trying to kill her with a heart attack."

"No! Of course not!" I said, rolling my eyes. "My parents have trusted us. It's got to be hard for them. I promise you if magic weren't involved, or this binding spell, I'm sure my dad would be chasing you off with a shotgun, or whatever else warlocks run would-be suitors off with."

"I'm positive you're correct on that matter," Vance replied wryly. "So why tell her you want to have sex with me? Doesn't that stir the pot?"

"No. It tells her I'm responsible enough to talk to her frankly about this kind of stuff. And it'll reassure her that their trust in you hasn't been misplaced."

"Don't count your chickens before they're hatched," I heard him mumble.

"What?"

"I'm saying you put too much faith in me. These are walls that could easily crumble. Trust me, the temptation is excruciating."

"And that's why I believe in you," I replied. "Because you're trying to stay away from temptation."

"And that's what I'm trying to tell you. I'm failing miserably. She's right, you know. If you were older, I'd be asking you to move on to a different stage in your life."

"But I'm not older, so I guess we're stuck making the best of our current situation. If we struggle to do things right for just ourselves, then let's try to do it for them as repayment for their faith in us."

"Like I said before, you're amazing."

Chapter 16

I was standing at the corner waiting to cross the highway. I noticed a woman driving a station wagon in the lane closest to me. Suddenly a dark clad figure on a motorcycle whipped around from behind and cut sharply in front of it.

The woman in the car jerked the wheel hard to the right to avoid a collision, and the vehicle popped up onto the sidewalk, coming straight for me.

I was paralyzed with a moment of fear.

"Run, Portia!" Vance's voice screamed into my head, and an image of us levitating together on the football field filled my mind.

I ran toward the vehicle, my left foot levitating on air, the right one actually touching the hood. I pushed off hard, sending my body into a roll as I coasted over the roof of the vehicle, only clearing it by inches. I landed in a crouch behind it and sank to sit on the ground. The station wagon hit a street light and came to a stop while the motorcycle sped off down the street.

I shook violently for several moments before the car door opened.

"Are you all right?" A shrill panicked voice filled the air, and a woman slowly exited her vehicle. She appeared to be several months pregnant.

"I'm fine." I hurried to reassure her, hoping she was okay too.

"I'm so sorry!" She rushed to my side.

"It wasn't your fault. It was the motorcycle." I noticed her trembling figure. "You should go back and sit in your car. I'll be okay."

By this time people were pulling over and running to help. I saw Grandma exit her store and run to cross the street.

"Somebody call 911," a man yelled out to the group of bystanders.

"Ouch!" The pregnant woman groaned, suddenly hunching over, grabbing her stomach.

"I'm fine! Help her!" I called to my grandma as she approached.

Grandma nodded and ran to the woman's side. I started to stand up to go help her, but the man who stood next to me told me to stay put.

"You could have injuries we can't see. Wait for the paramedics to check you out."

I felt stupid just sitting here, but it would be a lot easier to do that than to explain to him I was uninjured because I was a witch. I folded my arms around my knees and waited.

It shouldn't have surprised me that Vance made it to the scene before the police or ambulance, but it did. He was suddenly there next to me, running his hands all over my body, checking me out.

"I'm fine!" I said again, slightly exasperated. "Go check the other lady! I think she's in labor." I pushed his hands away.

He locked eyes with me for a moment, the fear in them apparent, before he nodded and went to help Grandma.

I could hear the wailing of sirens coming down the street. Soon a couple of police cars and an ambulance pulled up. One of the paramedics grabbed a trauma bag out of the back and ran toward the station wagon. The other came over toward me.

"I'm all right." I sighed. "The car didn't hit me. I just fell," I lied.

"Let me check you out real quick then," the young man said.

After taking my blood pressure, feeling my pulse, listening to my lungs, and giving me a general once over, he finally allowed me to refuse treatment. Grandma signed the release for me since I was underage.

I stood and watched as they strapped the pregnant woman to a backboard before wheeling her on a gurney to the back of the ambulance. Apparently, she was in full labor now. She kept apologizing to me as they loaded her. I reassured her I was fine and to concentrate on taking care of herself and her baby.

After the ambulance left, a police officer came over to question me about the accident. I told him about the motorcycle that fled the scene, and I hoped I made up a convincing enough scenario to fool anyone who had actually seen the accident. I said I jumped up onto the concrete base of the light pole, before jumping out of the way of the car. No one questioned me about it, and it was obvious to everyone I was okay, so I guessed it would stick.

The officer released me into the care of my grandma, and we walked across the street together while Vance got his bike, drove it over and parked it in front of her store.

"How'd you get out of school so fast?" I laughed as we approached him when he got off the motorcycle.

He didn't answer me. Instead he grabbed me in a

crushing bear hug and then kissed me hard.

"I was so worried." He ran his hands down my arms and over my stomach, then placing them on my head.

I knew he was checking me over again. I grabbed both of his hands in mine and pulled them away.

"I'm fine, Vance. Really," I stared into his concerned eyes. "The car barely touched me. Technically, I touched it. I'm okay."

"Let's go inside," Grandma said, and we followed her into the store, hand in hand.

"You didn't answer my question," I said to him.

"Hmm? What question?" Vance replied with a raised eyebrow.

"How'd you get here so fast?"

"I just ran out of the school, hopped on my motorcycle and came straight here. I'm sure my teacher will be calling Marsha to give her an earful about it. I'll probably be getting a detention too, I imagine." He grinned.

"You had to have known I was okay," I said with a slight shake of my head.

He turned me to face him. "When it comes to you, Portia, I don't take any chances." His eyes bore into mine seriously, before he glanced over to Grandma. "And I don't think this was an accident."

"What do you mean?" Grandma asked, a concerned look crossed her face.

"The motorcyclist—when he passed by Portia, I sensed something. He was gunning for her. He was trying to orchestrate an accident, and she was the target. It's why he fled the scene."

I felt numb. "Why would anyone want to hurt me?"

"I don't know. But I intend to find out," he said forcefully, and I could feel the anger beginning to brew inside him.

"We need to call the coven together this evening," Grandma said, heading toward the telephone.

"I think that would be wise," Vance agreed. "Something strange is going on."

"Well, there go our dinner and movie plans for tonight," I said with a little laugh.

"Portia, we've got to figure out what's going on. Someone tried to kill you today, or at the very least, hurt you significantly. We need to know why."

"I know. I'm just trying to lighten the mood. Self-preservation I guess." I suddenly felt like throwing up.

Vance wrapped his arms around me and rested his chin on the top of my head. "Yeah, and I have to figure out how to live the rest of my life without ever letting you out of my sight."

All the members of our coven came to the meeting that night. Everyone was very concerned, and things were discussed at length. No one could come up with any plausible reason why an attack would've been orchestrated against me. In the end, Vance insisted on having a powerful protection spell done. When the ritual was complete and the circle released, the meeting was adjourned and we all headed our separate ways.

Vance came home with me. It had been decided he would stay at our house, indefinitely, to help provide any extra protection needed. Mom made up the guest room next to mine for him, which I thought was funny since I knew she was aware he spent every night in my room. I guessed this was her way of keeping up appearances, or sending a not-so-subtle message to Vance, he now could be near me without being with me every night.

Marsha brought some of his things by a little while

later. She said there was an angry message on the answering machine, complaining about Vance running out of class without permission. She told us she would call them in the morning to tell them a family member had been in an accident and she'd sent him a text to let him know, causing Vance undue panic.

I felt bad about her having to tell a lie for my sake, but once again I figured there must be some leeway for being completely truthful when it came to magic. Even if she told the truth, she'd more than likely end up in a loony bin somewhere instead of helping things to get better.

After Marsha left, we went downstairs and ate dinner on the couch with Mom. She'd made chicken fettuccini alfredo while we'd been at our meeting, and it was delicious! We watched a little television while we ate, afterward helping Mom to clean up the kitchen before we headed off to bed.

Vance went into his room to change into a t-shirt and sweats, before he joined me.

"It's been a crazy day," he said, lying down next to me on top of the quilt as usual.

"Yes. I'm exhausted," I replied, not even trying to stifle a yawn.

"Well, get some sleep."

"I don't want to. I want to visit with you since I won't see you for most of the day tomorrow."

"You need your rest, baby." He stroked my hair. "I'll be here in the morning, then for lunch, and a couple hours after that I'll be home."

"I know. It's just that it's still hard for me when you're away. It still hurts."

"It's hard for me too," he said, continuing his stroking, trying to soothe me. "But we'll make it through this. I promise."

He reached over to place his hand on my forehead and began muttering soft words in my ear. Instantly my mind began to calm, and I was soon fast asleep.

When I woke up in the morning, I stretched out lazily and headed out of my room in search of Vance. I quickly paused by "his" bedroom and could hear he was in the shower, so I went downstairs to help my mom with breakfast.

"Morning, sweetie!" she said, flipping the French toast cooking in the pan.

"Morning, Mom." I gave her a kiss on the cheek. "What can I do to help?"

"There's some frozen orange juice in the freezer. You can mix it up if you want."

"Okay."

"I have to go into work early, so I won't be here all day," Mom said. "They're swapping my shifts."

"Is dad here?"

"No, he's out checking on some of his contacts this morning. He should be back sometime this afternoon."

"Great," I said, glumly. "A whole boring day to myself. I guess I could go to the shop with Grandma."

"I don't want you to leave the house, Portia," Vance said, entering the room and making my mouth water with the scent of his aftershave. "You'll be safer here."

"I agree," my mom said, further condemning me to my new prison by siding with him. "This house has protection charms all over it."

"That never kept Vance from getting in," I reminded her.

"True. But he's part of the coven. They were never meant to keep him out."

I was defeated, I could tell, so I let the subject drop.

Mom placed a steaming plate piled high with French toast in the middle of the table, while I finished stirring the juice. I carried the pitcher over and sat down just as she returned with a pot holder, placing a hot pan of freshly made maple syrup in front of us. We paused for a moment to bless the food, then dished things up.

"Wow! This smells great!" Vance said, looking over everything appreciatively. "Thanks, Mrs. Mullins."

"Please, call me Stacey—or even Mom," she replied. "Mrs. Mullins makes me feel so old. Besides, you're basically living here, and you're dating my daughter."

"My mom has to be one of the greatest cook on the planet," I said proudly to Vance, changing the subject. "I don't think there's a dish she can make that I wouldn't absolutely love."

"Well, maybe eggplant casserole," Mom said, correcting me with a laugh.

I groaned instantly at the memory. Mom tried a new recipe someone had given her that was supposed to be divine. It was the most horrible thing I'd ever tasted in my life. All three of us—Dad, Mom, and I—promptly scraped our plates into the garbage disposal. Mom even apologized to the garbage disposal for making it dispose of the dish.

"Yeah, that was pretty awful," I agreed with a shake of my head.

The chatter continued until we were all finished. Vance and I helped clear items, and I told Mom not to worry about the dishes. I would take care of cleaning the house so she could go get ready for work.

I followed Vance to the door when it was time to tell him goodbye. I hugged him tightly not wanting to let him go.

"I'm going to miss you today." I buried my head into his shoulder.

"I'll be back soon," he replied, hugging me tightly to him, and I knew instinctively he didn't want to go either. "Go take a nap or something. It'll go by a little faster for you."

"All right." I lifted my head so he could give me a kiss goodbye.

"I love you," he said as he stepped outside. "Be careful."

I leaned on the doorjamb watching him while he put his helmet on. Then he started his bike and took off. I closed the door with a sigh.

I went to the kitchen and tackled the morning mess we'd left behind. I was just finishing up the mopping when I heard my mom coming down the stairs.

"Smells great in here!" she said, entering the room, taking a big whiff of the pine-scented cleaner I was using. "You did a nice job."

She came over to give me quick hug and a kiss on her way to the garage.

"Be careful today. Call me if you need anything," she said.

"Don't worry, Mom," I replied. "If I die today, it'll be from boredom."

She laughed, grabbing her keys off the hook. "I'm sure it won't be that bad."

I watched with longing as she pulled out of the driveway and sped away. I turned back inside after the garage door had closed, making up my mind I was going to thoroughly clean the house for Mom today to help pass the time. There was only one problem. She'd been home all day yesterday, and there was nothing left to do. The house looked like a model home.

I decided to attack my room instead. It wasn't

really dirty, but I could go through my desk drawers and organize things.

I walked into my bedroom and plopped onto my desk chair with a sigh, opening one of the drawers. It was a mess. I didn't really feel like tackling such a project. Then a new thought popped into my mind.

"I'm a witch! I don't have to do things the old-fashioned way," I said out loud to myself.

This could be fun.

I immediately began calling out commands to the objects in my drawer. The trash separated itself from the important papers. My files stacked themselves, pencils rushed neatly into their holder, and spilled paper clips found their way back into the box.

I opened the other three drawers in my desk and did the same thing. This really was a blast!

After I was finished, I felt pleased with my success and looked at my clock. Five minutes had passed.

I groaned. What else could I do?

I looked around the room and settled on my dresser. I went through each drawer, magically rearranging all of my belongings. Then I moved on to my messy jewelry box using magic to help untangle my knotted chains and to hang everything neatly in its place. I progressed on to my closet.

It suddenly occurred to me, as I was arranging my pants and shirts, why Vance's room was cleaner than any guy's room I'd ever seen. He was using his magic as well. I didn't blame him. Doing jobs like this was a lot easier than the traditional way.

After I organized my nightstands, I looked around the room trying to think of something else I could do, and my eyes settled on my pale purple walls.

"I wonder ...." I stepped up and placed both hands on the wall. I thought of the color pink. Instantly the bright hue I'd pictured seeped out from under my hands and spread across the walls until the entire room was an awful, eye-popping shade.

I continued my experiment, thinking of several other colors, and each time the room changed to match the color I was pondering. However, I soon grew bored with my little game, so I thought of a whole bunch of colors at once and in a minute it looked like someone had tie-dyed my bedroom.

That quickly made me feel like I was on drugs having a hallucination, however, so I ending up settling for a soft shade of sage green. Then I went around flipping the fabrics to match. All the patterns stayed the same, just the colors were different.

After the fabrics, I concentrated on the pictures on the walls, and any other decorative items in my room to complement. Even the carpet wasn't safe from my mass remodel. When I was finished with those, I rearranged all the furniture. Finally, I plopped on my bed to survey the outcome.

"I should be an interior designer," I said with a satisfied smile on my face.

I turned to look at the clock. One hour had passed.

"Aarrrgh!" I groaned loudly. I plopped backward onto the bed, totally frustrated.

"Portia," I heard Vance whisper in my head. "I'm sorry, but I won't be home at lunch. The principal wants to meet with me and Marsha then."

"Great," I replied, the only bright spot in my day being ripped from me. "I guess I'll see you after school."

"Okay. Sorry, baby," he apologized.

At that moment I heard the doorbell ring, I sat up nervously wondering who it could possibly be.

"It's all right," Vance said. "It's your grandma."

Chapter 17

"I've come to spring the captive free," Grandma Mullins said with a smile as she stepped through the door. "Vance called me and said I better hurry, that a massive interior redesign was taking place, spurred on by boredom and magical experimentation."

So Vance had been keeping mental tabs on me from school during the morning. That made me feel good—even if he was spying without my knowledge.

"I'm quite happy with my work to be honest." I grinned. "Would you care to come have a look?"

"Sure, why not?" Grandma followed me up the stairs and into my bedroom.

"Wow. Green. That's a good color. When dealing with magic, green symbolizes balance and healing. It's a very good choice."

"Is that why you use it for the labels on the bottles in your store?" I asked, curiously.

"It is," she replied with a smile. "Is that where you picked up this color from?"

I nodded. "I've always loved your prettily labeled bottles."

"You must be naturally attracted to it. With all that's been going on in your life you probably could use some balance and healing … which actually brings me to my other reason for coming over."

"What's that?"

"I need to make some more things for the store. I was wondering if you wanted to come spend the rest of your time out of school with me. I could teach you how to make some of my favorite potions and lotions. Babs is going to cover the register for me. I figured we could work at my house where things might be a bit safer, since it has the same type of protection charms your dad has here."

"That sounds lovely," I replied with a sigh of relief. "I've been going crazy. The time passes so slowly. That's how all this experimentation began," I explained. "I was just trying to make it through until lunch, but then Vance said he wouldn't be coming back. I didn't know what to do with myself."

"Well, it doesn't look like it's been a bad thing. I'm glad you decided to try some things out. It's how you'll learn." She turned to walk out of the room. "I need to go get some herbs that your dad picked up for me out of his office. Why don't you grab some of your stuff and we'll get going. You might as well spend the nights over there too. Then we can work whenever we want and I won't have to worry about you being over here alone."

I packed a small bag of things for myself, while sending a mental message to Vance about what I was doing. He told me to have fun and said he would meet me at Grandma's after school.

When we pulled up in front of Grandma's house, we saw my dad had just arrived there also.

"Hello, Sean," she called to him with a wave as she exited her vehicle. "What brings you here?"

"Can we talk?" He inclined his head toward the house looking very serious. I felt a wave of apprehension wash over me. Something was wrong.

"Sure. Let's go inside," she replied. She led the way,

and soon we were settled in the living room, watching her light a couple of candles before she sat down across from my dad.

"Is there news, Sean?" She leaned forward in her chair, getting right to the point.

"There is. One of my sources has found some activity in the area of Albuquerque. I believe it may be the person we've been looking for. If it is, he's already moved on from this new location, but this puts him significantly closer to our position. I think we should call Marsha and Vance and see what we need to do from here."

"Definitely," Grandma agreed. "I'll call Marsha right now and have her and Vance meet us here after school today, unless you feel this warrants something quicker than that."

My heart began racing at epic speed, the thought of Vance being in imminent danger sending me straight into overdrive.

"No, no," my dad replied. "I think we're okay for the moment. We just need to readdress our current plan of action."

"Vance?" I called out to him mentally. "Are you all right?"

"I'm fine, baby. Just taking a calculus test. What's up?"

"Take your test," I replied. "I didn't mean to bother you. I'll talk to you after school."

I didn't want to distract him from his exam with news of his father. As long as he was at the school he was safe, and Marsha would be getting hold of him.

"Okay. See you later," he replied, and all was quiet once more.

After she placed the call to Marsha, Grandma, Dad

and I went downstairs into the basement to begin making some herbal lotions together.

I enjoyed learning about this process and discovering what things the herbs could be used for. I was also surprised to find my Dad was a pro at making these things. I'd never seen him do anything with herbs before in my life. Of course, I guess it shouldn't have surprised me to find out I didn't know something about him, since he'd fooled me into believing he was an encyclopedia salesman for my entire existence.

Grandma went through the whole procedure manually with the first batch we made. Then we played with magic to make the rest.

I really enjoyed that since I'd never really witnessed Dad doing actual spells, outside of past coven rituals, before. He seemed pretty impressed with me too. The rest of the afternoon flew by, and before we knew it Vance and Marsha were coming down the steps into the basement. I stopped what I was doing and ran over to wrap my arms around Vance's neck, thrilled he was safe and back with me again.

"Hey, baby," he said softly, hugging me back tightly. "I missed you today. Let's not stay apart that long again, okay?"

"Fine by me." I leaned my head back so he could kiss me softly on the lips.

"How did things go with the principal?"

"I'm off the hook. Marsha got a big lecture about the school policy on cell phones, but other than that, everything's okay."

We walked over to sit with the others at the table.

"So what've you found out?" Marsha asked.

Dad filled her in on the details he'd discovered, and I was surprised to see how nervous she looked.

"He's too close. It's time for us to move on." She

looked at Vance, and my stomach dropped.

"No," he stated harshly, and I could feel strong emotions running through him. "I'm not running again."

"Think about it, Marsha," Dad said, trying to help calm her. "You have safety in numbers here. We've promised to do all we can to protect both of you."

"I can't risk it." Marsha shook her head. "I swore to his mother I'd die before I let anyone get to him."

"I won't leave!" Vance shouted this time, pounding his fist down hard on the table, causing all of us to jump in response.

I'd never seen him angry like this, and I placed a slightly trembling hand on his shoulder attempting to calm him. The others stared at him with wide-eyed expressions.

"I'm sorry," he said, taking a deep breath. I could feel him trying hard to rein his anger back in. "You don't understand. I've already lost one home and one family because of this man. This is the first place that's felt like home since my mother ran away with me.

"And I'm with Portia now. I'm bound to her, and I won't leave her. I'm eighteen—this is my decision to make." He looked at Marsha. "Sorry."

Vance and Marsha stared at each other for a few moments before she gave a slight nod.

"All right," she said, conceding softly, but she didn't look too happy about it.

"I'm sorry I'm the reason all this danger's coming here," Vance said to Grandma and Dad. "If we have real proof he's getting too close, then I'll be happy to leave to help keep everyone else safe if that's what you wish."

"This isn't your fault in any way," Grandma replied. "We're glad you came here, and I think it's wise for you to stay regardless of how close he gets. We can protect you better if we know where you are."

"Plus we need to find out the reason your dad wants you so badly," my dad interjected. "He was obviously using you to strengthen his own powers. We need to know why, what he's planning, and why he's been recruiting more forces. That's definitely worrisome to all of us."

"I still hope we can find your mom out there somewhere too," I added softly.

Vance gave me a soft smile and placed his hand over mine.

"Thank you," he said. "I hope for that too."

The five of us spent the rest of the evening together, lost in our own thoughts, as we continued to make products for Grandma. At nine o'clock, Grandma called an end to the evening.

"We need to get these kids to bed," she said. "Vance has school in the morning. Portia and I can continue things once we get him off."

Dad and Marsha agreed. We quickly finished up what we were doing and put things away.

Vance grabbed my hand, and I followed him up the tiny set of stairs, through the closet and down the hall into the guest bedroom.

"I'm sorry I lost my temper earlier," he apologized, looking truly remorseful.

"You were fine," I replied, feeling badly for him. "It's understandable under the situation."

"It was wrong." He reached over to run his fingers through my hair.

"Do you really think it's wise for you to stay here?" I feared his answer.

He sighed in frustration. "I have to take a stand somewhere, Portia. I'm tired of running. I want a life, a real life—with you, to be precise." He rested his chin on the top of my head, moving his hands to run his fingers in lazy strokes up and down my back. "There's safety in numbers here. If I leave, we become weaker and so will the coven."

"I just don't want me to be the reason that keeps you in harm's way."

"Portia, I won't leave. I'd rather die than be parted from you. And honestly, under our current physical situation, it would probably feel like death to both of us if we were to be separated now."

I nodded, understanding the point he was trying to make. The separation of a few miles caused enough torture. I couldn't imagine him gone completely from my life. Just the thought gave me torment.

"Don't even think about it," he said, pulling me over to the bed. "It isn't worth the pain."

He turned back the bed covers, and I sat down. I flipped my shoes off, flopping back against the pillow. It was at this point I heard a scratching sound coming from the window.

"Looks like we have company." Vance chuckled and he lifted the window pane so Jinx could hop inside.

"Hey, pretty girl," I crooned, and she jumped up onto the bed, into my arms. "Did I leave you behind? I'm sorry. It wasn't intentional."

Jinx purred lovingly, nuzzling under my chin.

"Looks like I'll have to play second fiddle for your attention tonight," Vance said with a smile. He removed his shoes and sat down next to me on the bed.

"Not a chance." I grinned. "I can love you both. I'm talented that way."

The stresses of the day caught up with us quickly, however, and the three of us were soon fast asleep.

I was awakened sometime in the wee hours of the night when Jinx suddenly swiped my face with her paw, her claws grazing me slightly.

I let out a little squeal, sitting up in time to see her jump off the bed in the direction of the window. I gasped when I saw two red, glowing eyes staring in the window at me.

Instantly, Vance was up beside me.

"Don't move!" he ordered, jumping from the bed and running toward the window.

The red eyes suddenly disappeared, and Vance filled my view as he quickly crawled over the window sill in hot pursuit of whatever was out there.

Grandma came rushing into the room, flipping on the light as she passed the switch. "What is it?"

"I ... I don't know," I stammered, trying to catch my bearings enough to explain the sight I just beheld. "Something was at the window looking in at us. It had bright red eyes. Vance told me to stay put and ran off after it."

Grandma went to the window and slammed it shut, locking it tight.

"Come with me," she said, gesturing abruptly with her hand.

I followed her into the living room where we sat in the dark, in silence. I nervously ran my fingers over Jinx, who was curled up in my lap now. Soon we heard a tapping sound on the door.

"It's me," Vance called out.

Grandma didn't move a muscle, but the lock turned and the door opened slowly. Vance entered the room, and the door swung shut and relocked itself. I didn't know if he had done it, or if Grandma had.

"What did you find?" Grandma asked him.

"Nothing really," Vance replied, flopping onto the couch next to me. "Someone was out there, but whoever they were, they moved really fast. By the time I rounded the corner after them I couldn't see anyone at all. I ran another block just to be sure, but there was nothing. It was like they vanished into thin air."

"I think we're dealing with some very powerful magic here," Grandma said soberly.

"I agree." Vance sighed, sounding as if the weight of the world were on his shoulders. "Those eyes—they were demon."

"Uh, demon?" I said, sitting up straighter. "Could you elaborate, please?"

"A demon is a witch or warlock who's been exposed to the dark arts for so long that the evil they work with will actually begin to possess them," Vance explained. "The magic begins to take control of them instead of them controlling their magic. It's very bad since the witch or warlock can lose all sense and reason of what's right or wrong. It becomes all-consuming to them, causing them to do some very bad things."

"Were either of you ever going to fill me in on this little tidbit of information?" I asked doubtfully.

"Eventually," Grandma said with a sigh. "It isn't something we've had to worry about very often around here. I guess we kind of overlooked it. I wanted you to feel free to explore your magic without repercussion."

"You mean you were protecting me," I grumbled. "I'm not a little kid anymore, and I need to know what's going on."

"They think my dad is a demon," Vance said softly. "They've been trying to protect me, not you."

"How long have you known?" Grandma asked, looking surprised by his comment.

"For a while," Vance replied. "I first suspected when Sean started recruiting other witches to help be on the lookout. It was the only reason he'd think we needed the extra manpower. Plus, it was obvious that the path he's been on was headed in this direction."

"I guess we should know better than to keep things from you. You have a very quick mind, Vance," Grandma responded. "We weren't trying to keep you out of the loop. We just wanted you to have a normal life."

Vance snorted in disgust. "That's something that's never going to happen, no matter how much I desire it."

His melancholy words hung heavily in the air, and we all sat in silence a few moments longer.

"Shall we go back to bed?" I finally asked, not knowing what else to say.

"No," Grandma said. "Not up here at least. Let's go downstairs."

She stood up, and Vance and I followed her to the basement. She pulled a small fold-out bed from the storage room and set it up with the head of the bed against the wall. When she was finished, she placed her hand on the cot, muttering a few words, and I jumped back when it doubled in size into a luxuriously covered bed.

"Nice," I said under my breath, feeling a bit in awe over what I'd just seen.

Grandma went to the shelves that held the collections of crystals and gathered many of them together. She placed several around the bed, touching each one and whispering a small incantation. The crystals began glowing.

"Get some rest," she said, pointing to the bed. "I doubt we'll have anymore company tonight, but I'll keep watch upstairs anyway."

"What about your protection?" I asked, not wanting to leave her to fend for herself alone.

"I have some more crystals for my room upstairs. I'll be plenty safe," she assured me.

I gave her a hug and thanked her, and she headed up. I made myself comfortable in the bed while I waited for Vance, who had gone up with her to make sure things were all right. He was back shortly, and to my surprise he crawled under the covers next to me.

"I don't want anything to separate us tonight," he explained. "I want to know you're safe in my arms."

I shook my head in response. "You don't need to worry about me. I'll be fine," I said solemnly.

"What do you mean?" He looked confused.

"I don't think they're after me. I think they're after you."

Chapter 18

"His name is Damien Cummings," he whispered softly into my mind, and I knew exactly who he was talking about.

"How come his name is different than yours?" I asked out loud.

"My mom changed ours so it would be harder for him to find us."

I sat still, pondering this thought for a moment. It had never occurred to me he might be living under an alias. He was my Vance.

"Vance is my real name," he whispered as he decoded my thoughts. "And I'll always be a Mangum. I'll never take my old name back again."

"Where'd your mom get the name from?"

His face grew reflective for a moment, as if he were remembering back to a different time and place.

"We passed through a small little town in Oklahoma once that was called Mangum. We were only there for a couple of days, but Mom was charmed by the place. The people were so down to earth and very kind to us. She said someday she hoped we could live in a place just like that. I think changing our name to Mangum was her way of remembering places full of good people still exist."

"What a beautiful memory of her," I said.

"Yes," he agreed.

"You must really miss her."

"I do, but I understand why she did what she did. I owe her my life. If she hadn't run with me when she did, who knows what kind of disgusting creature I'd be now."

"She'd be so proud of you if she could see you now. You're such a good, determined man."

He sighed heavily, and I could see the subject was beginning to wear on him.

"Let's get some sleep," he said. "You need your rest."

"I'm not going to break, you know. You don't need to baby me," I replied with a small smile.

"Well, get used to it, because I'm not going to stop anytime soon," he mumbled into my hair.

It was the last thing I remembered before I closed my eyes.

The next morning when I awoke, Vance was already gone. I had no idea what time it was since there were no windows in the basement and no clock nearby.

I lay in the comfortable bed for several moments taking in the things that happened last night. Finally, I threw the covers back and placed my feet on the floor.

As soon as I'd finished standing up, the bed behind me immediately shrank back to its original form and folded itself up against the wall.

"I guess that's one way to get rid of company," I muttered to myself, staring in awe at the bed.

Walking in a circle, I picked up all of the glowing crystals and carried them over to the shelf, replacing them in their proper spots.

"Good morning, sleepyhead," Vance's voice chuckled in my head. "Or should I say afternoon?"

"Afternoon? What time is it?"

"It's noon." He laughed. "I'm upstairs. Milly's feeding me lunch."

I hurried up the stairs to meet them, combing my fingers through my hair and rubbing at any dark circles that might be under my eyes.

"Well, someone was tired!" Grandma laughed as I entered the kitchen.

"Sorry," I apologized. "I think it was that dark basement. I had no idea what time it was."

"That's just fine," she replied. "Vance said to let you rest because you'd tossed and turned all night."

"I did?" I asked, not remembering any such thing.

"You had your dream again," he said, in between bites of his sandwich.

"Really? I don't remember," I replied, surprised.

"It was a little different this time though."

"How so?"

"You were running toward something in the fog, not away from it."

"Hmm. That's interesting. Was I calling for you?"

He nodded.

"Well, thanks for helping me out again," I said.

"That's always my pleasure," he said, standing and coming over to give me a hug.

Grandma placed another sandwich on the table. "Come and eat, Lollipop."

"Thanks, Grandma." I went to sit at the table. "I'm sorry I've wasted half of the day away. I know you have things you wanted me to help you with."

"Don't worry about it. I worked on my project up here this morning. I actually got everything done already."

"I've got to go, baby," Vance broke in from behind

me, leaning over to place a kiss on my cheek.

"Already?"

"Just half a day, and then I'm all yours." He smiled reassuringly at me. "And you get to come back to school with me tomorrow."

"Who'd have ever thought I'd be excited about that?" I laughed, following him to the door.

He hugged me again before he left, placing a light kiss on my cheek, and I watched until he was out of sight.

"Finish up your sandwich, and then you and I'll have a little history lesson together," Grandma said.

"History?" I asked.

"Yes. It's time I introduce you into the world of the dark arts."

"Excuse me?" I choked.

"This isn't something I like to do, but knowledge is power, and with all the crazy stuff that's been happening, I figure you need to be aware."

"All right," I agreed, and I hurried to finish my food.

After we went back into the basement, Grandma pulled a very large, ancient looking book out of the storeroom and set it on the table in front of me.

I reached out for the book, but she stopped me. It was then I noticed there was a large leather strap surrounding it, and where it should open was covered with a giant lock.

"Do I need a key?" I asked.

"There is no key. It was destroyed. You're never to open the lock and read the book," she began.

I gave her a quizzical look.

"Okay. But I thought you wanted me to read it."

She shook her head. "You'll touch the book in the center of the cover, and its contents will be revealed to you. Never, ever, read directly from the text. This can initiate hidden spells and dark magic you're not aware of. Many a witch and warlock have been drawn into the dark arts by doing just such a thing."

I nodded, understanding her warning. This was obviously a very bad book.

"Whenever you're ready, just place your hand in the very center of the cover," she said, sliding the volume toward me.

I took a deep breath and hesitated for a moment, then placed my hand on it. As soon as my fingertips grazed the book, I felt a hard pull, as if I had stuck my hand into a massive vacuum cleaner.

My body went rigid, and my mind began to be racked with speeding images. Everything was moving so fast, zipping by at such high speeds I began to feel like I was on a roller coaster, but somehow my brain was able to keep up and comprehend it all.

It was a history of black magic, and the images in my mind were from the early days of man. There were pictures of people chanting, casting spells and sacrificing. Bits and pieces of text, spells, warnings, condemnations, and prophecies went unheeded by the people of the era in their thirst for more power, progressing until the era changed.

I continued to follow the black magic from its origins, throughout its journey through the ages, passing through the Christian era, Medieval, Renaissance, Victorian, all through time as it evolved and passed down from one hand to another. Horrifying images of curses, mutilation, and death leapt through my mind, sickening me with the depravity of it all.

I watched as witches and warlocks evolved with the dark magic too. As their power became stronger, they transformed before my eyes, beginning to sprout furrowed brows with small horn-like bumps, teeth that resembled fangs, nails that took on a claw-like appearance, and haunting blood-red eyes. They moved back and forth between features, looking completely normal at times in their appearance, but their looks changed the most when they were thirsty. It was then they would morph into their demon characteristics. I was surprised to see some of them physically preferred their demon looks over their human ones.

They were drinking blood—lots of it, feasting on the life source of other witches and warlocks, taking their magic to make themselves stronger. The blood exchanges turned their victims into the same demon-like creatures they were themselves. Once their captive had made the conversion, they found their demon blood to be polluted, so they moved on looking for someone new to feed upon. They grew stronger with each feeding, and some of the more powerful ones could actually shape shift into animals, or even look like other people.

They lived long lives, often training up a protégé to pass their magic on to when they were old. The larger their magical community, the stronger their powers were. They were recruiting, always recruiting. It was necessary for their survival.

The demonic societies searched out and preyed on those who were especially gifted, since these individuals supplied more power in their blood. There would be a feeding frenzy on these people, often taking them to the brink of death, before bringing them back again to build a new fresh blood supply.

On and on it continued, marching through the pages of time—every generation stronger and worse than the one before it. I saw whole covens of good witches and warlocks slaughtered as they tried to fight for their lives, but the demons always overtook them, allowing nothing to stand in the way of their thirst. And even though the demons always grew stronger, it was never enough. The thirst always deepened, they constantly craved more.

Something changed in me, shifting while I viewed them. I felt their desires, and I could feel the craving for a taste of the blood flowing through me, the unquenchable thirst and longing. I threw my head back and heard a moan escape my lips. I needed a drink now.

An image of Vance danced into my head, and all I could see was his blood pulsating through his veins. It called to me in a beating song so sweet I couldn't deny it. It was so powerful. I wanted to grab him and have just a little taste.

"Portia! Let go of the book!" Vance's voice pounded into my head.

Instantly, I was aware of Grandma tugging on my arms, trying to pull the book away, which I was now firmly grasping with both hands holding it up to my chest.

"No! Portia! No! No!" she was screaming at me.

I released it immediately, shocked, and stood up so quickly I knocked the chair over behind me.

Grandma grabbed the book and ran with it into the other room.

I leaned over the table, placing my shaking hands on it, while I stood there panting like I had run a marathon.

"I'm on my way!" Vance spoke into my pounding head, and I didn't have the strength to argue with him.

"What was that?" I said out loud, my voice trembling, but he didn't answer me.

Grandma re-entered the room and wrapped her arms around me.

"I'm sorry," she said, helping to right the chair and getting me seated once again. "I've never seen a reaction like this before. I would've never done it if I even knew it was a possibility."

She looked so upset that I placed my hand on top of hers, trying to comfort her.

"It's all right. I'm all right," I tried to reassure her, though I could feel the sweat dripping from my head. "What happened?"

"I don't know," she said, shaking her head. "Everything was fine, normal even. All of a sudden you grabbed up the book and started shaking and moaning. I tried to get the book away from you, but I couldn't. Your grip was too powerful. Even magic didn't help. You couldn't hear me."

I closed my eyes, and the images I'd seen danced faintly before them now, causing my pulse to still pound with an awful need.

"Just give me a second," I breathed in a whisper, bending to place my head between my knees. I knew it was one of the treatments for hyperventilation, and I felt pretty close to that right now.

I battled for control, trying to focus on anything besides the images I'd seen, while several minutes ticked away, my emotions swinging to and fro.

"Are you okay?" Grandma asked, finally breaking the long silence, and I slowly lifted my head to look at her.

"I was thirsty," I said sadly, shaking my head. "I needed a drink. I just wanted a small one, and I felt like I couldn't help myself."

"More precisely, she wanted a drink from me," Vance said, entering the basement at that exact moment.

I couldn't look at him, feeling horribly guilty. Hearing his voice and knowing he knew what I'd thought was all it took for my fragile front to break into pieces. I started sobbing into my hands.

"Baby, it's okay." He wrapped his arms around me. "You were being confused by the magic. I know you'd never hurt me."

I stood up briskly and pushed him away. He looked hurt for a moment, but then started toward me again. I held up a hand to stop him.

"I can still hear the power racing in your blood. It's like I can smell it or something. It makes me thirsty," I confessed, giving him tear-laden look. "You need to stay over there. Something has changed. Things are different between us."

"No. Nothing has changed. The effect of the book hasn't worn off you yet, that's all."

I turned away from Vance, unable to look at him without my mouth watering, and it was killing my heart.

"Why did I react differently than you expected?" I asked Grandma, wanting her to make everything right again.

"I don't know," Grandma said, still completely bewildered. "I've honestly never seen anything like it."

"I think I might have an explanation," Vance interjected. "Portia is linked to me. The bond between us is strong, and she's been able to experience my emotions before. I think the residual pull of the dark magic I still have from dealing with my father may have caused this intense reaction for her. As soon as her thoughts turned dark, I started having the cravings too. That's how I knew she was in trouble. My cravings didn't become as intense, but having had them before I recognized them right away for what they were."

This time he wouldn't let me push him away when he reached out and pulled me to him. He wrapped his arms tightly around me when I struggled against him, until I gave up and started crying into his chest. I grabbed up fistfuls of his shirt while he held me, and I tried to ignore the sound of his strong, beating pulse, brushing aside the thoughts of what his blood would taste like on my tongue.

"Well, whatever is happening here, we definitely need to figure out what's going on," Grandma replied from behind me. "This isn't good by any means."

"I think we may have seriously underestimated how strong Portia's powers really are," Vance said over the top of my head, still keeping his embrace strong even though I'd stopped struggling. "It's strange for someone who should be an apprentice witch to have such instant and strong reactions to magic. I think she's something special."

"She's a natural at it, for sure," Grandma agreed, continuing on as if I couldn't hear anything the two of them were saying. "I was just proud she was so good at everything. It never occurred to me she might be overpowered in a sense. Perhaps she's the one who's causing such a hard reaction to your binding spell. Maybe she overreacts to all magical influences."

"Great," I choked out between sobs. "Now I'm a dysfunctional witch too."

"No, not dysfunctional, just different," Grandma explained. "We need to study you a bit more, I think. Your powers are very mature and strong for your age."

"But not right now. Let's get you to bed and see if you can get some rest," Vance suggested.

"I've been asleep all day," I muttered in protest, my head still buried in his chest.

"That's all right," he replied. "You've had a pretty traumatic event. It's okay to take a little time for yourself to recover from it."

When I didn't reply, he gathered me up into his arms and carried me upstairs to the guest bedroom, laying me gently on the bed.

"Don't leave me," I said softly to him, though I was still too embarrassed to meet his gaze.

"I wouldn't dream of it." He sat next to me while he stroked my hair away from my tear-streaked face. He didn't say anything more and neither did I. I chose to stare at the ceiling instead of looking at him.

Several minutes later, Grandma came in with a steaming cup of herbal tea in her hands.

"Here, Lollipop. Drink this. It'll help calm your nerves," she said, handing the cup out to me.

I sat up so I could take it from her and I drank the tea down quickly. It wasn't long before I felt the chamomile working its magic as soothing warmth spread throughout my body. When I was done with the tea, Vance removed the cup and saucer from my hands and placed them on the nightstand. I snuggled back down into the pillows, and he continued to stroke his hand through my hair.

I was happy to discover I didn't have any kind of craving coursing through me anymore. I closed my eyes and just enjoyed the relaxing comfort of Vance being next to me, while I listened to the thoughts trailing through my head.

"Your father's recruiting," I said, breaking the silence.

"Yes," he agreed softly.

"And he wants you so he can feed himself and his coven," I replied, even though the words made me feel sick to my stomach.

"Yes."

"He's going to find you this time." I looked straight at him, searching his eyes for a hint of anything like fear.

"I know," he replied, his face unchanging.

"What then? Will he try to kill you?" I asked, scared.

"No. He'll try to turn me into one of them."

"How do you know that for sure?" I felt a streak of panic run through me at the thought of Vance becoming one of the monsters I'd just witnessed.

He let out a big sigh. "When I was young he had a nickname for me. He called me his 'little protégé.' I think he's planning on grooming me to take his place."

Chapter 19

"You have to run!" I insisted, sitting straight up on the bed so I could face him directly.

He shook his head. "I won't leave you."

"Vance. It'll mean nothing if he finds you and makes you into something like him. You have to go," I pleaded.

"No!" he shouted, his answer firm.

I knelt in front of him, placing my hands on either side of his face and stared straight into his eyes. "Vance, please! I'll even come with you. We can run away together! We'll get married and go somewhere he'll never find us," I begged him in earnest.

He pondered this for a moment, looking deeply at me, before he spoke again.

"Portia, I'd love nothing more than to run away and take you as my wife, but we'd always be running. I want to have a life with you—a real life, one that's full of love, laughter, and someday children too. If I don't face him, we'll never be able to have that. He's always been able to find me somehow. Sometimes faster than others, but I'm always looking over my shoulder, waiting for him to reappear. It's time for me to make a stand now."

"And if you lose?" I asked, feeling scared over the

possibility.

"I don't plan on losing," he said stubbornly.

"Things don't always go the way we plan, Vance! I'd rather live a life on the run than have you gone completely!"

"You're going to have to trust me, Portia," he said quietly, searching my eyes.

I dropped my hands from him and flopped back over onto the pillow in defeat.

"I don't like this," I sighed. "I've had the tiniest exposure of this dark magic today, and it almost consumed me. I can't allow that to happen to you."

He reached over and took my hand in his, massaging my fingers with his own.

"I love that you care so much," he said with a small smile. "But I managed to escape his influence once before. I'm banking on being able to do that again. I'm stronger than I was then."

"Well, I hope that you're right this time, Vance." I knew I was going to have to trust him because I couldn't force him. "I can't live without you. You know that, don't you?"

He stretched out next to me and gathered me up into his arms.

"I'll never leave you, Portia, and that's a promise. Please try to understand me."

We eventually had to agree to disagree on the subject, tabling our discussion until the meeting with the coven that evening. Grandma had called another get-together after my experiences of the afternoon and the previous night.

After much discussion, everyone agreed things out of the ordinary were definitely happening, but since no one had actually spotted Damien Cummings, or any of his followers, we were all cautioned to just be extra careful and alert toward anything that might seem unusual somehow.

Grandma reminded that there was safety in numbers

and whenever possible to travel with companions from the coven when we were out and about. My dad said he would alert some of the neighboring covens to the possibility of a demon cult being in the area and ask them to keep watch also.

When the meeting was adjourned, I rode back to my house with Vance on his motorcycle. He stayed silent until after we were safely behind closed doors in my bedroom, steering me over to the bed.

"Sit down," he said with a sigh. "I have something I need to tell you."

"All right," I replied, feeling nervous butterflies in the pit of my stomach. "What's up?"

"Well, I've been keeping something from you on purpose." He looked at me a bit warily. "I didn't want to upset you."

"Tell me," I responded with a little too much force.

"It's about Shelly. She hasn't let up. She's been all over me at school."

"All over you how, exactly?" I asked through clenched teeth.

"Hugging me in the halls, rubbing up against me whenever she gets the chance, she's even tried kissing me again."

"Apparently a broken nose wasn't enough to get my message across," I grumbled.

"She seems to be doing remarkably well with her nose," Vance commented. "Other than some slight bruising beneath her eyes and a piece of medical tape over it, she looks almost normal. Well, at least her 'new' normal."

"So does all this attention turn your head?" I asked, and he snorted.

"It's quite annoying to be honest with you. I wish

she'd grow up."

I giggled at that comment. "Well, I guess it's time for me to step up my game then."

"How do you intend to do that?" he asked, his interest piqued.

"I have an idea in mind."

Instantly, he was in my head probing around until he found what he was looking for.

"You don't play fair do you?" he said with a chuckle.

"Not when it comes to you," I returned with an innocent looking smile.

"I like this idea," he said, his eyes lighting up. "I can't wait to see it in action."

When we pulled up at the school in the morning, I took a deep breath and prepared to get a lot of stares.

"You look great! Don't even worry about it," Vance said with a reassuring grin.

I threw my thigh-high-leather-booted leg over the motorcycle and stood up. I looked down to straighten the pleats of my black micro-mini skirt over the two inches of white fishnet tights that were showing. Smoothing my hands over the black-and-white-striped, scooped-neck shirt, I reached down and pushed the sleeves of my leather jacket to my elbows.

Removing my helmet, I shook out the luxuriously curled hair that had been piled beneath it. Then I put on my giant silver hoop earrings I'd carried during the ride in my jacket pocket.

"There. How do I look?" I bent over to look in the bike's rearview mirror.

I checked my carefully applied make-up, which was much heavier than I had ever worn it before.

Vance made a low whistling sound next to me.

"You should be a felony, baby. It's got to be a crime for a girl to look this good." His eyes trailed up and down my body as he spoke.

"Shelly's always felt superior to me when it's come to looks. She doesn't think I'm worthy of someone like you. That's why she's always flaunting herself when you're around. I'm just giving her a dose of her own medicine."

"Well, you always look good to me." He smiled. "But today you're going to knock their socks off!"

"I look like a hooker." I laughed shakily.

"Sometimes a guy might not think that's a bad thing," Vance said with a boyish grin. "Remember, baby, it's all about the attitude. Work it."

He gave me a playful slap on the rear, grabbed my hand and led me toward the school.

"How long do think it'll be before I end up back in the principal's office?"

"Don't worry. I'll protect you."

I laughed. "You didn't think I was going to wear this get up all day, did you? This skirt is a serious violation of the dress code."

"You're going to change?" He sounded deflated.

"Just a little. I'm swapping the skirt for a pair of skin tight leather pants before first hour."

"Skin tight, huh? I think I can live with that." He gave a grin that flashed his dimples. "I can't wait to see how those look on you."

"You're such a guy."

"True. But that's why you love me, right?"

"Only one of the reasons," I replied with a smile. "It's definitely a plus for you though."

This morning turned out to be a basic repeat of Shelly's dramatic entrance into the school after her makeover. People stopped in the busy halls just to stare at me.

Vance squeezed my hand for support as he led me through the throng, until he stopped right in front of Shelly at her locker. He turned and grabbed me up into his arms and kissed me with such intensity I thought my lungs might burst before he stopped.

"You're right, Shelly," I said, running a red-painted finger down the side of my lips. "He does taste like butter and honey. And I'm going to taste him again, and again, and again."

Vance gave me a wicked grin right before he plastered another scorching kiss on my lips.

I heard Shelly give a loud huff as she pushed by both of us to get away, but I didn't see her expression since Vance was commanding all my attention.

The crowd in the hall broke up, and I could hear laughing and whispering in the background.

"Dude, that was harsh," Brad's voice broke in, followed by a short laugh. "She deserved it though."

Vance quit kissing me and glanced over at Brad.

"Sorry. I know you have a thing for her, but I couldn't take it anymore," he explained with a slight shake of his head.

"No apology necessary. She needed to be knocked down a notch or twelve," Brad responded.

"I agree wholeheartedly!" I added. "How are you by the way, Brad?"

"I'm all right." He smiled at me. "It's nice to see you back at school. And, I might add, you look smoking hot today!" He looked me over with new appreciation lighting in his expression.

"Hey! Take it easy there, Brad," Vance said, narrowing his eyes at him. "I might have to beat you down a bit."

"No worries." Brad laughed, blowing off the fake threat. "I know she belongs to you."

"You have it all wrong." Vance smiled, looking back over at me. "I belong to her." He squeezed both of my hands.

"Well, the two of you are lucky. Don't take it for granted," Brad said, continuing on down the hall.

"I'll never let that happen," Vance said in a whisper directed only at me.

The following Saturday was one I'd been greatly anticipating. I felt we needed a break from everything and had planned a little surprise for Vance.

When I discovered his yearbook, I vowed to keep my promise to him about getting a camera and taking some pictures. I'd gone to the bank and drawn out some of my money I earned from working at Grandma's store. I gave the money to my mom, asking her to purchase the nicest camera she could get with it.

I had the camera now, all gift-wrapped in a small box. It was making a nice little bulge in my jacket pocket while I was sitting astride the back of Vance's motorcycle, zooming up to our special place in the canyon. I asked him if he would take me there, but I hadn't told him why, and I hoped he hadn't picked up on any of my thoughts racing through my head.

We soon reached our parking place and trekked off to the big rock that overlooked the creek. The trees below us that still had leaves were in various stages of yellows, reds and browns, though lots of dead leaves blew around on the ground, littering the forest floor and crunching under our feet as we walked.

"So what's up your sleeve?" Vance asked casually as we stood holding hands looking out at the scene before us.

"What do you mean?" I asked innocently.

"I mean you've been acting like a giddy school girl all morning. I figured something was up." He smiled at me.

"You peeked into my head, didn't you?"

He shook his head. "No. I figured you'd tell me when you were ready."

I released his hand and wrapped my arms around his neck, standing on my tiptoes to place a light kiss on his lips. He returned the favor with a little look of amusement on his face.

"I have a present for you," I said, rubbing the end of my nose against his.

"Really?" He seemed genuinely surprised. "What is it?"

"It's in my pocket. But you have to find which pocket," I said with a devious smile.

He grinned widely. "I'm up for this task, but are you sure you are?"

I just laughed at him and I didn't remove my arms from around his neck when his hands began moving over me. I sighed in disappointment when he located the bulge he was looking for rather quickly.

"That was way too fast."

He smiled. "Guess you'll have to hide it better next time," he said as he pulled the box from my pocket. "Wow. It's wrapped and everything."

I released him, stepping back to give him a little room to open it.

"You do know my birthday is a long way off still, right? It's not until April." He laughed, and I nodded.

"I know. Open it," I said impatiently, eager to get on with it.

"All right." He gave a sly grin, and he began to remove the paper very slowly.

I knew he was trying to taunt me. "Just rip it off!" I almost shouted, grabbing for the package, determined to do it myself.

He jerked it out of my reach with a laugh before I could grab it though.

"Take it easy!" he teased, with a shake of his head, clicking his tongue. "Who knew you could be so impatient!"

I rolled my eyes, letting him play his annoying little game with me. He kept shaking the box and offering absurd guesses, before carefully opening another bit off the package. After what seemed like an unreal amount of time, he finally removed the paper completely.

"You got me a camera!" he said, looking at the box in true surprise.

"Yep." I smiled. I was very excited I'd been able to keep it secret from him. "I told you before, I'd work on getting you some new pictures of me. I thought maybe we could take some of us together."

"I like that idea," he said, snaking an arm around me and pulling me in for a quick kiss on the lips.

"I even put the batteries in it for you," I said, laughing, when I pulled back.

"Well then that deserves another kiss," he stated and kissed me again, but I pushed him away when he started getting too intense. "Hey! Come back here," he said, reaching for me.

"No. You're getting distracted!" I went running away from him.

He, of course, chased after me, and soon we were romping and climbing through the woods and cliffs, taking candid shots of us laughing playfully together. After a while of being crazy and impulsive we found a colorful spot in a grouping of trees. We placed the camera on a fallen log and set up the timer so we could take several posed shots.

When we were done we collapsed in a heap on a pile of soft leaves. Vance looked so handsome lying there propped up on his elbow staring at me. I took the camera and snapped a few more pictures of just him. I wondered if the lens would be able to capture the love I could see in his eyes and the emotions he was conveying to me there.

I lowered the camera to look at him.

"I love you so much," he said, continuing to stare. "I wonder how I ever lived without you."

"That doesn't matter anymore," I replied, running a hand down the side of his chiseled face. "We have each other now."

"I know, and it makes me really happy. I could never leave you, Portia." He wrapped his arms around me, pulling me down next to him, and he kissed me.

"I wouldn't let you," I said, laughing, when he was done.

"Good!" he replied. "I'd have to be a fool to risk anything that would cause me to lose you."

"You'll never lose me." I laughed and threw a handful of leaves in his face.

"Oh! You are on!" he said, pouncing on me and rolling me into the leaves, getting them all stuck in my hair.

I laughed and squirmed as I tried to get away from him unsuccessfully.

"I give up!" I hollered, throwing my hands in the air and surrendering in exhaustion.

"I told you I wouldn't let you get away." He laughed at me, and I decided right then I needed to win this one after all. I used my magic to scoop up a bunch of leaves and dropped them over his head.

"Hey!" He grinned through the shower of falling leaves. "That wasn't fair!"

I just shrugged my shoulders, and soon we were rolling about in a tornado of color as a magical battle ensued.

Chapter 20

Thanksgiving finally rolled around, and I began to help my mom with the preparations for it. She'd invited the entire coven to come and eat with us this year.

Vance helped me put out some seasonal decorations in our formal dining room, and together we transformed the space.

The dining room table was laden with a beautiful cornucopia, flanked with taper candles in crystal holders. We finished polishing all the silver from the china cabinet, carefully putting each one in its formal place setting. Vance carried the china dishes over from the cupboard and helped me to set them with a fancy folded napkin. The table glistened when we were done.

Vance went outside with my dad to bring in some wood to build a fire in the fireplace, while I went into the kitchen to help mom out with the rest of the food preparations.

"Mom?" I walked over next to her, breathing in the wonderful aromas filling the air. "How come you never let us use magic to help you out with things like cooking?"

"Cooking is an art," she replied with a smile. "It isn't something that should just be thrown together. Besides, it's my own little type of magic around here. I need to be valued for some reason."

"Mom!" I laughed and reached out to hug her. "You're always appreciated! Don't ever think otherwise!" She reached out to pat me affectionately. "What can I do to help out?"

"Well, I guess you're worthy enough to take on the relish tray this year," she replied with a grin.

"Oh! Thanks so much, your Majesty, for bequeathing me with such a noble assignment!" I teased her back, and she laughed at me, giving me a shake of her head.

I got out the serving trays and the cutting board and began to cut the vegetables. The two of us continued to visit while we finished making the last of the meal together.

The dinner ended up being a huge success, and it was wonderful having all of our "family" there with us. We ate until we were stuffed, and when we were done, we cleaned up and gathered around the piano for a sing-a-long.

While several members of the coven were certainly musically gifted, the singing got significantly wilder as the evening progressed. I thought it was due directly to how much wine was been consumed by the older members of the coven.

Vance and I watched them, laughing at some of their crazy antics. He finally stood and asked me if I'd like to take a stroll in the night air with him.

I thought that sounded like a fabulous idea, so we got our coats on and headed out the door.

"It's a little nippy out here tonight," I said, when we stepped into the courtyard.

"Don't worry, I'll keep you warm." Vance smiled and wrapped an arm around me, pulling me close to him.

I blew my heated breath into my cupped hands and rubbed them together briskly to warm them up a little, then shoved them deeply into my coat pockets.

We walked slowly together down the dimly lit street, looking at the houses we passed. Many had their windows aglow with home fires burning while other families celebrated their holiday also.

"Today was great," Vance said, breaking the silence.

"You really enjoyed it?" I'd worried if all the extra people around would make him feel nervous.

"This is one of the first Thanksgivings I can think of in a long time that I've had so much to be thankful for. I really felt like part of a family tonight."

"You are part of a family," I said. "You're my family."

"I know," he continued, trying to explain. "It's just I've never been surrounded by that many people, with that kind of warmth for an occasion like this."

"Well, get used to it," I replied, smiling up at him. "I plan on spending many more celebrations with you in my lifetime."

He smiled back at me and gave me squeeze.

"I'm looking forward to that, too."

Monday morning returned all too soon, and it was time to go back to school once again. We pocketed away all the wonderful memories of the weekend and prepared to buckle down with classwork once more.

Marsha had let Vance drive her Audi that day. We'd been rewarded with our first light snow of the winter overnight, and the roads were a bit too icy for the motorcycle. When we arrived at the school, there were numerous kids running around outside involved with some pretty intense snowball fights.

Vance and I decided to bypass the front of the

school to avoid the mayhem, and worked our way around to one of the back doors to the building. We walked down the hall together, reaching the door to Vance's classroom first. He kissed me goodbye, and I walked over to the science hall where my chemistry lab was.

I was surprised to see Shelly near the doorway when I entered. She stopped next to me.

"You'll never win," she said with a glare, before pushing past me and continuing on her way.

I watched her for a second, wondering what she was up to, before I went in and sat at my assigned table. I took off my hat and scarf, hanging them, along with my jacket, on the back of my chair.

My lab partner was Maggie Pratt. We usually had a fun time mixing the ingredients in our assignments together. I'd always thought science was fun, and now that I knew about magic, it even took on more fascination to me.

We were using chemicals on the Bunsen burner for today's class. Maggie already had our protective goggles laid out, as well as masks to prevent inhalation of the fumes. The beakers we were using were all lined up in a row, and the large labeled bottles of chemicals were next to them.

I dug my pencil out of my bag while Mr. Fisher passed out the handouts and gave us an explanation of the assignment.

After roll call, everyone buckled down to get the experiment done. Maggie and I chit chatted over recent events and gossip going on at school while we worked.

"How do you like the snow this morning?" she asked me.

"I always love the snow," I replied, waxing a little wistful. "It's like the world becomes all fresh, kind of clean again. You know what I mean?"

"Yeah." She laughed. "Except for when it all melts and

everything turns filthy from the mud."

"That's so true," I said, agreeing with her.

"So are things any better with Shelly?"

"Not even close," I muttered back, with a shake of my head. "I don't know what the deal is with her."

"I tried to talk to her, to ask her about an assignment this morning," Maggie told me. "She wouldn't even look at me. It was like I didn't exist."

"Well, don't take it personally. I think that's the way she treats all of her old friends now. I don't know what her problem is."

When we were done preparing the chemicals, we fired up the burner and began to add the ingredients.

All of a sudden, there was a horrible explosion. The next thing I knew I was being blown across the room. I slammed into the opposite wall hard and crumpled to the floor. I groaned loudly, looking up just in time to see the ceiling buckle and begin to cave in.

Instinctively, I raised my arms over my head just as a shielding ray of power shot out from the talisman hanging at my neck, forming a magical barrier around me. Debris rained down hard against it.

"Portia!" Vance yelled loudly into my mind. "Hang on! I'm coming!"

I could hear screams filling the hall outside as a cloud of dust swept through the room, completely blinding me.

"Maggie?" I called out, choking on the silt thickened air, since my mask and goggles were no longer on my face.

I tried looking over some of the debris piled all around me, and as the air cleared a little I could see the entire outer wall of the classroom was blown away, exposing the outdoors. The roof was gone completely, burying my classmates on the floor beneath.

I shivered as the cold air swept into the space.

"Maggie?" I called again with a cough, before trying to climb out over the rubble.

An excruciating pain went through my back, and I screamed out loud.

"Oh, Portia!" Vance's frantic voice swept through my head. "Don't move! I'm almost there!"

I started to weep, choosing to lie still on my stomach, waiting for him to arrive. I wasn't prepared for what happened next.

"No! *No*!" Vance's voice pelted through my brain, and suddenly he was gone. His mind had shut like a steel trap. He was no longer there, and I knew it.

"Vance!" I screamed with every fiber of my being, my heart flooding with true terror. Then the intense physical crushing pain came throughout my entire body. The kind of pain I only ever experienced when he was moving away from me. Pain like we used to experience during the early days of our binding spell. This time, however, was the worst I'd ever experienced, and it was crippling.

I lay on the pile of debris and sobbed, the faint wail of several sirens beginning to fill the air.

"Maggie?" I called out again hoarsely. There was no sound coming from the wreckage, just the sounds of people running through the halls, evacuating the building.

"Vance?" I called mentally. "Where are you?"

Nothing. Not even a hint of his presence.

"Can anyone hear me?" I recognized Mr. Holland's voice shouting over the din coming from the direction of the outer wall.

"Yes," I whispered.

"Can you hear me?" he shouted louder again. "Anyone?"

"Yes!" I tried to say a little more forcefully.

"Who am I talking to?" he shouted back.

"Portia Mullins," I croaked out, my mouth feeling like it was filled with layers of dirt.

"Portia, can you see any of your classmates or teacher?"

"No. They're under the roof." I started coughing, and I cried out as some more shocks of pain radiating through my back.

"Do you know where you are?"

"I think I'm somewhere near the hall doorway. I hit the wall," I said through my tears.

"Hang in there, Portia! Help is on the way! Try to hold still, okay?"

"Hurry!" I said, shaking violently. "It's getting harder to breathe."

Chapter 21

It was a long time before I was pulled from the building. The rescuers had to secure the scene before they could even enter. Firefighters worked hard to shore up unstable areas of the building before any of the paramedics were allowed to come in.

Finally, one firefighter made his way to my side, coming in from the blown-away hall door. He edged his way down the wall carefully, over the piles of debris, and knelt down next to me.

"Are you Portia?" he asked gently.

I nodded.

"Portia, my name's David. I'm a firefighter paramedic. I'm going to ask you some questions, and I need you to answer me with a yes or a no. I don't want you to move your head or body at all. Do you understand?"

"Yes," I wheezed, and he slipped a small monitor on the end of one of my fingers.

"I'm going to place an oxygen mask over your nose and mouth to help you breathe better now," he said after looking at the monitor, and he gently placed a soft plastic mask with a bag hanging off the end if it over my face.

"This bag down here's an oxygen reservoir. It's just

there to help you breathe better," he explained.

I inhaled deeply several times, letting the cool air rush into my lungs.

"How old are you, Portia?" David asked me while he pulled more equipment out of the large canvas bag he'd brought with him.

"Sixteen," I replied through the plastic mask.

"Do you know what day it is today?"

"Monday."

"Good," David said. "Do you know where you are?"

"At the high school," I responded.

"Very good. Portia, can you tell me where you hurt?"

Everywhere, I thought. "My back," I said out loud. "I was slammed up against the wall."

"Do you remember what happened?"

"I only know we were getting ready to mix our chemicals together in the burner when there was a horrible explosion from the front of the room. I was looking down though, and I didn't see anything."

"That's okay. I'm going to examine you real quick now. You'll feel my hands pressing on your body. You need to tell me if you hurt anywhere I touch, all right?"

"Okay." My teeth chattered uncontrollably.

David began to run his fingers over me. When he reached the middle of my back, I sucked in a painful breath and cried out.

"I'm sorry," he said. "I didn't mean to hurt you. Are you okay?"

"It's all right. I'll be fine." I gritted my teeth, tears leaking from the corners of my eyes at the white hot pain radiating from where he'd touched.

David's face was full of concern while he watched me for a moment before he spoke again. "I'm going to continue now." His hands resumed their palpating down the rest of my back side.

"Portia, can you push your feet against my hands?"

I pushed them against him like he'd asked.

"That's great," he said. "Now I'm going to check your arms."

"Ouch!" I said as soon as he started, wondering what was wrong now.

"You have a lot of tiny shards of glass embedded in the undersides of your arms and your hands. I'm not going to check them anymore, but since you can't squeeze my hands, can I get you to wiggle your fingers for me?"

I slowly wiggled my fingers.

"That's good." He lifted his head to look over the top of me. "Over here!" he called to someone I couldn't see.

"My friend Maggie was right next to me," I said, still worried about her.

"Maggie?" David asked. "What's her last name?"

"Pratt," I said. "Do you see her?"

"I haven't seen her, but don't worry. There are a lot of people here to help out. We'll find her."

I could still feel the tears trickling down my face, leaving cold watery trails as they traveled along. I started to shiver even harder, I couldn't control it.

"Portia, my partner is here now. His name is Kevin. He's brought a backboard we're going to put you on to help protect your spine and any other injuries you might have. It's probably going to be very uncomfortable for you, but it's necessary."

"All right," I said, and a new face floated into my view.

"Hey, Portia, I'm Kevin. I just want to give you a few instructions. When we move you, we need you to let us do all the work. Don't try to move anything yourself. Do you understand?"

"Yes."

"Okay. I'm going to place this board up next to you, and David and I are going to turn you on your side against it. Are you ready?"

"I'm ready."

I felt one of them lift my arm and lay it gently up by my head.

"Keep your arm right here," Kevin instructed. "Okay, Portia. We're going to turn you on the count of three now. One, two, three."

They rolled me in unison onto my side.

I clenched my teeth to keep from screaming out, but was unable to suppress the sound.

"You're doing great!" David said with a reassuring smile. "We're going to do the same thing one more time, only this time we will lay you back onto the board. Ready? One, two, three."

It was then I realized a third person had been there holding the backboard, while Kevin had held my head and David had rolled me.

"Hello, Portia, I'm Pam," the female firefighter said to me. "Kevin's going to continue holding your head while we get you strapped in now."

She produced several belts and a roll of duct tape, as well as some sort of cardboard thing she snapped together. She held something up to my neck.

"This is a c-collar. It's to protect your cervical spine. I'm going to wrap it around your neck now."

While she was placing it on me, David was crisscrossing several buckling belts over my body and securing them to the backboard.

After they were done, they slid the cardboard thing

around my head.

"We're going to tape your head down with this to keep it from moving. It's just a precautionary measure to protect your spine as well," he explained.

I soon felt like a mummy, wrapped up in a papoose.

"We're ready to move her out!" Kevin called to someone out in the hall.

I felt myself being lifted up into the air, and I was carefully carried over the great piles of debris. They moved me out of the classroom door and into the hallway. Someone came up and put a blanket over my freezing body after I was placed on a gurney. I was strapped down again, and then wheeled down the hallway.

As we rolled along, I noticed several of the light fixtures were busted and hanging from the ceiling. Foam tiles were missing too, leaving gaping holes up into the dark space above. When the doors opened to the outside, I had to shut my eyes against the light of the bright, cloudy sky.

I was rolled to a waiting ambulance, and when they were putting me inside, I opened my eyes, catching my first and only glimpse of the school.

There was a giant gaping hole where my classroom had once stood, and rubble spilled out of the building. Policemen were swarming the grounds with dogs.

I noticed at least three long black bags lying in a spot on the snow-covered grass. Body bags, I realized. That meant people were dead, people who were my classmates. I started crying again.

"Hey, Portia, you're doing great," David said, reassuring me again as he climbed in to sit on the seat next to me, while Kevin slammed the doors shut behind him.

I didn't answer.

"I'm going to start an I.V. on you now. This is just in case I need to give you any medication or if you were to need surgery or something. Kevin's going to be driving us to the hospital, and you'll be hearing the sirens. There are a lot of bystanders and heavy traffic out on the road, so we need them to get through everyone."

"Okay," I said, hearing the loud wailing sound of the vehicle as we began to move.

David started the I.V. in the back of my hand, since the other side of my arm was covered in glass.

"All done!" he said, when he had the I.V. securely taped. "Hey, Kevin? Can you patch to the hospital for me while I take her vitals?"

"Sure thing," Kevin called back from the front of the ambulance.

A minute later he called back to David.

"Verde Valley has requested that we defer to Flagstaff Medical Center under the circumstances. They said they have a chopper on standby at their facility if we need it."

"Yeah, let's do that. I don't want to have to bounce her all the way to Flag in this weather."

"My mom's a pediatric nurse at Verde Valley," I said then.

"Really? What's her name?" David asked me.

"Stacey Mullins. She's working today."

"Kevin!" David called up to the front. "You'd better get Verde back on the horn. This is Stacey Mullins's kid."

My mom was standing at the emergency room door when the ambulance backed into the bay, and a flight crew was standing there with her.

"Portia?" my mom called out to me, and I could hear the worry straining her voice.

"Mom!" I choked back, emotion at the sound of her voice flooding me, and I started crying again.

She started to reach for my hand, but David stopped her.

"She has glass embedded in her hands and arms, Stacey," he warned, and she pulled her hand back to her chest.

"How is she?" she asked him, though her eyes never left my face.

"Let's talk while we walk," David said, motioning to the flight nurse that he was ready to give his report.

The flight nurse began writing everything David said on his clipboard. Even though I could hardly understand any of the medical jargon he was saying, my mom seemed to be getting the gist of it all.

"We have a sixteen year-old female, Portia Mullins, who's the victim of a possible chemical explosion at Sedona High School. Portia was thrown across the room, unknown how far, and slammed into a brick wall. The ceiling of the classroom fell in completely on top of the occupants. She was found up against the wall lying on her stomach over a pile of debris and is complaining of severe back pain in the lumbar spine. Deformity is noted in the same area."

I heard my mom gasp.

"Patient is able to move all extremities at this time with good pulses and capillary refill. Full c-spine precautions and one hundred percent O2 by non-rebreather were initiated on scene. An eighteen gauge I.V. was started in her left hand enroute to this facility via ambulance. Pupils have been equal and reactive to light, and patient is alert and oriented. Initial O2 sats were at ninety percent on room air, and patient is now saturating at ninety-eight percent on one hundred percent oxygen. Pulse is up a little at one hundred and ten. I was unable to get a blood pressure due to the shards of glass in her extremities."

"Very good," the flight nurse responded, glancing over at me. "We'll take her from here."

David and Kevin helped to move me from the gurney and loaded me into the helicopter.

"Good luck, Portia," David said, resting his hand gently on me. "We have to go back to the scene now, but we'll check in on you later when we get the chance."

"Thanks," I said, to them, watching them walk away while the flight crew tightened all my restraints.

"Hi, Portia. My name is Scott," a male voice said. "I'll be your flight nurse from here to Flagstaff, along with my partner today, Mary Ann. She's a paramedic. Your mom is coming with us. She's going to sit up front with the pilot. His name is Stan."

"I'm right over here, honey. Daddy's on his way to Flagstaff to meet us," my mom called out to me.

I couldn't see her, but it was comforting to know she was still here with me.

"Portia, we're getting ready to start up the chopper. It'll be very loud, so we'll be placing a headset down through your cardboard brace to cover your ears. There'll be a microphone too so you can talk to us if you need to. We'll be wearing the headsets also."

"All right," I said.

Scott soon had me set up with the head gear, and I could see the helicopter's blades begin to whirl in the air outside my window. Pretty soon they were moving at a very fast pace.

"Here we go," Scott's voice cut in through the headset.

We lifted off the ground easily, and I could hardly tell we were moving through the air. It was kind of like being in a giant bubble.

"I'll just be checking your vitals again while we're in the air," Scott said, his voice clicking on and off through the headset. "The flight to F.M.C. is very short. It'll take about ten or fifteen minutes. Are you doing okay?"

"Yes." I closed my eyes and thinking I wasn't okay at all. I was terrified for Vance.

True to Scott's word, we soon began our descent onto the helipad, down to the heavily snowed roof of the hospital.

"We're here now," Scott explained. "We'll wait a minute for the chopper to shut down, and then we'll get out. After that we'll be putting you on another gurney and then taking you on an elevator down to the emergency room on the ground floor."

"You're doing great, baby!" my mom's voice came over the headset, trying to reassure me.

I was soon unloaded from the helicopter. Mom walked by my side as I was wheeled into an elevator where we were met by a trauma nurse and an E.R. doctor.

Scott gave them his report, and I was wheeled into one of the trauma rooms and switched over to another bed.

"The doctor will be right in," the trauma nurse said to my mom while hooking me up to a bunch of monitors.

"Thank you," she replied, coming to stand next to the bed and finally, for a few moments, we were alone.

"Momma," I cried in a whisper. "Something happened to Vance."

"Was he with you?" she asked, looking concerned.

"No. He was running to help me, and then ... I don't know. He just disappeared."

"What do you mean he disappeared?"

"Everything's gone. I can't reach him. Mentally there's nothing, and the farther we flew from Sedona, the worse my pain got."

The doctor came into the room at that moment.

"I'll let your dad know immediately," Mom reassured me.

I spent the next hour answering all the same questions over and over again, before I was finally wheeled in to get a cat scan.

The backboard, with me on it, was slid into the giant machine, and I could hear it whirring loudly as it took the pictures. Thirty minutes later I was wheeled back into the trauma room where my mom, dad, and grandma were all waiting for me.

"Hey, Pumpkin. How are you hanging in there?" my dad asked, bending to give me a kiss on the forehead.

"Not so great, Dad. Has anyone heard from Vance?"

I noticed him exchanging a worried look with Grandma over my head.

"Just concentrate on you right now, honey," he said, evading the question.

"Dad. Ninety percent of the physical pain I'm in right now is because Vance isn't with me. If you know something, then please tell me. I don't know how much longer I can survive this."

He stared at me for a few seconds, working his jaw a bit before he spoke.

"It's bad, Pumpkin. Really bad," he said, sadly shaking his head. "Are you sure you're up for it?"

"Please just tell me." All sorts of horrible thoughts began running through my head.

"Babs went to tell Marsha about the explosion at the school," he began speaking. "When she got to Marsha's house she found her there. She's dead, honey. Someone killed her. All of her belongings were strewn everywhere, and all of Vance's things are missing. The police are still there."

I gasped at the news. "They don't think Vance is responsible, do they?" I replied in shock, my heart breaking into a million pieces as I realized he'd lost another family member.

"No. He was at the school, so he has a good alibi. Sweetheart, Vance is missing though. No one has heard from him, and no one can find him since the explosion happened. I'm beginning to think the whole thing at the school may have been orchestrated as a cover to kidnap him."

He was right, and I knew it. I felt as if everything inside me had died, and I began sobbing hysterically, unable to keep the terror at bay any longer.

The nurse ran into the room. "What's wrong?" she asked, looking at me with concern.

"She's in a terrible amount of pain," Grandma said, covering for me, but it was the truth.

"Her scans are back now." The nurse looked at me compassionately. "I'll get the doc in here and see if we can't give her something for the pain."

I tried to control my tears when the doctor came in a few minutes later and started explaining my current condition to my family.

"The scans look good around her head," he said. "However she does appear to have a serious fracture in one of the lumbar vertebrae in her spine. There's a significant amount of swelling around the fracture though, so we'll need to wait for it to go down and then we'll probably have to operate."

"What'll the operation be on, specifically?" my

mom asked.

"We need to stabilize the vertebrae so it won't slip and do any damage to the spinal cord. We'll watch her for the next twenty-four hours and re-evaluate things from there."

"Okay," Dad said.

"I've already sent her papers to admitting," the doctor added. "The nurse will be in shortly to give her something for the pain."

"Thank you, doctor," my dad replied, reaching out to shake his hand.

"Dad, I can't stay here," I complained, the moment the doctor couldn't hear us anymore. "I have to go find Vance."

"Let us worry about that," my dad replied. "You have to get better first."

"Dad, he's a healer. If we find him, he can fix me. Please! You have to take me with you!" I was starting to feel more than a little desperate.

The nurse entered the room now. "Here's some pain meds for you, sweetie." She picked up my I.V. and administered it straight into one of the ports. "If you start feeling nauseated, just let me know."

It was amazing how fast the medicine moved through my system. I could taste it in my mouth before she was even done pushing it all in. I felt a wave of dizziness and a heavy sensation passed through my neck.

"Daddy, don't leave me," I pleaded once more as I fought the medication. "I have to find him!"

"Honey, the police are doing everything they can." I knew he didn't really mean the police, but the nurse was still in the room.

I could feel the medication begin to ease all my pain, and I turned to my Grandma.

"Gram. Please," I slurred in desperation, but the room started spinning, and I was suddenly so very tired.

I closed my eyes and drifted into blissful unconsciousness.

Chapter 22

I spent the next twenty-four hours in and out of awareness. I welcomed every single pain shot when it came, for it offered me a mental release from my anguish. The doctor had been in to visit with my parents again, and I was scheduled for surgery first thing in the morning, if the second scan showed I was ready. They were going to put some titanium around my vertebrae to help keep it together properly.

Grandma had gone back to Sedona and was heading up the search for Vance with the remaining numbers of our coven. I knew our powers were greatly diminished with our loss of Vance and Marsha, as well as Dad and me not being there.

Mom said the police were still looking for Vance as well. He was the only one who hadn't been accounted for from the school. All the kids in attendance had been shuttled down to the football field after the explosion, and every single one had been interviewed by police before being turned over to their loved ones.

My mom cried when she told me I was the only survivor from my class, and I cried for an hour straight after that.

Everyone at home was calling my escape a miracle, but I knew the only reason I'd been spared was because of the magical shield that protected me from the falling debris. I felt undeserving.

All I could think about was how Maggie and I had been laughing one minute and she was dead the next. She had probably been buried right next to me. I imagined her lying under the rubble while people walked over the top of her to get to me, and the guilt was excruciating.

Dad kept telling me it wasn't my fault and Maggie was probably already dead before the rescue people even arrived. It didn't help me feel any better.

Grandma called to say the school was going to close early for the holidays. Christmas was just two and a half weeks away, and the school board felt the kids needed the next month to get through the trauma they had just experienced. It would also give them the time needed to repair the school. Grief counselors were going to be available to anyone who needed them and would be stationed at Verde Valley Medical Center.

Grandma also said she located a witch in Phoenix who had healing powers. She said the woman was on her way to Flagstaff to offer her services and her name was Sandy. Dad thanked Grandma profusely and said he would keep an eye out for her.

When the woman arrived, the nurse's station called my room saying I had a visitor, and my dad went to get her. I liked her immediately, as soon as she entered the room. She was an older woman with short salt and pepper hair. She had lots of smile lines around her kind eyes, and there was just an air of goodness about her.

"I'm so glad I could come and help you," she said, reaching for one of my bandaged hands that had recently had all the glass picked from them.

"Thank you for coming." I smiled.

"Oh! I see you have quite a lot of pain and not just from your injuries either."

"Yes," I replied, my thoughts going instantly back to Vance.

"Well, let me see what I can do."

She began running her hands all over me, similar to the way Vance had done before. Every time she hit a sore spot she lingered a little longer. Then she reached underneath me and placed one of her hands under my broken spine.

I groaned at the pressure.

She placed her other hand on my stomach, and I began to feel a change as a white light started glowing from beneath her hands. Instantly, soothing warmth flowed through me, and I knew without a doubt the bone had been repaired. There was no more pain from my injury.

She removed her hands. "I left the cuts in your skin, but removed the pain. I figured one miracle would be enough for the doctors to fuss over."

"You're wonderful," my mom said, getting up to grab the woman by the hand with unshed tears of appreciation in her eyes. "How can we ever repay you?"

"No repayment is necessary," Sandy said with a smile, clasping my mother's hand in both of hers. "I was devastated to hear about what happened to all those poor kids. I'm only too happy to be of some help."

"We'll always be in your debt," my dad spoke.

"Yes," I added. "If there's ever anything I can do for you …."

"Just be happy and live your life." Sandy reached out to pat me.

The nurse came into the room shortly after my dad had left to walk Sandy back out to her car.

"I just wanted to let you know that someone from

radiology will be here to get you soon. It's time for your second scan. The doctor wants to check you over one more time before surgery, just to make sure you're ready."

"Okay," I replied with a nod, hoping they would be quick about it so I could get out of there.

"You look a lot better to me today." The nurse paused to glance over me. "You aren't nearly as flushed as you were a while ago."

"I'm feeling much better," I said, honestly.

"Well, that's good," she smiled. "Hopefully it won't be too much longer before they come. Let's get you well!" She checked my vitals and my I.V. before leaving the room.

"I just want to go home now," I said mournfully to my mom.

"Patience, darling. Hopefully you'll be able to leave by this evening. These things take time."

"Ugh," I groaned. "I don't have time for this. I need to find Vance."

The x-ray tech came in then. "Hi. I'm John," he announced in the same manner of every medical person I'd met during this whole experience. "I'm here to take you for another scan of your injury. Just lay back and enjoy the ride."

He wheeled my bed out of the room and back into radiology, where we repeated the same procedures we had done the night before. After a while he came out from behind his equipment looking a little confused.

"I have a few questions about the scans I just took, so I'm going to retake them so I'm sure the doctor gets a good picture."

"No problem." I tried not to smile to myself, and we went through the whole thing again.

I hadn't been back in my room for very long when the doctor came in looking a little strange.

"I have good news, I guess," he started, reaching up to scratch behind his ear. "Either there was some sort of mix up with our scans yesterday, or we're witnessing a miracle, but I can't find anything on these scans that remotely resembles a fracture. Would you mind if I examine you?"

"Not at all."

"Are you in any pain?" he asked, looking me over a bit warily.

"No," I said. It was mostly true. The pain I had was nothing a doctor could fix for me.

"Can you carefully roll to the side?"

"Sure." I complied easily with his request.

The doctor ran his hands up and down my back repeatedly.

"Let's stand you up now."

I did so effortlessly, though I felt a bit groggy still from my pain medicine. He had me move, slowly at first, and then ended up having me bend and stretch.

After several minutes of doing everything he'd asked, and me beginning to feel a bit like a circus monkey, he told me to sit back down.

"Young lady, I have no explanation for what has happened here, but you seem to be fine. I see no reason to keep you here any longer. If your parents are in agreement, I'll start the papers for your discharge."

"If you're sure she's okay, we're fine with it," my dad replied, smiling. He and Mom both thanked the doctor, who left the room still scratching his head.

One hour later I was free. I was showered, dressed in clean clothes, and in the car headed back toward Sedona. My heart became lighter and lighter with each mile we drove closer to home, and I started laughing.

"What is it?" Mom turned to look at me, perplexed

at my attitude.

"He's still here somewhere," I said, unable to contain my relief. "The physical pull hurts less and less the closer I get. He has to be alive somewhere in Sedona."

"Well, don't get your hopes up too high, Pumpkin. There's a reason we haven't found him yet. He must be being held captive, or he would've shown himself by now." my dad said.

"I know." I started to cry, my previous moment of joy being shattered with despair. "I can't take it anymore! I have to find him. If only I could hear him."

We pulled into the driveway when the first wave of agony hit me.

"*Aaahhhh*!" I screamed, doubling over in pain, grabbing my wrist.

"What's happening?" my mom called to my dad. She unbuckled, jumping up to lean over the seat, looking at me in fearful concern.

"*Aaahhhh*!" I screamed again, this time grabbing at my other wrist. "The pain! Make it stop! Please!"

Dad threw the car into park and turned around. He started grabbing the bandages at my wrists, ripping them away from my body. As he exposed my skin, both he and my mom gasped together.

Though the skin wasn't broken, angry red slash lines began to appear all over my arms, followed by what looked like bite marks.

"What is it?" my mom yelled frantically as I cried out yet again.

"We have to get her to my mother's," Dad said, turning back behind the wheel and throwing the car in reverse. "They've started feeding on Vance!"

I lay moaning on a cot, surrounded by what was left of

our coven. The rituals had been ongoing for most of the night. My physical connection to Vance was obviously as strong as ever.

He had been fed on several times in the last few hours. The slashes and bite marks would appear on me while it was happening to him. Following the feedings we began to notice gray marks starting to creep up my veins.

My dad said this was happening because they were feeding him their blood to help replenish his. He explained to me that this was how the exchange happened, how Vance would eventually become a demon.

I curled myself up into a ball and cried inconsolably for hours on end. I cried until there were no tears left to cry, yet still I sobbed, while my body was wracked with uncontrollable spasms. I cried until I fell into exhaustion. Then they would start feeding on him again, and the whole cycle started over.

I was losing him. I could feel it. I could taste the poison as it slipped through his body, and I didn't want to live anymore. I just wanted to die.

"Portia, you've got to fight this," Grandma said, as my dad lifted my limp body so she could pour some type of herbal concoction down my throat.

"I don't want to live," I groaned in agony. "Not if I can't have him."

"Drink some more of this," she commanded, shoving the drink back into my face. I tried to take a swallow, but I began vomiting.

"Now what?" my mom said in frustration from where she was sitting in the corner.

"Vance's body is trying to reject the blood they're giving him," my dad explained. "He's the one who's causing her to vomit."

"I can't take this anymore," she said, getting up and storming from the room.

"Where are you going?" Dad called after her.

"To pray at the church." She slammed the door behind her.

Dad looked over at Grandma, and she shrugged.

"Every little bit helps. This doesn't seem to be working. Maybe God can step in."

"Well, something better work!" he shouted angrily at her. "This has been going on for three days!"

Three days? I thought to myself. Apparently, I hadn't been conscious the entire time. That was when I started noticing the appearances of the other coven members. They were haggard, unwashed, unshaven, and their clothes had been rumpled from overuse. They were tired, and I immediately felt pity for all of them.

"Tell them to go home," I whispered.

"What?" Grandma asked me, leaning in closer so she could hear me better.

"Tell them to go home. They need sleep. They'll work better with it." I gave a great sigh. "Let them eat and get showered. Nothing is working right now. I'll be fine while they tend to their needs."

"She's right," dad said with a short nod. "We need to let them get some rest while they can. Who knows where this might lead."

Grandma agreed and called the others together. They all refused to go, so Grandma pulled rank and ordered them, as their high priestess, to leave and take care of themselves.

I watched them depart, one by one, until they were all gone. It wasn't long before Grandma and Dad were slumbering on two cots on either side of me.

Lying still in the dim silence, I looked at my arm. The

gray streaks had now progressed to my elbows.

I had to find him. It was up to me now. The man I loved was being destroyed, and I couldn't give up without trying.

Slowly, I pushed my lethargic body into a sitting position and sat there breathing heavily for a minute before I attempted to stand. I was very dizzy when I did, so I made my way over to the wall, leaning against it, and carefully crept out of the room.

I managed to get up the stairs, through the house, and then out under the night sky. I didn't know which way to go once I made it to the street, so I just turned left and started walking, albeit a bit haphazardly.

I hadn't walked very far when I noticed my pain seemed to be increasing. I stopped. I must be going the wrong way.

Turning around, I walked in the direction I had come from, and the pain began to decrease slightly.

Realizing I'd discovered a major tool in helping me find him, I totally centered myself on listening to my body. If the pain became more intense, then I would do a course correction until I felt better.

I had to pause to rest several times, sometimes from fatigue or during an attack on Vance. I stopped anywhere I could find a place, leaning on a fence post, sitting on someone's porch swing, and even lying on the hood of someone's car. As I was able, I would stand up and begin walking again.

It was a slow way to travel, but eventually I found myself across town and in an old business section. I disturbed a couple of alley cats in the misty night air when I stumbled over a garbage can left lying on the ground, and they screeched at me as they ran off.

It was just the adrenaline rush I needed. It perked

me up a little. I kept trying to tell my body this was all just an illusion. These things weren't really happening to me, only to Vance. Unfortunately, it seemed to only want to listen to the pain it was experiencing.

I rounded the corner out of the alley and stopped to stare at the sight ahead of me. Across the street from where I stood was the bar Vance had been tailing Shelly to. Instantly, the pieces of the puzzle began to fall into place.

I remembered Shelly coming out of the chemistry lab as I had been going in.

"You'll never win," she'd said before shoving past me.

Then the explosion had happened. She had meant for me to die in the blast, so she could take Vance. That meant she was obviously a witch, or a demon for that matter.

All of a sudden I knew exactly where Vance was.

Chapter 23

Rage boiled through my veins, giving me a sudden burst of power, which heavily fueled my adrenaline. I crossed the empty street and flung the door to the bar wide open, stepping inside, only to see the bartender cleaning up after closing.

"We're closed," he said automatically, before looking up.

I was over to him in a flash. "Where are they?" I said, grabbing him around the neck with my hand and lifting him off the floor with a little push of power.

"I can't," he choked out, his face reddening under my grip. "They'll kill me if I tell you."

"And I'll kill you if you don't," I snarled back at him, feeling angry enough in that moment to actually do it.

His eyes darted away from me, and I followed his quick glance toward the back of the bar. I butted his head against the shelves, and he sank to the floor.

Quickly, I made my way toward the storage area and peeked around the corner.

I could see one of Shelly's groupies leaning up against a door, smoking a cigarette. He hadn't heard me because he was listening to the ear buds he was wearing. I could hear the music from here. He was facing away from me, so I snuck up behind him and tapped him on the shoulder. When he turned around, I punched him with all the magical force I had, right in the face. I felt bone crunch beneath my fist, and he sank to the floor.

Pushing him out of the way, I opened the door to reveal a wooden staircase that descended into the black earth. I couldn't see any kind of light at all, and I had no idea what was down there.

Quietly, I tiptoed down the stairs, making as little noise as possible. I levitated over three stairs at a time and pushed off the fourth. Finally, I reached the bottom, finding myself in a dark narrow hallway.

I walked toward a dim, glowing red light I could see coming from what looked like the crack at the bottom of a door. When I reached it, I stopped outside and listened, holding my breath.

I could hear nothing.

There were only two choices left for me now. I could go through the door or go back the way I'd come and call for help.

Slowly, I turned the handle of the door, and silently swung it open. My eyes took a second to adjust, and then I gasped at the sight before me.

Vance was sitting in the middle of the dimly lit room under a small red light bulb hanging from a string. He was bound in irons and strapped to a chair. I could easily see the manacles holding him in place were magically reinforced.

He had been stripped to the waist, and his head was drooping over his chest. There were slashes and bite marks all over his arms, and his veins were pitch black all over his body, running up his neck toward his face.

"Vance?" I called out in a choked whisper, repulsed by the damage done to him.

His head slowly lifted toward mine, and his glowing,

blood red eyes stared straight into my soul.

"Run!" was all he said, and I covered my mouth with my hands to stop the scream that was there.

I did run—toward him, throwing myself at his feet and trying to find a way to loosen his bonds. He slumped over in the chair again.

"Hang in there, Vance," I said frantically, hoping no one could hear the noise I was making, but then I heard a sound behind me.

I jumped up, swinging around to come face to face with Shelly.

"He's mine now!" she spat out viciously.

"I don't think so!" I flung my hand out with a burst of magic and sent her flying across the room.

She hit the wall hard and crumbled to the floor like a broken doll, not moving. I tried to still my rapid breathing as I watched her, making sure she was down and out before I turned back to Vance.

I needed to figure out a way to get him out of the irons. I grabbed and I pulled, trying to think of a spell or something that would free him, but I couldn't make it work.

I placed my hand on his arm, while I paused to rack my brain. He was so hot to the touch.

"Think, Portia, think!" I said out loud. I was about to cry in frustration when suddenly an idea popped into my head.

I remembered our first outing together, when Vance had taken me to his secret place. He made a fireball in his hand, and I had frozen it. I grabbed the manacles and thought of that moment.

Right away a cold wave flowed out of my hands and over the iron binding him. I kept pushing that power into the metal until I began to hear cracking sounds. I didn't stop, continuing to force the magic into it and soon the cuff just fell apart into jagged pieces on the floor.

Giving a little exclamation of glee at my success, I quickly went to work on the cuff binding his other arm. When it was destroyed, I moved on to the ones at his feet until, finally, I set him free.

Someone started clapping slowly behind me, and I looked over to the corner where Shelly was still collapsed in a heap.

Cautiously, I stood and turned around, tensed to face whomever I would find there.

Someone was standing in the shadow of the door, but I couldn't make out who it was.

"Bravo, Portia! I didn't think you had it in you," an unfamiliar female voice said to me.

"Who are you?" I asked, standing my ground.

She stepped inside, but kept herself well hidden in the shadows around the perimeter. She didn't answer me, choosing instead to work her way around the room until she stood behind Vance, with me in front of him.

All of a sudden she leaned over into the light and slapped Vance twice, hard on the face.

"Wake up, son! We have company!" she rasped.

I took two involuntary steps backward.

Krista Mangum!

"Surprise!" she said, laughing at my expression. "You weren't expecting to see me, were you?"

"It's been you all this time?" I shook my head in denial. "Why? How?"

"I'm guessing you got the whole sob story from Vance about how I ran away with him," she said, her red eyes never leaving my face. "Well, his daddy caught up with me and showed me what I was really missing. All that power—who could resist it? Damien and I have been looking for him ever since."

"But why?" I asked, unable to wrap my head around this. "You worked so hard to get him away!"

"I just didn't understand the truth back then. Power is everything. And my son has plenty to spare!"

I pushed the pain I felt for Vance at this discovery aside, and tried a different tactic.

"I can't imagine Damien will be too happy with you. Where is he? After all, you've been feasting on his prize."

"Don't you worry your pretty little head about that!" She laughed. "Damien sent me for Vance, and I've bottled up plenty of blood for him. I'm taking Vance to him later. It's much easier to travel with him as one of us, than against us."

We were slowly moving around the room now, making a wide circle around Vance as we spoke.

"How'd you get Shelly involved in all this?" I asked, still stalling while I desperately tried to come up with a plan.

"Who? That twit in the corner?" she said barely glancing in Shelly's direction. "She's not even a witch! Just my little puppet on a string. It was easy to place a spell on her and then channel my magic through her. She had no control over her own mind."

While I was relieved to hear that Shelly had not done any of this of her own free will, I didn't have the time to ponder its meaning. I had no idea how I was going to get out of this mess, let alone take Vance with me. Krista was like a hawk guarding her prey.

He started to move in his chair.

"Son! It's time to wake up! There's work to be done," she called out again loudly.

Vance slowly opened his red eyes and stared at me.

"Isn't it fitting that you'll be his first kill, the one that'll help him complete his change?" She laughed, and I watched as her face transformed before my eyes.

Her brows furrowed, small horns popped from the top of her forehead, and her teeth sharpened into uneven rows. All the while her glowing eyes continued to mock me.

"Time for dinner, son. Trust me, you don't want to pass up a fresh blooded witch. It will taste better than anything you've ever had before." She licked her own lips even as she encouraged him to attack me.

Vance slowly stood from his chair, and I realized with horror I'd unwittingly set my own killer free. He began walking slowly toward me, and I unknowingly crept backward. One step for every step he took forward, until I abruptly found myself up against the wall with nowhere to go.

I could tell I was being hunted, and I could also see the hunger in his eyes that never left mine. I couldn't look away from him. He was magnificent, and I both loved him and feared him at the same time.

He continued to move toward me until he was pressed completely up against me, pinning me with his body against the wall. He ran one of his hands slowly down my right arm and grasped my hand, raising it up over my head. Then he did the same with the other, lifting it too, until both of my small wrists were captured under his right hand above me. His left hand, he placed behind my head, twisting his fingers into my hair, pulling my face closer to his.

I wasn't expecting the kiss when it came, his mouth slanting over mine, kissing me hard and passionately. Even now I couldn't resist him, knowing it would be our last time, so I kissed him back. Then I started to cry.

"Finish her!" his mom yelled.

He pulled away, looking at me, and I saw his teeth

lengthening into fangs.

"I love you," I said, wanting it to be the last thing he heard from me.

He yanked hard on my hair, pulling my head over to the side. Then he leaned in and bit into my neck like I'd seen in a dozen vampire movies.

I wanted to scream when I felt the searing pain. I felt my blood bubble up to the surface, rushing from my neck into his mouth. He sucked hard on me for several moments, and then unexpectedly, he released me and turned toward his mom who was still chortling across the room from us.

Shock overwhelmed me when he threw his left hand out and a large arc of flame shot from it, completely engulfing her in fire, incinerating her on the spot while she screamed in horror. When there was nothing left but ashes, he turned and slumped against me, sliding roughly to the floor in a dead faint.

I raised a trembling hand to my neck, pressing hard to try to stop the bleeding, and I shakily ran out the door and up the stairs to the bar above. I grabbed the phone from behind the counter and dialed the number to my grandma's with my blood-slicked fingers.

"Hello?" her frantic voice answered on the first ring.

"Come quickly. I found him, but there isn't much time," I shouted into the receiver, giving her the address.

"We're on our way!" she said and slammed down the phone.

I dropped the phone without bothering to hang it up and ran back downstairs to where Vance was still unconscious on the floor. I wanted to try and wake him, but I was too afraid. I didn't know how much control he really had, and I worried other demons were lurking close by.

I heard a soft moan in the opposite corner, and I ran over to check on Shelly.

"Portia?" she said, opening her eyes with a confused look on her face. "What're you doing here?" She stopped to look around. "Where is here exactly?" she added, glancing at me and then down at herself. "And what am I wearing?" she moaned, and that's when I knew she'd be okay.

"There's no time to explain right now," I said in a rush. "We're in a terrible situation, and I need your help to get Vance up the stairs."

"Vance?" she asked blankly, her expression puzzled. "What's the matter with Vance?"

"I promise I'll explain everything if you'll just help me first," I pleaded with her, trying to show her the desperateness of the situation.

"All right." She grabbed my outstretched hand, climbing to her feet. We went over to where Vance was lying on the floor.

"Just wrap his arm around your neck," I instructed, showing her what I meant as I wrapped his other arm around mine.

We got him into a sitting position, and I reached back to grab his belt loop, using a little levitation magic to pull him to his feet, causing Shelly's eyes to widen, but to her credit she didn't say a word.

The two of us maneuvered Vance up the stairs and out into the bar area, where I directed her to help me slump him into a nearby booth.

"Someone's here," Shelly said, her head jerking up when we heard a car pull up outside.

"It's okay. It's my family," I explained, as my dad came

running into the bar.

"He's over here," I called out, motioning to him.

"I've got him. Go get in the car!" he replied, moving to grab Vance.

"Go ahead," I told Shelly. "I have one more thing I've got to do first."

I ran back into the storeroom and looked around. The refrigerator was in the corner, and I ran to it, pulled the door open, and found what I was looking for. Pint after pint of blood filled every shelf in the whole icebox.

Flinging my hand out at the contents, I sent a burst of magic, shattering the glass jars in every direction, spraying blood all over the fridge and myself. I slammed the door shut, turned and ran out to the car.

"Are you okay?" Grandma called to me from behind the wheel, seeing the blood all over my clothing.

"I'm fine!" I jumped into the backseat next to my dad and Vance. "Let's move it!"

The tires made a squealing noise as we peeled out from the parking lot. We sped through town, thankfully not passing a soul, and soon we were back at Grandma's.

Several members of the coven were there waiting for us when we arrived. They helped to get Vance into the house and downstairs where they'd prepared a containment area in the ritual room. Vance was gently placed on a cot behind a magically charged glass wall before the coven members stepped out and sealed it up behind them.

"Is it necessary to move him from one prison to another?" I asked, feeling like a traitor for doing such a thing.

"Yes it is, honey," Grandma said seriously. "If we can save him, and that's a big if, he's going to go through some serious withdrawal. He'll be a danger to all of us now, even you," she warned.

I didn't care. He was back, and he was with me. He was still my Vance.

"Let's have a look at that neck," my dad said, lifting his hand cautiously toward my wound. "Did he bite you?"

"Yes. But he did it to save me. His powers were drained, and he needed my strength to help defeat his mother," I replied, silently adding to myself that I hoped it really was the reason he'd done it.

"His mother?" Dad and Grandma said at the same time, their confusion written on their faces.

"Sit down and tell us what happened," my dad said.

I sat on a cot outside the cell and explained everything that had happened since I left the house this evening, up until I made the phone call.

"That was very risky, Portia!" Grandma chastened me. "You shouldn't have done this without the rest of us! You could've been killed!"

"That would be better than living without him." I sighed, rubbing my hands at my temples. My poor mind didn't need this lecture right now. "I need to go talk to Shelly now. I promised her an explanation." I got up and left the room, going upstairs to find her.

"Did you see my hair?" she asked when I walked into the room, from where she was huddled under a blanket on the couch. "It's black! Tell me please how I ended up with black hair!"

I plopped down next to her. "Shelly. I have something to tell you, and you probably won't believe it," I began, wondering how to tell her exactly what was going on. About an hour later, and a few magical examples to boot, she finally believed me and I thought she actually comprehended the things I was telling her.

She didn't remember any of it. Her mind was a completely blank void when it came to her life over the past few weeks. She cried and cried when I told her about the explosion at the school. I assured her it wasn't her fault, she had been used.

"What about Brad?" she asked finally. "Is he okay?"

"As far as I know." I gave an exhausted sigh. "I'm going to have to explain all this to him too, I guess. He's been coming by here for days asking to see me, Grandma says. He's going to wonder what's going on."

"I'd better call my parents," Shelly said with a dejected look. "I wonder if they were under a spell too. They would never let me get away with all this stuff."

"That actually makes sense. Vance commented at one time they seemed to be acting strangely."

My dad came up the stairs and offered to take Shelly home to check things out there.

"You should go change. You're covered in blood," Dad reminded me, stopping to look at me on his way out the door with Shelly.

Bruce, from the coven, went with him just to make sure everything was all right with the Fontanes.

I headed down the hall and into the guest bedroom, pulling out a pair of boxers and an old tank top from the dresser. I headed into the bathroom to take a shower.

I let the hot water run over my body, washing the dried blood on my neck down the drain with it. I shampooed my hair, shaved my legs, and washed up real well with thick soapy bubbles before I finally lost it and broke down. I slid down the wall, huddling in the corner while the water sluiced over my skin, and I cried my eyes out.

Chapter 24

Everyone had gone home except for Dad and Grandma, and they were asleep in the upstairs bedrooms.

I'd been lying for hours on a cot I pushed up against the glass wall that separated Vance from me. I wanted to be as close to him as I could get.

He hadn't awakened since he'd passed out in front of me at the bar. He was still slumped over on his side, in the exact position they'd put him in on the inside of the chamber. I would've worried he was dead, except I could see he was breathing deep and evenly.

I still couldn't hear anything from his mind. It was completely shut off to me. I kept trying to reach him mentally off and on, but so far I'd had no luck.

Reaching out, I traced one of my fingers over the divider, making tiny sparks in the magical current running through it. It didn't bother me at all, but then again, the magic wasn't meant to keep me out, but to keep him in.

The need for sleep began to threaten me, and I yawned. I continued to watch him for as long as I could, until my eyes grew too heavy to keep open, and then I fell asleep.

I found myself standing in the beautiful field of

flowers again when I entered my dream state, and I turned around, expecting to see him standing there next to me. The field was empty, however. I sighed and sat down in the tall waving foliage, staring off into the serene space for a long while.

"Portia," I heard him whisper my name on the breeze.

I jumped to my feet, looking all around trying to spot him.

"Vance?" I called out, my heart racing. "Where are you?"

"Portia. I need you!" he replied again. This time it sounded like he was right next to me. I turned around quickly to face him, but he wasn't there.

"Portia!" he growled. "Wake up!"

Instantly, my eyes popped open, and I was face to face with the demon red eyes that had been haunting me.

"Help me!" he said, placing his hand on the glass. I saw the current was shocking him, but he didn't move away.

"You're awake! That's wonderful!" I said with a sigh of relief coursing through me.

"Please, Portia. You have to help me," he pleaded with me again.

"What do you need me to do, Vance?" I wished I could just take down this barrier and hold him in my arms.

"I'm thirsty. I need a drink."

"We left water for you over on the stand beside your bed." I pointed over to it. "There's food too if you're hungry. I'm sure you're feeling very weak now."

"No!" he rasped again. "I'm thirsty!"

"So go get a drink!" I replied, becoming frustrated that he wasn't listening to me.

He stood up and angrily went over to the tray flicking it across the room with his hand, spraying the contents everywhere.

I stood up against the glass, lifting both of my hands to rest on it. "What're you doing?" I asked in irritation.

He strode back over to the partition and placed his hands against mine on the other side, leaning heavily on it. I could see he was trembling.

"I need a drink, Portia. Please! Just come in here with me. I promise I won't take too much."

I suddenly understood what he meant. He was thirsty, and he needed a drink of blood. He was asking me to let him feed on me.

"I'm sorry, Vance. I can't do that."

"Bull!" he yelled, clenching his hands together and pounding his fists against the glass.

I gasped and took a few steps backward.

"Let me out of here, Portia!" he continued, the heat in his eyes flaring.

When I didn't move or say anything, he pushed away from the glass and began pacing around the small space like a feral cat.

I watched him as he moved, wringing his hands, rubbing his arms, running his fingers through his hair. He continued on that way for several minutes before he came back to the divider.

"I'm sorry." He looked at me with pleading eyes. "Please come back over here."

I walked over and stood next to the pane.

"Portia, I need to have some blood. I'm getting sick."

I shook my head. "No, Vance. It's the blood that's making you sick."

"You don't understand." He turned his back to me, then sliding down the wall to the floor. He grabbed his hair in his hands. "If I don't get any, I'll die."

This pierced straight to the center of my heart, and

I couldn't bear it. The thought of losing him again was more than I could stand.

"Portia! Don't even consider it!" my dad's voice came strongly from behind me. "He's just trying to trick you."

Instantly Vance was on his feet, pounding at the barrier with all his might.

"Let me out!" he screamed, exposing his teeth in a snarl.

My dad reached out for me and pulled me back, away from the wall.

Vance stepped backward and starting throwing fireballs at the partition. One after another they burst out of him as he threw with both hands. The magic field easily absorbed the shock, but he didn't stop.

"Let him get it all out," my dad said.

I cried as I watched him. I hated not being able to help him.

Vance finally wore himself out and slumped onto the floor against the bed.

"I thought you loved me," he said weakly, hanging his head and refusing to look at me.

"I do love you, more than you can comprehend right now," I tried to explain. "That's why I'm doing this."

He gave a huff before he rolled over on the floor with his back to me. He didn't say anything else, and after a while I could tell he was sleeping again.

"Let him sleep," Dad said. "That's the best thing for him."

I nodded, my guilt over not being able to help him threatening to overwhelm me.

"Why don't you come upstairs and get something to eat now?" he suggested. "You need to keep your strength up too."

"I can't leave him, Dad," I said with a sigh.

"All right," he said, choosing not to try and argue with me about it. "I'll see if I can find something for you to eat and bring it down here."

He left the room, and I walked over to my cot and sat down. I didn't think I'd ever be able to eat again—my stomach was too tied up in knots.

Lying down on the cot, I continued to watch Vance until I fell asleep.

Sometime later I was awakened by a soft nudge on my shoulder, and I opened one sleepy eye to see my mother standing over me with a plate of food. She gave a nod, gesturing for me to follow her. I did, and we went into the supply room where she had the table set up.

"I thought you could use some real food." She set a plate of her steaming enchiladas in front of me. She left another plate on the table for herself.

The food actually smelled wonderful, and I realized with surprise I was starving. I picked up a utensil, digging right in, and we ate together in silence for several moments before she spoke up.

"I've been really worried about you."

"I know, Mom."

"Things have been crazy. Too crazy for a young girl like yourself." She looked me over carefully.

"I'm stronger than you think," I replied, and I placed another forkful of enchiladas into my mouth.

"I know you're strong. I've never doubted that. I just hoped you would have the opportunity to enjoy being a kid for a while."

"Life has a funny way of messing those things up." I shrugged. "I've learned to deal with it and do my best to move on."

We ate a few more bites before she continued. "What'll you do if he dies?"

"I can't think about that," I said, dropping my fork to my plate, my appetite vanishing immediately.

"You need to be prepared, Portia. I know it's awful, but there are only two ways this thing can go. Either he dies from not feeding, or you'll feed him and he makes the change, not to mention he'll probably kill you during the feeding. Either way you'll lose him!"

"I don't know what I'm going to do!" I shouted, standing up and pushing away from the table. I placed my hands on both sides of my head and squeezed hard, wishing I could stop the incessant pounding going on inside. I felt like my mind would explode!

My mom stood up and came over to wrap her arms around me. "I'm sorry, precious. I don't mean to be harsh. I just want you to be prepared, that's all."

"Dad said you prayed for me at the church," I said, pushing away from her.

"Yes, I did," she replied, searching my eyes.

"Keep praying, Mom. I'm hoping for a miracle."

I left her there, walking down the hall and back up to the glass divider in the ritual room.

He was still sleeping.

I watched him for a few moments, knelt down on the floor next to my cot and took my own advice.

"Please, God," I prayed with all my heart. "Help us." I knelt there for a long time, wishing for some sort of a divine answer—something, anything, that would tell me what to do. But there was nothing.

I heaved my tired body up off the floor and crawled back onto the cot. I let the silent tears fall as I cried myself to sleep once again.

When I finally woke up, I looked at the clock next to me and realized I'd slept through the entire night.

I rolled over to check on Vance and found him to be awake, huddled in the corner with his legs pulled up to his chest. His head was resting on his arms, on top of his knees, and he was shaking violently. I jumped up and hurried over to the corner where he was, sliding down the wall until I was settled next to him.

"Are you okay?" I asked, placing my hand on the glass.

He didn't acknowledge me at all.

I stayed there quietly for several minutes, not knowing what to say.

"Is there anything I can do for you?" I asked, instantly regretting it, because I knew what he wanted me to do for him.

He raised his face to me this time, and I was surprised to see the tears streaming down his face, his red eyes glowing at me with a cynical look.

"Vance. Please try to understand," I begged him.

He let his head droop back down.

"I love you more than anything. If giving you my blood would cure you, I would happily do it. It'll only make things worse though."

He didn't answer, or even acknowledge me, for that matter.

We stayed like this for hours, without speaking, while he shook uncontrollably. I was beginning to think we were going to sit that way forever, neither of us willing to bend to what the other needed.

When he finally moved, it was to crawl away from me slowly, back over to the bed. I watched him with horror written all over my face. I hadn't realized how weak he had actually become. As it was, he didn't even get into the bed, instead reaching up to grab the thin blanket there, pulling it over himself.

"Vance. Talk to me please," I begged him. "Don't shut me out. I don't know what to do."

"There's only one thing you can do, Portia, and you aren't willing to do it," he said, not making eye contact with me, his voice shaking. "It doesn't matter anymore anyway."

"What do you mean, it doesn't matter?" I said, slapping the glass hard to get his attention.

He slowly turned his gaze toward me, staring at me with half-lidded red eyes as if he were too tired to keep them open. Huge gray circles were now underneath them, giving them a sunken look.

"I wasn't lying to you, Portia. I'm dying." His voice was a whisper, and I strained to hear him.

I believed him. Even though my head told me not to, my heart knew he wouldn't lie to me about this, and the pain was excruciating.

"I'm sorry. I want to help. I just don't know how." Tears began slipping over the rims of my eyes.

"It's too late for apologies," he muttered, closing his eyes.

"What do you mean, it's too late?" I shouted, slapping at the glass again to get his attention. "Answer me, dang it!"

"I mean my time is running out. I won't be able to hang on much longer." I felt like I was going to vomit.

I scrambled to my feet, turning to run out of the room and up the stairs.

"He says he's dying!" I blurted out, huffing into the kitchen, where my dad and grandma were sitting at the table. "Help him, please!" I pleaded.

The two of them exchanged a knowing glance, before my dad stood up.

"Portia, sweetheart," he said, coming to wrap his arms

around me. "We've been researching everything we could get our hands on. There's just nothing else we can find to do."

"So, you're just going to let him die?" I yelled, shoving my dad away from me and staring at both of them.

"We expected it would happen," Grandma explained, with pity in her eyes. "We just hoped for some sort of a miracle, though."

"*No*!" I shouted at both of them.

"Portia, honey, let's try to let him go as peacefully as possible, okay? He doesn't need any more heartache than he's having already," my dad said softly. "Give him some dignity."

"You want me to sit here and let him die? Let him die while he thinks we're the ones doing this to him? I can't let that happen." I ran back downstairs.

"Portia! Come back here!" my dad called after me.

I didn't stop until I was standing outside the glass looking at Vance. I watched him for only a brief second before I knew what I had to do. I placed both of my hands firmly on the force field and pressed as hard as I could, letting my magic flow from me and into it.

A hole began to melt into the partition, widening until it was large enough for me to step through. I went into the chamber and quickly reinforced the field from the inside, sealing myself into the small cell with him.

I turned and knelt over him. "Vance! Wake up, please!" I called out to him, just as Grandma and Dad entered the room.

"Portia! What're you doing?" Grandma called out in alarm to me, and my dad raced over to the glass.

"Don't try to stop me!" I said, before turning to shake Vance again.

"Take the barrier down now!" my dad yelled to Grandma, and they both leaned up against it, pushing with their magic.

I knew I didn't have much time.

"Vance! Wake up!" I shouted at him, slapping him hard across the face.

He groaned and opened his demon-colored eyes to look up at me, and I glanced up to see there was a significant-sized hole melted in the glass now.

"Hurry!" I pleaded with him. "We don't have much time!"

I lifted him into a sitting position, moved my hair out of the way. I cradled him against me, pushing him toward my neck.

"Portia! Stop!" my dad yelled at me.

"I'm sorry, Dad," I said to him, right as Vance bit hard into my neck.

I stiffened, crying out in pain, and the blood began to flow freely from me and into him. At first he just swallowed what poured into his mouth, but I could tell when he suddenly became stronger, because he started sucking hard against me.

I shook and began slowly sinking as I felt my strength depleting. He moved then, grappling to change positions with me without removing his mouth, so he was now holding me in his arms.

My eyes watched the horrified looks that passed over my dad and Grandma's faces. They finally breached the barrier and came rushing inside to grab me.

Vance raised a hand, and a force field shot out around us. He continued to feed on me, drinking heavily, not letting them get any closer.

"It's too late, Sean," I heard Grandma say, and she grabbed my dad, pulling him back toward the opening. "We need to seal them both in and see what happens. We can't let them out."

She had to drag him out as he kept hollering toward us, calling Vance all sorts of names and cursing the day he'd allowed him anywhere near his daughter. He helped Grandma repair the cell wall, and when they were done, Vance dropped the shield around the two of us.

He ravaged me now with a hunger I didn't think he would be able to ever stop, gulping my blood down with relish.

I felt so weak and tired. My mind started to feel hazy, and I knew I needed to speak to him before it was too late.

"I love you," I said, with great effort. "More than anything, please remember that."

He released my neck suddenly and pulled back so he could look at me. His eyes were flaming now, his blood raced through his veins, filled with the strength of my powers. He was strong again, I could feel it.

"Don't leave me," he said, holding me tenderly as he shifted me in his grasp, and I flopped like a rag doll.

"I feel too weak." I tried to keep my eyes open so I could look at him as long as possible.

"It'll get better, I promise. Your blood will regenerate, and you'll feel better."

"And then what? You and I will feed off each other until we're both demons?"

"As long as we're together, that's all that matters," he said, his view distorted once again.

"I won't live like that, Vance. I let you drink from me, but I won't drink from you. I won't make the change," I said sadly.

"You'd rather me make the change while you die

and leave me here alone, after all you just did to save my life?" Confusion flickered in his eyes.

My heart hurt, and I felt like I was on the brink of falling into an abyss. "I'm sorry. It was the only thing I could do to save you. I needed to give them more time to find a cure for you."

"I won't let you leave me," he said forcefully, the alpha male in him demanding my compliance. "I'll force you to drink if I have to."

I didn't answer, instead closing my eyes in exhaustion.

"Portia! Don't you dare sleep now!" he yelled, shaking me roughly.

I opened my eyes and looked up into his.

"Listen to me, baby." He stroked his hand through my hair, rocking me in his arms. "It won't be that bad. We can both make the change. We'll be able to be together, in every way. We can make love with one another, just like we always wanted to do. We'll be strong and powerful. You'll see. Please, baby, see what I'm saying."

He pulled me to his mouth, kissing me hard and desperately, trying to stimulate a response in me, but I was too tired.

"I want to *be* with you, Portia. I want to make you mine in every sense of the word," he whispered into my hair. "Come on, baby, today could be our day."

He shook me hard again when I didn't respond.

"Do you hear me, Portia?" he yelled at me. "Do you hear what I'm asking you to do?"

His stare bore into mine, and I knew what my answer had to be.

I lethargically lifted both of my hands, placing them gently on either side of the face I loved so much, and slowly began to speak.

"Vance Mangum, Blessed Be.

I give now, my heart to thee.
My soul is yours to bind and take,
My love for you will never shake.
I promise to always keep you pure,
And never into evil lure.
Let Heaven be our destiny,
I love you Vance, So Mote It Be."

As the words to our binding ritual filled the air, a white light began to emanate from both of my hands. The light grew until it had completely encased Vance and then spread over me also. I could feel he was shaking violently.

When I was done reciting the words, I let my hands fall away and finally slipped into unconsciousness.

Chapter 25

I was dreaming. I felt safe … I was safe, dancing around in my field of flowers. Suddenly someone's arms reached out and snaked around my waist.

"You did it, baby," the voice whispered in my ear. "It's going to be all right now. I promise."

I turned toward the sound of the voice I loved more than anything else in the world.

"What did I do?" I asked Vance innocently, staring into his bright blue eyes.

"You saved me. It worked!" he replied with a wide smile.

"What worked?" I was confused, unable to figure out what he was talking about.

"The binding spell, the healer's magic. All of it." He laughed and hugged me tightly to him.

"Healer's magic?"

"You've proven to be a very powerful healer witch."

"Then why am I still sleeping?" I asked suspiciously, narrowing my eyes at him.

"You still need to rest for a while. Your body was very depleted." He leaned down to nuzzle his face into the crook of my neck. "I'm sorry about that."

I wasn't sure what he was talking about, so I just relished the feel of him for a few moments, too happy to try and straighten things out in my head. But I became very tired all of a sudden and wanted to go to sleep. I closed my eyes.

Wait a minute, wasn't I already asleep?

I started to feel the physical pain that only happened when Vance was away from me. I opened my eyes to look at up at him, but he wasn't there.

"Vance?" I called out. "Vance! Where are you?

My heart was pounding in my chest, and I twirled in a circle, searching for him.

When his voice finally came to me, it was in a distant whisper.

"I'm leaving you for a while, baby," he said apologetically.

"What? No! Don't go!" I ran in the direction I thought his voice had come from. "Don't leave me!"

"I have to—just for a little while. I'll see you again someday though. I promise! I love you!"

I knew he was gone then because I couldn't feel him anymore, and I sank to the ground beneath me. I curled up into a ball and allowed the tears to overcome me until I fell asleep.

When I awoke again, I was still lying in a heap in my field of flowers. I sat up and looked around, the breeze in the meadow blowing gently over the top of me.

Voices tinkled softly in the air that moved around me, but I could only catch snippets of what they were saying while I tried to recognize them.

"Is she okay?"

"...don't know if..."

"...hasn't woken up since..."

"No, he's gone..."

I tried talking to them to get their attention. "Hello? Is

someone there?"

"...just moved..." came the reply.

"Maybe she is..." another voice answered.

I concentrated real hard on the sound of those voices.

"Grandma?" I called out, thinking I recognized one of the voices as I heard more of the mumblings. "Shelly!" I shouted when I recognized her voice out of the blue, but there was no reply from either of them.

I got up and wandered around when I realized the curious conversation had stopped. I walked around the edges of my meadow, examining the beautiful flowers that dotted the landscape, but I soon tired and lay down once again to rest.

The next time I opened my eyes, I found myself situated in Grandma's guest bedroom, lying on the comfy bed with blankets tucked nicely around my body.

I blinked several times at the bright light that filled the room.

"Oh! You're awake!" an exuberant voice at my side exclaimed, and I turned my head to see Shelly jump up from the chair. She tossed a book onto the nightstand and came to sit beside me on the bed. I was happy to see her appearance was back to the old Shelly I had known and loved my whole life.

"Hey," I said, my voice cracking a little from lack of use.

"How're you feeling?" she asked me, a concerned look on her face.

I did a quick mental check before replying. "Fine, I think. Where is everyone?"

"They're not here. I volunteered to sit with you while they all went to the funeral," she replied.

"The funeral?" I asked, and horror streaked through my body. "Where's Vance?"

"I'm sorry, Portia," Shelly replied with a sad expression. "I forget you don't know everything that's going on. You've been out of it for a while."

"Shelly!" I groaned, struggling to sit up. "Where is Vance?"

"He's gone," she replied, and I sucked in a sharp breath, a sob caught in my throat.

"He died?" I asked, everything in my whole world crumbling to nothingness.

"What? Died? No!" Shelly responded in a rush. "I'm sorry. I'm really botching this up, aren't I? It's Marsha. They're all at Marsha's funeral."

It took a moment for her words to sink in.

"He's not dead?" I gasped, and I fell back onto the pillows in exhaustion, my hand clutched over my pounding heart.

"No. But he is gone. He left."

"He left?" I asked, still confused. "Left where? To the funeral?"

Shelly got up off the bed and walked around to where a white envelope was lying on the nightstand. She picked it up and brought it to me.

"He said to give this to you when you woke up," she explained, handing it to me.

My hands trembled slightly when I took it from her, carefully opening the envelope and reaching in to pull out a folded paper from inside. When I opened the paper, several pictures fell out, tumbling before my eyes into my lap. They were our photographs from the day we had been in the forest.

I held up the images one by one, looking at our smiling faces. Some were funny, others were serious, and we were kissing in several of them. I paused on the last one I had taken of him that day, propped up on his arm as he looked at me with all the love in the world.

I gently placed the pictures on my stomach, picked up his letter and began to read:

"Portia, my love,

I'm breaking my word to you by even writing this letter. Please don't hold it against me.

First of all, I ask your forgiveness for all the heartache I've caused you. I can't even imagine what I must've put you through. Thank you for believing in me and not giving up. It means more to me than you will ever know.

I assume it's been explained to you by now that you're a healer witch. Without the gift of your blood, and power, I would most certainly have lost my life in this battle. Your mother said you wanted a miracle, and you got it. A healer witch has never been able to heal someone in demon transition before. As usual you've proven your powers far exceed what anyone ever thought they could do.

It was the words of our binding spell that finally brought sanity back to my head. Thank you for helping me to remember.

Second, as I'm sure you've noticed, I'm no longer there. I cannot and will not let you live a life where something like this could happen again. I'm going to go find my father and finish this once and for all. If I'm successful, I'll return to you as fast as I can. If I'm not, then please know I love you more than anything in this world, and I will be waiting for you to join me in the next one.

Please live your life and be happy. I hope to see you again soon!

My Heart Will Always Be Yours,

Vance

To say that my blood began to boil would have been an understatement. I was furious!

"What the heck is he thinking?" I yelled at Shelly, and she took an involuntary step backwards. "He's going to get himself killed!"

I tried to push myself up out of the bed so I could stand up.

"What're you doing? You're too weak to get out of bed yet!" She hurried over and tried to push me back down onto the pillows.

"Move out of my way!" I said, grabbing her hand.

"I'm supposed to be taking care of you, though," she pleaded with me.

"I can't live without him, Shelly. He has no support, no help, nothing! He's running to his death!"

"What do you need me to do?" she asked then, sighing in resignation.

"Bring your car around," I said firmly. "I'm going after him."

ABOUT THE AUTHOR

Lacey Weatherford has always had a love of books. She wanted to become a writer after reading her first Nancy Drew novel at the age of eight.

Lacey resides in the White Mountains of Arizona , where she lives with her wonderful husband, six beautiful children, one son-in-law, and their energetic schnauzer, Sophie. When she's not out supporting one of her kids at their sporting/music events, she spends her time writing, reading, blogging, and reviewing books.

Visit the official website
http://www.ofwitchesandwarlocks.com
http://www.laceyweatherfordbooks.com
Follow Lacey on Twitter at:
http://twitter.com/LMWeatherford

Also From

Moonstruck Media

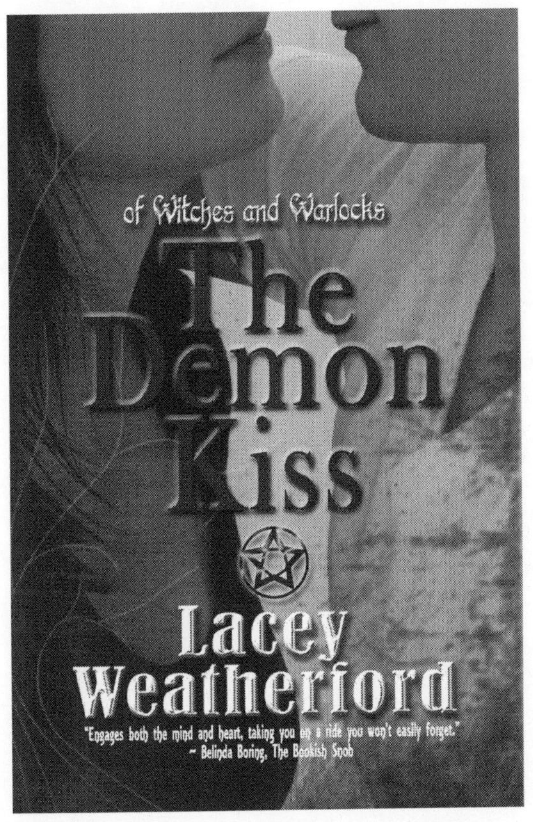

Of Witches and Warlocks
The Demon Kiss
Lacey Weatherford
"Engages both the mind and heart, taking you on a ride you won't easily forget."
~ Belinda Boring, The Bookish Snob

After being drained of nearly all the blood in her body, novice witch, Portia Mullins, wakes up to find that her warlock boyfriend, Vance Mangum, has fled in search of his demon father. Determined to keep him from facing the evil alone Portia follows after him, unknowingly setting herself on the path of a new adventure that will take her, Vance, and their coven over international borders, into a foreign place where they will discover that the black magic which awaits them is far worse than they ever imagined. Portia finds herself tangled up in a web of lies and deceit in another's quest for demonic power in the excitingly romantic second paranormal novel in the bestselling *Of Witches and Warlocks* Series, *The Demon Kiss.*

Made in the USA
Lexington, KY
10 September 2012